Julie Wassmer is a professional television drama writer who has worked on various series including ITV's *London's Burning*, C5's *Family Affairs* and BBC's *Eastenders* – which she wrote for almost 20 years.

Her autobiography, *More Than Just Coincidence*, was Mumsnet Book of the Year 2011.

Find details of author events and other information about the Whitstable Pearl Mysteries at:
www.juliewassmer.com

Also by Julie Wassmer

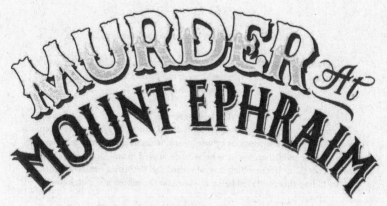

MURDER AT MOUNT EPHRAIM

A Whitstable Pearl Mystery

JULIE WASSMER

CONSTABLE

CONSTABLE

First published in Great Britain in 2022 by Constable

Copyright © Julie Wassmer, 2022

3 5 7 9 10 8 6 4 2

The moral right of the author has been asserted.

A CIP catalogue record for this book is available from the British Library.

ISBN: 978-1-47213-446-2

Typeset in Adobe Caslon Pro by SX Composing DTP, Rayleigh, Essex
Printed and bound in Great Britain by Clays Ltd, Elcograf S.p.A.

Papers used by Constable are from well-managed forests
and other responsible sources.

Constable
An imprint of
Little, Brown Book Group
Carmelite House
50 Victoria Embankment
London EC4Y 0DZ

An Hachette UK Company
www.hachette.co.uk

www.littlebrown.co.uk

For the Dawes family of Mount Ephraim

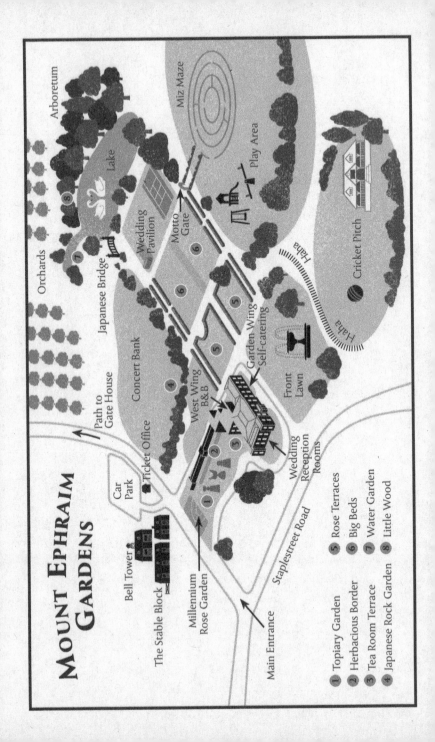

MOUNT EPHRAIM GARDENS

- 1 Topiary Garden
- 2 Herbacious Border
- 3 Tea Room Terrace
- 4 Japanese Rock Garden
- 5 Rose Terraces
- 6 Big Beds
- 7 Water Garden
- 8 Little Wood

Arboretum

Orchards

Lake

Miz Maze

Play Area

Cricket Pitch

Ha-ha

Ha-ha

Japanese Bridge

Wedding Pavilion

Motto Gate

Concert Bank

Garden Wing Self-catering

West Wing B&B

Front Lawn

Wedding Reception Rooms

Path to Gate House

Ticket Office

Car Park

Bell Tower

The Stable Block

Millennium Rose Garden

Main Entrance

Staplestreet Road

PREFACE

From: amy_y@travelbird.com
Sent: 4th August 2022 18:52
To: pearl@thewhitstablepearl.com; pearl@
nolansdetectiveagency.com
Subject: Summer Surprise

Dear Pearl,

It's been so long since we last saw one another and I know
it's my fault for the break in contact, but keeping in touch
has proved quite a challenge while on the other side of
the world – until now.

Could you please reply ASAP and let me know if you
might be free for a few days soon?

I can explain more once I fly out of Bangkok on Friday.

I'm coming home, Pearl, and for a very special reason.

With love.

Your old friend,

Amy ❤

CHAPTER ONE

The day was deceptively bright with a clear blue sky, and Whitstable's estuary waters remained undisturbed by waves as they lay stretched out beyond Pearl Nolan's home at Seaspray Cottage. Nevertheless, as was so often the case on the north-facing Kent coast, there was a chill to the air, sufficient for Pearl to close her latticed window before turning back to find her mother holding aloft a small, framed painting.

'So, what do you think?' asked Dolly Nolan, beaming as she waited for an opinion. For a moment, Pearl was lost for words as she noted that the seascape in her mother's hands had been created in Dolly's favourite medium, '*objets trouvés*' – a sophisticated term for the flotsam and jetsam Dolly was apt to collect on her beach walks: dried seaweed, fragments of bleached timber and tiny pieces of ancient glass polished by the tide.

'It's . . .' Pearl struggled for a suitable adjective. 'Unique,' she said finally, 'and very kind of you to do this for Amy.'

Dolly gave a shrug. 'Well, as there's no wedding list I thought a personal gift might fit the bill. It ticks all the boxes.'

'Boxes?' asked Pearl as she zipped up the travel bag she had packed that morning.

'The old rhyme,' said Dolly, 'to bring a bride good luck on her wedding day. Something old,'—she indicated the painting's antique gold leaf frame—'something new'—She paused to remind Pearl: 'It's a brand-new piece of work. And as to "something borrowed",' she went on, 'a friend lent me some brushes for this piece, and I haven't yet given them back.' She offered a mischievous smile then. 'Something blue? Well . . .' She allowed her daughter to guess for herself.

'The sea,' said Pearl, pointing to the azure band above a mass of oyster shells affixed to the canvas. She returned Dolly's smile. 'I'm sure Amy will really appreciate this. A reminder of home?'

Dolly considered the painting. 'Yes,' she said thoughtfully, 'though not quite the tropical climes she's used to. You said she's been living in Thailand?'

Pearl nodded. 'And we might be short of waving palm trees here, but Whitstable has its own charm – as has your gift,' she added, before checking her watch and noting it was almost midday. 'I'd better get going.'

'What's the hurry?' asked Dolly. 'The wedding's not until tomorrow.'

'I know, but as the guests have all been invited to stay at the venue for the whole weekend, I was hoping to arrive reasonably early today to catch up with Amy.'

Pearl grabbed a white linen jacket from the back of an armchair while Dolly began carefully wrapping her painting in a sheet of silver gift paper. Pearl watched her and flipped her long dark curls from the collar of her jacket as she mused, 'It's true there's no wedding list, but it's usual these days to have one, isn't it?'

Dolly shrugged. 'I presume they're not in need of much,' she commented as she continued wrapping. 'Guy Priddey's a very wealthy man.'

Pearl reacted to an element of disdain in her mother's voice. 'Successful,' she said.

'An adventurer,' said Dolly with conviction before she pushed back her fringe, which had recently been coloured a bold magenta – a return to her favourite shade after a period of sporting a strong turquoise. Pearl knew it wouldn't be long before her mother chose another attention-grabbing hue. Vivid colour was a weapon in the armoury Dolly used against age, as evidenced by her shockingly bright clothes. Dolly was sixty-five but going on sixteen and committed to growing old disgracefully. She finished wrapping the painting and remarked, 'I can quite see why Amy's been swept off her feet by him.'

'Can you?' asked Pearl.

Dolly looked back at her daughter as she secured a gold bow to the wrapped painting then stood up and smoothed the folds of her Technicolor artist's smock.

'Of course. Quite aside from his money, Priddey's a free spirit – just like Amy – though he needed to be more than that to salvage that precious cargo from the South China Sea.'

'*And* sell it for a small fortune,' said Pearl.

'Not so small,' remarked Dolly knowingly. 'It raised over five million at auction.'

'That much?' Pearl asked in shock.

Dolly gave a nod. 'And I wasn't in the least surprised. It was the finest Ch'ing dynasty porcelain.'

Pearl suddenly felt out of the loop. 'How d'you know so much about it?'

Dolly preened before declaring: 'I made it my business to find out. I read a few articles about the whole operation. I'm a ceramicist, remember?' Pearl paused before humouring her. 'Of course,' she said, failing to point out that her mother's shabby-chic platters hardly resembled priceless Chinese porcelain – though they did come in handy for oyster displays at the High Street restaurant that bore Pearl's name – The Whitstable Pearl.

'There again,' said Dolly tentatively, 'we mustn't think that having all that money makes Priddey any more attractive to Amy than he clearly is.'

Pearl eyed her mother before setting the record straight. 'Amy's in love,' she declared. 'She called me from Bangkok and talked of nothing else *but* Guy. They may only have been together for a short while but they're both old enough to know what they feel for one another.'

'Good,' said Dolly, seemingly satisfied, 'though why Amy, or any other woman, feels the need to get married these days remains a mystery to me.' She gave a sidelong glance at her daughter to which Pearl failed to react, then added: 'Especially when you're in your forties.' She now offered the wrapped gift to Pearl, who gaped at her in shock.

'Like me, you mean?'

'You're not married.'

'Yet,' said Pearl. 'But I am engaged.'

'Yes,' said Dolly with a confused frown. 'But what does that actually mean? You're promised to one man and therefore unavailable to any other?' She gave a pinched look. Pearl grabbed the wrapped painting from her and said, 'McGuire proposed.'

'And you accepted,' said Dolly quickly, raising a finger to stress her point. 'So now you're neither single nor married, but in a form of . . . purgatory? You're not even living together.'

'This cottage is too small for us.'

'It was big enough for me and your dad,' said Dolly, 'and now that Charlie's moved out, you have a spare—'

'I'm not getting rid of Charlie's room,' said Pearl quickly, before picking up her travel bag.

'Why not?' asked Dolly. 'Charlie's in his twenties and managing to pay rent on his own place in Canterbury – finally,' she added, aware that Pearl had been subsidising him for quite a while.

'And what if something goes wrong?'

'If Charlie knows you're keeping his slippers warm at home, it most certainly will,' said Dolly. 'He'll be bouncing back here instead of learning to stand on his own two feet. But if he does ever need somewhere to stay in Whitstable there's always my place – if I don't have any guests staying.'

'You've *always* got guests staying,' said Pearl, knowing that Dolly's Attic, the Harbour Street apartment situated above her mother's home and the shop from which she sold her ceramics and artwork, was one of the town's most popular holiday haunts.

'Then he can sleep on the chaise longue in my conserv-atory,' argued Dolly before she paused and considered her daughter. 'There again . . . if you're looking for a reason *not* to settle down with McGuire—'

'I'm not,' Pearl insisted. 'We . . . just haven't had time to discuss wedding plans, that's all.'

Dolly watched as Pearl hitched her bag over her shoulder, then she paused and came closer. 'So . . . this is really what you want, is it? Marriage?' Somehow she made the word sound deeply unattractive.

'Would I have said yes otherwise?'

Dolly took a moment to consider this. 'Lots of women get carried away with a proposal. There's nothing wrong with having second thoughts.'

'You mean cold feet? I haven't got them.'

'After all these years of independence?'

'What's that got to do with it?'

'You'll be giving up the life you've carved out for yourself – your routines. We settle into middle age like a pair of comfy slippers.'

'Forty is *not* "middle-aged".'

'You're over forty now, Pearl.'

'So?'

'So, I'm just saying . . . our needs change as we grow older. When I was young, I'd have given anything for love.'

'And now?' asked Pearl, curious.

'Now, it's a foot spa.'

Pearl gave a heavy sigh. 'Is it marriage you're trying to put me off – or McGuire?'

Dolly gave a shrug. 'It's really nothing personal.'

'You just don't like the idea of having a police officer in the family, is that it?'

It was true that Dolly Nolan had always shown a disregard for all authority – including members of the police – though she had warmed to Pearl's fiancé, DCI Mike McGuire, evidenced by the fact that she no longer called him 'the flatfoot'.

'Now that you mention it,' mused Dolly, 'we could do with a useful profession in the family.'

'"Useful"?'

'Like a plumber,' said Dolly. 'With the money they charge these days, I'm going to have to remortgage just to get my old boiler overhauled.'

Pearl gave up. 'Why don't I find a brain surgeon and get *you* overhauled?'

'Uncalled for,' said Dolly. 'I'm just pointing out the obvious, that's all: you hardly have time to see one another as it is, what with McGuire on call at the police station and you at the restaurant – or embroiled in trying to solve someone's problems.'

'Cases,' said Pearl. 'Nolan's is a detective agency – not a knock-and-drop-in centre.'

'Whatever,' said Dolly dismissively before beginning again. 'I've always wanted what's best for you, Pearl. You need to invest time in a marriage for it to work.' She gave a knowing look. 'As for Amy,' she went on, 'why on earth would she want to give up a dream job like hers, jetting all over the world and writing about interesting people?'

'I told you – she's in love.'

'She was in love with her job.'

'Work isn't everything.'

'It is to you and McGuire.'

'Well then,' said Pearl. 'Things will have to change.' The finality of her tone seemed to serve as a punctuation mark to the conversation. Dolly got the message and finally softened.

'At least you've got a nice break to look forward to.' She plucked an invitation from its place on Pearl's mantelpiece. It featured an aerial photograph of a country manor house nestled in stunning grounds. Dolly gave the card an approving nod. 'Very tasteful,' she said, eyeing the silver lettering against its stylish dove-grey background before checking the back of it. 'Thompson's of Faversham,' she noted. 'Nice work. They've done Mount Ephraim proud with this. It's a beautiful venue,' she said, 'for a special person.' She looked over at Pearl as she suddenly recalled, 'Poor Amy had a lot to overcome as a child, didn't she? Can't have been easy losing her mum as she did, only for her dad to fall under the spell of Madame Meadows.'

'The Stepmonster,' said Pearl. 'That's what Amy used to call her.'

'And I'm not surprised. Barbara Meadows squeezed herself into Geoffrey's life like an octopus into a bottle.'

'Yes,' said Pearl, pained by the thought. 'She completely displaced Amy.'

Both women reflected on this for a moment before Dolly remarked, 'She must have been so unhappy. Perhaps that's why she always looked so . . . otherworldly?' She thought for a moment then added, 'As though she was trying to . . . absent herself from life.'

'She certainly always hankered after getting away from Whitstable,' Pearl commented. 'I missed her when she left, but now she's back. To get married,' she added pointedly. 'And I, for one, am very grateful for my invitation.' She plucked the card from Dolly's hand then picked up her travel bag, moved to the door and threw a glance back to where her two tabby cats lay sprawled on the sofa. 'You will look after Pilchard and Sprat for me?'

'Of course,' said Dolly. 'I'm Cat Woman of Whitstable,' she purred. 'They'll be in safe hands with me – as will the restaurant.'

'No need to worry about that,' said Pearl, grateful that her young chef, Dean Samson, could more than cope in her absence. 'Charlie can cover some shifts if needed.'

'As can I,' Dolly insisted.

Pearl smiled, aware that while her mother was no cook, Dolly Nolan's spirited presence front-of-house was always a boon at The Whitstable Pearl – unless she had to talk about the town's most famous delicacy – oysters – which she despised.

'In any case,' Dolly went on, 'you'll only be gone for the weekend. Back on Monday?'

Pearl nodded. 'Right.'

She moved towards the front door then eyed her mother, asking hesitantly: 'Did you . . . really mean what you said?'

'About?'

'Me getting married?'

Dolly looked uncomfortable and carefully gathered her thoughts. 'Look,' she began, 'in my day, you got wed because you needed a bit of stability before starting a family. You already have a family – unless, of course, you're thinking of—'

'I'm not,' said Pearl firmly.

'Then you won't be needing a spare room.' Dolly smiled again – triumphantly this time. Pearl decided to let the matter drop. Instead, she leaned forward to kiss her mother before finally heading to the front door.

Once outside, Pearl hurried over to her Fiat, which was parked nearby on Island Wall, a long street that ran parallel to Whitstable's coastline. A row of seagulls perched on the roofs across the road appeared to observe Pearl carefully as she placed her travel bag in the boot; once they were sure there were no food scraps forthcoming, they lost interest and returned to basking in the pale sunlight. Pearl got into her car and settled Dolly's wedding gift carefully on the passenger seat beside her. Opening the driver's-side window, she saw her mother was already waving from the doorstep. 'Have fun!'

Dolly blew a kiss at her daughter and Pearl called back: 'Don't worry, I will!' Then Pearl put the Fiat firmly in gear and drove off, leaving Dolly gazing after her, confident that her daughter was about to enjoy a well-earned, peaceful break.

CHAPTER TWO

Ten minutes after leaving home, Pearl found herself in a heavy flow of traffic on the dual carriageway heading in the direction of London. Putting her foot hard on the accelerator, she recognised she was not only responding to the general road speed but to the faster pace of life that existed beyond Whitstable. Pearl's hometown on the North Kent coast had been something of a backwater, most famous for its oysters and a fishing industry that had existed since Roman times, with the estuary waters providing the perfect shallow mix of salt and fresh water in which the molluscs thrived. At the start of the twentieth century, during the 'glory days' of oyster fishing, more than a hundred boats had been involved in local dredging, and oysters had been so plentiful they had been considered not an expensive delicacy but the mere cheap padding of a steak and oyster pie. Now, for the most part, Whitstable's famous native oyster had been replaced by its larger grey-shelled competitor, the

Pacific rock oyster, which could be eaten all year round and was therefore now farmed, not fished, in industrial proportions on a proliferation of metal trestles which stretched out for some distance along the foreshore to become visible at low tide as the estuary waters receded.

The rock oyster was also now considered to be an invasive species as it had escaped its local containment to spread along the Kent coastline at such a rate that it threatened other sea life. Local fishermen talked of rock oysters weighing more than two kilos – monsters taking over the local marine ecology – and environmental groups were working hard with volunteers to destroy the species, likening the farming of rock oysters for profit to growing Japanese knotweed in polytunnels. In other coastal areas, a similar programme of removal had been put in place, not least because the razor-sharp shells of the Pacific rock oysters, which sat vertically rather than horizontally on the sea bed, were sharp enough to penetrate the soles of rubber boots and injure the feet of sailors jumping out of their boats at low tide.

There were parallels between the threat from the rock oyster and Whitstable's other non-native 'invasive species': the DFL – the acronym locals used for the 'down from Londoners' – who were snapping up second homes for themselves in what they considered to be a quaint little fishing town less than an hour's drive from south London. They had pushed up property prices so that a whole generation of young adults could no longer afford to remain in their hometown. Charlie was one. He had first moved into student accommodation in Canterbury while studying graphics at the university, but he now seemed permanently settled there, secure in the knowledge that he would be unable to manage the rent on even the smallest Whitstable apartment. To Pearl's chagrin, her son had now made his home in a university city filled with tourists, bars and chain stores – a contrast to all he had ever known in Whitstable. The fact that Charlie had become a city boy continued to unsettle Pearl, whose own haven remained the estuary coastline which was now fast receding out of her driver's-side window.

The sea was in Pearl's DNA, gifted to her by her fisherman father, and his before him, from a bloodline of men whose harvests were gathered from the seabed itself. The estuary waters coursed through Pearl's veins – ebbing and flowing with the beat of her heart – so much so that even following the traffic on its way to London made her slightly uneasy. Relief finally appeared in the form of a road sign which offered an exit just before those for the creek-side haunts of Faversham and Oare. Pearl moved into the slow lane destined for local traffic and followed a signpost for the hamlet of Fostall.

Bordered by orchards and farmland, the winding road was in fact little more than a country lane, and it was a welcome contrast to the busy dual carriageway as it carried Pearl uphill through glades of overhanging trees until another sign came into view, this time informing her that she was nearing the village of Hernhill – twinned with the French town of Vis en Artois. From a landscape of rolling farmland, a tractor appeared, which hindered Pearl's progress but allowed her time to appreciate the pretty cottages that lined the road. The tractor slowed to a halt, forcing Pearl to do the same just in front of The Red Lion, a centuries-old inn that looked out on to a village green where an ancient oak tree stood guard over the old church of St Michael's.

As the tractor waited to turn into a nearby farm, Pearl stared across at the pub's half-timbered exterior, graced with colourful window boxes and the date, 1364, above the door. A chalkboard menu was displayed outside, which Pearl took the opportunity to investigate as the tractor continued to block her path. It soon became clear that the old country inn had long since exchanged 'pub grub' for a more sophisticated bill of fare which included starters of crispy salt and pepper squid, Chinese five spice duck rillettes, and a *chevre* cheese cheesecake on walnut sable. Vegans were catered for with a Buddha bowl salad of mixed grains, nuts and spiced corn, and a vegetable risotto with a garlic-oil confit. Within the Pub Classics section, even the beef pie was 'handmade', and there was a selection of chef-inspired desserts and an extensive cheeseboard that included quince jelly. Seated at tables shaded from hazy sunshine by parasols were a mixture of locals and visitors – the latter easily identified by the photographs they were taking, not only of the pub's good food but of an old set of stocks that stood near the door.

Pearl glanced across to the village green, which on one side was home to four pretty cottages built on a site which centuries ago had housed the old vicarage and a tithe barn. But as she considered the medieval church, she found herself reflecting on Dolly's comments about her engagement to McGuire. While she had so often been a guest, if not bridesmaid, at the weddings of her friends, she had never walked down a church aisle as a bride. It was true her independent spirit had a lot to do with that, and the fact that for two decades Pearl's son, Charlie, had remained the most important man in her life. But then she had been brought into contact – and conflict – with Mike McGuire, a Met CID detective seconded temporarily to Kent to work out of Canterbury, and fate had ensured that Pearl and McGuire had crossed paths. McGuire's blonde good looks contrasted with Pearl's dark beauty, and yet the old cliché of opposites attracting had proved to be accurate. The pair were yin and yang – even in the way they approached a case. Pearl relied on her instincts to solve the crimes that came her way at Nolan's – the small detective agency she had started up in part to assuage her empty-nest syndrome – while McGuire preferred formal procedure to satisfy the demands of the CPS. He and Pearl were distinct but ever connected – two sides of the same coin – even as partners in crime.

Although McGuire wasn't exactly a closed book, he played his cards close to his chest, which meant Pearl had learned little about his life before his move to Kent.

If McGuire preferred to keep his past undisclosed, so did Pearl. The complexity of crime had brought them together, but it was McGuire's proposal, posed as a simple question on Whitstable's beach at full tide, that had finally moved their relationship on. In that instant, all Pearl had been aware of was the look in McGuire's blue eyes that matched the colour of the sea that hot summer afternoon, and his need for certainty and assurance, which she had given in a single word – 'yes'.

Since then, time had moved on, and Dolly was now posing the questions Pearl had asked herself. What was it that she had actually agreed to that day? To becoming Mrs Mike McGuire, shedding her name and her own identity as Pearl Nolan while giving up the home in which she had brought up her son – a home filled with decades of memories? Staring across at St Michael's Church, she realised that a walk down an aisle also constituted a leap of faith – as it clearly did for her old friend, Amy Young, who had remained single for as long as Pearl had. Would the two friends' faith in their new loves – and lives – prove justified? Before Pearl found an answer, a loud horn sounded behind her, and in her rear-view mirror she caught sight of a disgruntled driver indicating the clear path ahead of her as the tractor turned off the road. Pearl set her Fiat back in gear, relieved to be moving on – and leaving behind a trail of anxious thoughts.

It wasn't long before the entrance to Mount Ephraim

came into view, marked by a pair of imposing wrought-iron gates decorated with the entwined letters that formed the initials of the family members who had occupied the estate for three centuries. At the end of a serpentine driveway stood the elegant two-storey red-brick manor house, but before Pearl had a chance to properly take in her surroundings, a figure appeared. A young woman with cropped red hair, like burnished gold in the bright sunlight, was standing at the main pillared entrance – perhaps having seen the Fiat turn into the driveway. Pearl parked on the gravel forecourt while the young woman remained quite still, as though standing to attention, giving Pearl the impression she might be a member of staff. Finally, she approached, and as she did so, she seemed vaguely familiar to Pearl – a ghost from the past.

'Good to see you, Pearl,' she said with a warm smile.

Taken aback, Pearl was unsure if her mind was playing tricks on her. 'Emma?' she asked. 'Is it really you?'

The young woman nodded. 'It's been a while, hasn't it?'

Pearl quickly took stock. 'Ten years, or more,' she recalled. 'I hardly recognised you – which is not to say you look—'

'Older?'

'Different,' said Pearl. 'Your long blonde hair?'

'Long gone,' smiled the young woman. 'A new style for a new life.' As Pearl opened the boot of her car, Emma reached forward to take Pearl's travel bag. 'Here, let me . . .' But at Pearl's hesitation, she explained. 'It's okay. It's my job. I work here, but when I saw your name on the list of guests, I asked Amy to leave it as a surprise.'

Pearl smiled at the thought. 'It's certainly that,' she said as she allowed Emma to take hold of her bag. 'How long have you been here?'

'Eighteen months. I manage the accommodation and catering, and my partner, Ryan, helps with the gardens.' She glanced around. 'It's idyllic, isn't it?'

Pearl turned around to take in her immediate surroundings: an expansive central lawn with a circular fountain and two magnificent trees partially obscuring the view of what appeared to be a cricket pitch with a white pavilion a few hundred metres from the house. Turning back to Emma, Pearl smiled. 'Was it too much to expect that you might have stayed working for me at The Whitstable Pearl?'

'It was good of you to take me on in the first place,' said Emma. 'I was a juvenile delinquent in those days. A bolshie teenage kitchen hand.'

'At first, maybe,' said Pearl, 'but you were always a natural chef, Emma. I could tell that from the way you made every dish your own.'

'Even though they weren't always a success?'

'Some people need a rule book. Others learn by trial and error.'

'Like you?'

Pearl shrugged. 'Maybe. But I didn't mind you making a few mistakes in the kitchen as long as my customers didn't have to eat them.' She smiled again and added sincerely: 'We missed you after you left.'

'Really?' Emma asked with surprise.

Pearl nodded. 'We still have some of your postcards on the noticeboard in the office. All those glamorous places around the Med? It looked like you were living the high life.'

Emma smiled. 'I took a summer job cooking aboard a yacht.'

'How was it?'

'Hot – and hard work. But it was good experience and I put everything that I learned from you into practice. When the season ended, I took a job at a little restaurant in the hills around Antibes. Then I studied everything I could about French cuisine. It's stood me in good stead.'

'I bet,' said Pearl, impressed. 'I'm sure you could teach me a thing or two now.'

The women shared a smile before Pearl looked back at the house. Emma indicated a flight of stone steps leading to a balustraded terrace surrounding a wing of the old house.

'Is this where I'm staying?' asked Pearl.

Emma nodded. 'It's known as the garden wing and was built later than the rest of the main house, which connects to it. Most of the guests will be staying here – but some will be based in the west wing.' She nodded to the other section of the house across the terrace.

'And . . . is everyone here?'

Emma shook her head. 'Only two other guests so far,' she explained. 'Friends of Amy's: Tess and James.

They've just gone into Faversham. James is a playwright and Tess is an actress, so they wanted to take a look at the local theatre – the Arden. Amy has a few things to sort out with the florist and the celebrant, and Guy's in town too – soon he'll be picking up some more guests from the station. You can take your time and get settled before everyone comes back.'

Pearl followed Emma up the steps and said, 'I can't believe you've been here for so long and you haven't once come and eaten at The Whitstable Pearl.'

'You're always fully booked,' said Emma. 'Besides,' she added, 'we've had our hands full here. Apart from helping with the grounds, Ryan's always busy with odd jobs. You wouldn't believe how much there is to maintain.' She paused. 'It's strange, but . . . it's sometimes easy to forget that there's another world beyond here.' She considered this for a moment before she explained, 'The owners are away at the moment on a cruise. The house and estate have belonged to the same family for hundreds of years and amazingly there are only two gardeners, but the family are very hands-on with the estate's upkeep. It's their home, after all.'

'And yours now too?'

Emma nodded. 'Ryan and I have an apartment near the tea terrace.'

A bell tolled the hour and Emma smiled. 'That's the old clock tower. Thankfully, I've got used to the chiming now.'

Arriving on the terrace, Pearl noted how it wrapped

around the end of the garden wing. An antique wrought-iron table and chairs were situated at the best vantage point, offering a view of the central lawn and a series of neatly clipped yew hedges which enclosed some of the gardens. Following Emma to the door, Pearl saw that a courtyard in a basement area remained in shade, bordered by dust-covered windows that peered blindly from the building, unable to view the magnificent grandiflora magnolia blossom that shrouded the upper terrace.

'What's down there?' Pearl asked, curious.

'The old service wing,' Emma explained as she produced a set of keys from her pocket. 'It's disused now, apart from storage, but once upon a time it would have been the kitchen.'

'Shrouded in darkness . . .' mused Pearl, noting how little sunlight reached the area, but in the next instant Emma opened the door to the garden wing to reveal a bright welcoming hallway with parquet flooring. The shelves of a long wooden dresser housed a large selection of books as well as several vintage port bottles and what looked like a couple of grouse feathers. Setting down Pearl's bag, Emma opened a door to a cosy drawing room with an antique desk, sofa and a pair of comfortable-looking armchairs. Windows offered different views of the terrace: one looking straight out at the wrought-iron table and chairs while the other looked back on the magnolia blossom.

'The sitting room's through here,' Emma said, moving back into the hall and on to an elegant room, its own dual aspect looking out onto the central lawn in one direction and further grounds in the other. Noting the enormous stone fireplace, Pearl commented, 'I'm sure I could fit the entire ground floor of Seaspray Cottage in here.'

Emma smiled. 'Wait till you see the kitchen and dining room.'

She led Pearl along a corridor to an open door, and Pearl caught her breath at the sight of an enormous kitchen and dining room, its table set with a dozen chairs.

'An Aga *and* a cooker,' Pearl noted, before putting her head around another door to find a well-equipped scullery. She looked back at Emma. 'What I wouldn't give to have this space at The Whitstable Pearl.'

'Well, there'll be no need for you to cook this weekend,' Emma replied. 'I'm your chef, and if the weather holds we'll be eating outside on the terrace this evening. But I'll prepare everything in the west wing to give you all some privacy.'

Glancing around, Pearl's attention was drawn to an imposing iron door at the side of the Aga. She looked back at Emma, who shrugged. 'An old strongroom,' she explained. 'No longer used – just another bit of history that comes with the house – like that.' She pointed above the door to an antique bell system for summoning staff, then she gestured towards the other side of the room, saying, 'Those two double doors beyond the dining table lead to the games room. Come on, I'll show you.'

Again she led the way, this time opening the doors to an enormous room dominated by a full-sized billiard table overhung by a frame of lamps. A long sofa lined a wall, together with some well-stocked bookcases and a large painting of a ship, the SS Ruahine, a reminder for Pearl that the owners of the estate had been a shipping family. An antique scoreboard also hung on a wall near a bank of tall windows. A piano stood at the far end of the room. 'Do you play?' asked Emma.

Pearl shook her head. 'Not a note,' she said. 'But my snooker's not bad.' She smiled and, for a moment, allowed herself to imagine playing a game with McGuire – if he had only been able to spend the weekend with her.

Emma noted Pearl's thoughtful reaction and went on. 'How are Dolly and Charlie?'

'Both fine,' said Pearl, recognising the years that stood between herself and the formerly troubled girl who had once worked in her kitchen but who was now managing such an impressive establishment.

'We've actually crossed the threshold into the original house,' said Emma, 'and the far door near the piano leads into it but it's kept locked most of the time, so if we head back into the hallway I'll show you to your room upstairs.'

Pearl followed Emma as they climbed a wooden staircase to an upper corridor. On the right-hand side, several doors faced a large window which looked out on to the opposite section of the house.

'The west wing?' said Pearl.

Emma nodded. 'There are six bedrooms in this part of the house. Amy is in the main suite.' She nodded to the first two doors they encountered. 'Tess and James are next door in the blue room.' She then indicated the open door to another room which Pearl could see was tastefully decorated in dove-grey tones. 'Ingrid, Amy's agent, will take that room, and'—she moved on to the fifth door—'Amy chose this one for you.'

Throwing open the door, Emma revealed a charming room decorated in a muted pink shade. 'I think it has the best views,' she added, gesturing towards the room's two windows.

'Amy's quite right,' said Pearl. 'I love it.' Looking back at Emma, she noted, 'But you've . . . mentioned only four bedrooms?'

'That's right.' Emma nodded. 'There's a shower room at the end of the corridor and a bathroom next to this, and there are two more bedrooms through the door at the end of the corridor. They're actually situated above the games room.'

Pearl took stock of this. 'And you said that some guests are staying in the west wing?'

Emma smiled. 'It's tradition for the groom to spend the night before the ceremony in the Sir Edwyn Suite, so Guy's there and Amy will join him after the wedding. The west wing is now bed-and-breakfast accommodation but it used to be the old servants' quarters, so the rooms are all named accordingly. Guy's sister, Sarah, and her husband, Toby, will have the Cook's Room, and another friend of Amy's will take the Gamekeeper's.' She handed Pearl a set of keys. 'I'll leave you to settle in, Pearl, but

28

would you like me to bring you a drink and a sandwich?'

Pearl shook her head. 'I'm fine, Emma. But I'm ashamed to say I haven't actually visited the gardens here at Mount Ephraim since I was a child, so I wouldn't mind taking a short walk and getting reacquainted with them.'

'Of course.' Emma reached across to the dressing table. 'Here's a map.' She handed it to Pearl and said, 'You'll soon get your bearings using this. If you take the steps down from the terrace, you'll find a path that leads to the Japanese rock garden on your left and the rose terraces to your right. Below that are two other grass levels with a tennis court at one end and the wedding pavilion at the other – that's where tomorrow's ceremony will take place.' She smiled and nodded her head towards one of Pearl's windows. 'The lowest terrace leads down to the edge of the lake.' She indicated this on the map and Pearl suddenly caught the fragrance of Emma's perfume – something familiar and aromatic which Pearl couldn't quite identify but which she associated with North African countries like Tunisia and Morocco – Neroli, perhaps, she thought. Oblivious to Pearl's distracted expression, Emma continued to trace a route on the map then looked back at her. 'It's quite a back garden, isn't it?'

'It certainly is,' Pearl agreed, 'and a perfect setting for a wedding.'

'You're right. I have a feeling this is going to be a very special weekend.' For a moment Emma seemed to reflect on this before she finally moved to the door. 'I'm sure everyone will be back soon, but in the meantime make

CHAPTER THREE

After unpacking, Pearl changed into walking shoes and headed out to explore the gardens. Taking the flight of steps leading down from the terrace, she paused for a moment, noticing a cavernous space below it; a recessed porch half-concealed by the blossom-laden branches of the grandiflora magnolia. The space beckoned invitingly to Pearl, and, stepping inside, she found a door which she assumed must lead to the old storage area Emma had mentioned. Four cobweb-covered panels of glass offered only a glimpse into what looked like a dark, narrow corridor and a series of rooms that seemed to lead off it on the right-hand side. Staring around the porch, Pearl saw that its plaster ceiling and walls had seen better days. In fact, in stark contrast to the rest of the wing, the area seemed abandoned – a fact that piqued Pearl's curiosity. As she reached for the door handle, she was reminded of a painting which hung in the Beaney Museum in Canterbury, a portrait by Harriet Halhed, *The Little Girl at the Door.* The painting showed a young girl, dressed in a black hat, winter coat and polished boots, her hands clenched around the brass doorknob of an imposing grey door as she looked back towards the viewer, unsure perhaps of what, or whom, she might find on the other side. Down through the years, the image had intrigued Pearl, not least because the door in the painting remained forever closed. Countless times throughout Pearl's childhood she had imagined what the girl might have encountered if it were to open. Now, she thought how much she resembled the young girl in Halhed's study, forever trying to open the closed door, forever needing to solve the unsolved mystery . . .

Pearl tried the handle but found it locked. Turning away from the cobwebs, she headed out through the overhanging magnolia branches into the daylight and Mount Ephraim's grounds.

As Emma had described, a path appeared beyond the steps – an avenue bordered by tall yew hedges on either side. At its foot, a stone bench offered a peaceful place for contemplation while Pearl noted on her map that a series of rose terraces were laid out beyond the yew hedges. A bell tolled, and Pearl checked her watch, recognising it was again sounding the hour. Heading down the path, she found it littered with pinecones stripped of seeds by squirrels. Summer had now fully taken hold, and the memory of a harsh winter had fast receded with the sight and scent of so many new blossoms. Pearl hardly ever walked in the countryside – the beach was her usual retreat for solitary thought, and her own small garden backed on to Whitstable's prom, offering a coastal view that constantly changed with the weather. A beach hut in her garden, set on a handkerchief of lawn, had become her agency office in which clients discussed the cases they needed investigating. It was to Pearl they came to confirm or erase suspicions concerning spouses; to run checks on employees; to seek missing relatives; and to investigate thefts and other crimes – even murder. A psychologist might have characterised Pearl's love of order, and her need to find solutions and tidy up all loose ends, as a counterbalance to a childhood which, for the most part, had been carefree and unrestrictive. It was true that, twenty-odd years ago, Pearl had thrived within the framework offered by her basic police training, but during her probationary period she had also shown that she was someone who engaged well with the public and displayed a sharp, instinctive understanding of people in general. It was this skill, above all, that had singled her out as a potential candidate for criminal investigation, until a positive reading on a pregnancy test had prompted her resignation. Dolly quietly celebrated this turn of events, infinitely more comfortable with the idea of her daughter as a single mum than a 'lackey of the State'.

'Sometimes dreams are best left as that,' Dolly had said at the time, but Pearl had revisited her old dreams to start up Nolan's Detective Agency – and that, in turn, had shifted fate by putting Pearl together with McGuire.

Perhaps, she thought now, it was fate that had determined their relationship – as it had also done with her old friend, Amy Young. Their alliance had coincided with a troubled period for Amy, following her mother's death. Back then, Pearl had failed to fully appreciate how traumatic that loss had been for teenaged Amy, though she had thought about it since – and she found herself reflecting on it now. In fact, it seemed to Pearl that as a girl, Amy had been set adrift and was only now returning to a safe haven, on the eve of her wedding, in a magical setting.

Heading beyond the stone bench, Pearl became aware of the gentle sound of trickling water flowing from what she identified on her map as a series of cascading pools that formed a feature of the Japanese rock garden. The banks were lined with decorative plants and trees – ferns, lupins and colourful shrubs – and punctuated by a series of stone lanterns which also adorned a curved stone bridge that appeared like a feature from a Blue Willow pattern. Pearl hurried on to the bridge and observed the cascading pools opening to form a wider stream beneath her. It was a peaceful spot, but romantic too, and one that Pearl imagined had been used as the backdrop for numerous wedding photos. She paused on the bridge and took a deep breath before the sound of her ringing mobile phone broke into the sense of calm. Answering it quickly, she heard McGuire's voice on the line.

'Are you there yet?'

'I am,' she replied. 'Just getting my bearings. Is everything okay?'

At that moment, McGuire was sitting down on a bench in Canterbury's Dane John Gardens, having ordered a bite from a little South American eatery that served food from what had once been an old tea hut. With the gardens situated on the other side of the city wall from Canterbury Police Station, McGuire usually found it a suitable spot to cut off from work, if only for a hastily snatched lunch break. He paused thoughtfully before he replied: 'Nothing's okay,' he said, 'because I'm going to miss you.'

Pearl smiled. 'You mean, you're not missing me already?' She leaned across the bridge and reminded him, 'You could have come too if you'd only asked for some time off.'

'Too short notice,' said McGuire. 'I couldn't get out of this weekend shift. Staff shortages—'

'As usual,' sighed Pearl.

'Yeah,' McGuire agreed as he sipped his coffee. 'But I thought most people planned big weddings months in advance?'

'I guess so,' Pearl replied, 'but then my old friend, Amy, isn't "most people". And the wedding, as such, isn't big – just the venue. She seems to have had an offer she couldn't refuse.'

'The stately home, you mean?' McGuire took his tablet from his pocket and switched it on.

'It's a country house,' Pearl explained, 'albeit a grand one. Amy happens to know the owners and they've let her have the place for the weekend.'

'*Very* grand.'

'Sorry?'

'I'm just looking at it now,' explained McGuire as he scrolled through photos on a website. 'It mentions eight hundred acres here.'

'That's the whole estate,' said Pearl. 'There are actually ten acres of gardens – and they're very beautiful too.'

'Exactly how many are you going to be?'

'Nine guests, the bride and groom – and an estate manager.'

'Twelve?'

'If you'd managed to wangle some leave it could have been thirteen.'

'Unlucky for some.'

'Only if you're as suspicious as Mum,' said Pearl, recalling the traditional wedding rhyme for brides. 'I was just thinking about an old saying she reminded me of this morning.'

McGuire hesitated as a kitchen hand brought a dish of empanadas to his table, then asked, 'Absence makes the heart grow fonder?'

Pearl smiled. 'There again, familiarity breeds contempt?'

'Is that why you've left me?'

'I'll only be gone for a couple of days.' She paused. 'But I wish you could be here right now. It's very special.'

'Tell me,' he said. 'Paint a picture for me.'

'Well,' Pearl crossed the bridge and moved on. 'Right now, I'm looking at a lake. It's straight in front of me.'

'Careful!'

She smiled and looked out across the water. 'There are plenty of ducks and flag irises on the banks, a magnificent willow tree one side . . . and on the other, a little wooden shack.'

'Shack?'

Pearl frowned. 'Maybe it's a boathouse. I can see a lifesaver attached to the wall.' She rounded the lake and approached it. 'If only you were here . . .' she began.

'Yes?' said McGuire in anticipation.

Pearl smiled. 'You could be fishing.'

McGuire almost choked on his lunch. 'I've never been fishing in my life.'

'It's never too late to start! I could teach you. We'll go out in my dinghy.'

As a landlubber, McGuire usually did his best to avoid sailing trips with Pearl, but he said, 'Maybe one day.'

Silence.

'Pearl?'

'Hold on a sec.' Having moved closer to the shack, Pearl had noticed a series of hosepipes leading down into the water. The door to the shack was padlocked, but through a missing panel in its wooden exterior, she could spy inside using the torch on her smartphone. 'Ah,' she said finally, spotting the hosepipe ends attached to an electric pump that was whirring softly. 'This is some kind of pump house. There must be a system that takes a supply of water from the lake to feed the pools of the rock garden.' She stared out across the water then quickly back into the shack; in a far corner were two small, upended

ULIE WASSMER
boats, along with a supply of chicken wire, boxes of fish food – and a smell of damp.

'Pearl?' repeated McGuire as she fell silent again.

She pulled away from the broken panel to answer him, but as she did so she suddenly caught sight of a flash of yellow moving quickly on the bank. She squinted against the sunlight, unsure now if she had imagined it or perhaps witnessed only the branches of a false acacia tree disturbed by the sudden breeze, its lime-coloured leaves still shimmering in the summer air.

'Pearl? You still there?'

'Yes,' she finally answered. 'But—' She broke off and murmured to herself, 'perhaps someone else is too.'

'What?' said McGuire, struggling to hear properly.

'Don't worry,' she replied. 'I'll call you back in a while, but in the meantime . . . keep on missing me.'

With that, she ended the call and McGuire found himself staring down at the image on his tablet, a website photo of a happy bride and groom in the grounds of Mount Ephraim. The image slowly faded – along with his tablet's battery.

Returning her smartphone to her pocket, Pearl hurried on beyond the acacia to check out the bank which rose in a steep slope away from the lake. Reaching its summit, she found she was staring across a small wood – an arboretum occupying a raised mound with views to the unmistakable form of St Michael's Church at Hernhill in the far distance. Behind her, closer to the house,

lay something which was referred to on her map as a
Miz Maze – a labyrinth formed not of hedges but tall
flowering plants – based on a circular design that had
once been used by medieval monks when walking in
meditational prayer.

Staring back around her, Pearl could see nothing
more than the acers, gums and birches spread before her.
Thinking that perhaps she was alone after all, she began
to head back to the house and was approaching a bank
of tall trees when a chill came to the air. The branches of
old oaks began swaying in the breeze and a loud shrill
noise suddenly cut through the silence. She moved to take
another step forward, but the raucous squawk of rooks
caused her to halt in her tracks. Looking up, Pearl spotted
a few old nests still perched high up in branches from
which the birds' young would surely have long flown. But
the din continued – not the usual calling that took place at
roosting time, but a strange raw cry, almost human in tone.
A cry of alarm, as if the creatures were issuing a warning
to leave their territory. The call was a stark contrast to the
gentle birdsong in the Japanese rock garden; distinct and
piercing, it ceased only as Pearl hurried on, away from the
rookery and down towards the lake, steadying her path
using a handrail constructed from chestnut poles.

The rail led down to yet another bridge. Not decorative
this time, but made of wood and wholly functional,
marking the entry of water into the lake from a spring
in an adjacent meadow. Along the swampy banks rose
a distinctive fetid smell, reminding Pearl of the skunk

cabbage with its strange odour and bright yellow pod-like blossoms that resembled something from a science-fiction movie. The odour was repulsive, like that of rotting flesh, but always an attractive perfume to the bees and butterflies that usually hovered in clouds among the plants. Pausing on the bridge, Pearl could see no such blooms but gave an inward shiver before she looked back at the rookery trees and finally crossed the wooden bridge, leaving behind the smell of decay. She mounted the opposite bank and encountered the terrace on which a hard tennis court stood, with the wedding pavilion at its far end. Without investigating it, she hurried on ahead to the Miz Maze and discovered at its threshold an isolated stone gateway with a wooden door within it. The breeze still held its chill as Pearl looked up to read the words carved into stone above the gate:

> *Keep your face always*
> *Towards the sunshine*
> *And the shadows will*
> *Fall behind you.*

The wooden door creaked in the breeze, and she stepped through it to find another motto carved on the other side:

> *Whichever way the wind doth blow*
> *Some soil is glad to have it so.*
> *So blow it east or blow it west*
> *The wind that blows is always best.*

The Miz Maze beckoned, bordered on either side by tall plants over two metres high: rudbeckia, its flower resembling a brown-eyed Susan, and the wildflower Pearl knew only as joe-pye weed. The latter matched its partner for height but distinguished itself with a pale lavender bloom swaying in the breeze. Pearl took a step forward, but before she had a chance to enter the maze, a loud 'ping' marked the arrival of a text on her phone. Checking it, she saw it wasn't from McGuire. Just four words:

Pearl, where are you?

Pearl recognised Amy's number and replied with some relief, *On my way!*

Turning her back on the maze, she headed back to the comfort of the house.

CHAPTER FOUR

'Sometimes I have to pinch myself to realise I'm back here. It's been such a long time.' Amy Young stood at one of the tall windows in the master bedroom of Mount Ephraim's garden wing, staring out at the grounds below before turning back to Pearl, who was sitting on the room's huge bed, trying not to spill coffee onto its satin coverlet. In that moment, it seemed to Pearl that something in Amy's expression had remained unchanged from the young girl she had befriended almost thirty years ago. Nevertheless, the years now lay between them, and the girl was now a woman. Amy's straight dark hair was styled in an elegant bob at her jawline, emphasising a slender swan-like neck. She wore little make-up, just a slick of pale pink lipstick which contrasted with a glowing tan.

Glancing around the room, Amy added, 'And I certainly never imagined that one day I'd be staying here on the eve of my wedding.' She shook her head and explained, 'Decades ago, I used to come to Mount Ephraim and help with the ponies. The old paddock is now a meadow planted with wildflowers, but years ago I used to muck out the stables pretending that the ponies belonged to me and that this was my family home.' She smiled at the thought. 'I think the family here knew it too, that I was a dreamer. They were kind and treated me like a surrogate child. But it was difficult,' she explained, 'after Mum died and Dad got together with—'

'Your Stepmonster?'

Amy seemed brought up short by the term. 'I used to call her that, didn't I?' she said. 'So unkind of me.'

'You had your reasons.'

Amy shook her head. 'It was a long time ago. I was jealous, insecure . . .'

'And grieving,' Pearl added. 'You were only thirteen and you'd just lost your mum.'

'But I'm all grown up now,' said Amy. 'And that's all in the past. In fact,' she continued brightly, 'since Dad died, Babs and I have got on rather well.'

'Babs?' echoed Pearl, surprised by the endearment.

'Yes,' Amy said. 'She's actually my last remaining relative – not by blood, I know, but she did legally adopt me when she and Dad married. And though she can still be as demanding as ever, she now has Simon to look after her.'

Seeing Pearl's curious expression, Amy explained, 'Simon Mullen. He's her companion – and an angel. He's Irish, and he worked as a trained nurse in Dublin, so

44

he's quite capable of keeping on top of Babs's medication. She's not exactly ill,' she added quickly, 'but she does have a number of ailments. Still, you know what they say: a creaking door hangs longest.' Her smile faded as she checked her watch. 'I hope their train isn't delayed. If it is, she won't be very happy.' Amy frowned and took a deep breath to dispel her anxiety before turning again to Pearl. 'I just know you're going to love Guy.' Her smile returned as she went on, 'It's an extraordinary thing, but I've actually been on my own since I left Kent – though that's not to say I haven't met some fascinating people and had some wonderful relationships with some lovely men, but . . . things just always seemed to peter out.'

'Like they did with Ian Soutar?'

Amy frowned. 'Ian, yes . . . we were together for some time, weren't we? But we were also very young.'

'First love?' asked Pearl.

'Perhaps,' said Amy enigmatically. She turned away and seemed to reflect on this for a moment. 'Maybe it was my fault things didn't work out. I've always liked my own space. Being alone, but not lonely. That's not to say I didn't hope to find someone special – to be . . . in the right relationship at last, and to experience what everyone else seems to have. Do you know what I'm trying to say?'

'Yes,' said Pearl, knowing exactly.

'My agent, Ingrid Davis, got a commission for me to write a magazine feature about Guy, but I can't say I had any expectations about it. I happened to be in Thailand at the time, writing about the elephants in Chiang Mai, and Guy had just returned after the London auction for the cargo.' Amy shrugged. 'It was just another job as far as I was concerned. I knew about the salvage operation because it was hot news in Thailand and Malaysia, but . . . well, I'd already made an assumption that Guy was a spoilt rich playboy. You know the type – out to prove himself with feats of bravado. He comes from a very wealthy background. His father was Frank Priddey, the banker. Frank made all his money in the States, where he married Guy's mother, Dorothy, a beautiful socialite. There's quite a history of rich young men trying to outdo the achievements of their successful fathers, isn't there?'

'Is that what Guy did?' asked Pearl.

Amy paused for a moment. 'No. He rebelled against his father, who disinherited him. The family home was lost and Guy's since made his own way in the world.' She smiled then went on. 'Guy had dual citizenship through his mother, and he served in the US Navy for a time. When he left, after failing a medical, he dropped out, bought a boat and used his diving knowledge to start up a good business in Phuket – trips around the islands for tourists. But he was already researching wrecks; there are quite a few in those waters – Dutch, mainly. I looked into it all before the interview and realised that Guy had pulled off something quite amazing, not least because he needed to negotiate with the Thai and Malaysian authorities, who were both trying to lay claim to the cargo.'

Amy gave another wistful smile. 'I was given an hour for the interview, Pearl, but it was as if time stood still. We ended up spending all afternoon together on the Chao Phraya River. Another adventure. I forgot all about the magazine commission and we connected in a way I've never done with anyone else.' She turned away from Pearl to stare out of the window again as if reliving that moment – seeing not the verdant grounds of an English country house but the famous Thai river. When she turned back again, the smile was still on her face. 'The French call it a *coup de foudre* – a thunderbolt? But really it was more like being struck by lightning. What I felt really shook me to my core. I absolutely knew that nothing could ever be the same again. Suddenly I knew who I was and who I could be – with the right person.' She came closer to Pearl. 'I know you understand what I mean. You're getting married too – to someone very special.'

Pearl nodded. 'Yes, McGuire *is* special,' she admitted, though she was becoming aware that she didn't quite share the intense focus of desire that Amy had been describing.

Amy sat down beside her friend. 'I realise I am springing this on you, Pearl, but there's something I'd like you to do for me. Would you mind saying a few words at the ceremony tomorrow?'

'Me?' asked Pearl, shocked by the request.

'I don't expect you to write anything at such short notice, but you were always the poetry buff at school, and I was sure you could come up with something appropriate. A few lines to quote? You've known me for so long.'

Pearl considered the expectant look in Amy's eyes – and finally smiled.

'Of course.'

'Thanks,' said Amy sincerely, her eyes scanning Pearl's face as she went on. 'It's been a long time since we've seen one another, but there are some people you meet in life who never leave you. Wherever I've gone, I've thought about you, Pearl. It was a special time . . . at that age . . . growing up together.'

Pearl understood. 'Formative years?'

Amy nodded. 'Exactly. I've never needed lots of friends. I've enjoyed my independence – and my friendships have always been defined by quality, not quantity.' She smiled. 'That's why there won't be too many of us this weekend, just a small group. To be honest, Guy and I probably wouldn't be having this ceremony at all if I hadn't been offered Mount Ephraim for the weekend. But it's a chance for me to get to know Guy's family; his sister, Sarah, and her husband, Toby, are coming. And my agent Ingrid, of course – she's like family to me after all the years she's represented me. Then there's Tess and James, if they ever get back from Faversham. And Ian, of course.'

'Ian?' asked Pearl.

'Ian Soutar,' said Amy. 'We were just talking about him.'

Pearl frowned, taken aback. 'You've . . . actually invited him to the wedding?'

'Why not?' asked Amy with surprise at Pearl's tone. 'Like you, he's been a big part of my life.'

'Maybe,' said Pearl, 'but he was in love with you.'

'I know,' said Amy, 'and I'm sure I felt the same at one time. But like I said, we were young and we both moved on. Ian met someone else, remember?'

Pearl nodded. 'Kate Parsons.'

'That's right.' Amy smiled but Pearl's frown remained in place as she said, 'They were engaged for some time, but I heard things didn't work out between them.'

'Ian told me,' said Amy thoughtfully. 'Such a shame. He really deserves someone special.'

Pearl paused before asking tentatively, 'And how does Guy feel about Ian coming?'

Amy looked back at her. 'He's absolutely fine about it,' she said quickly. 'Why shouldn't he be?' On Pearl's silence, Amy finally gave a long sigh. 'Pearl, it *is* possible to remain good friends with someone you once loved.'

'Is it?' asked Pearl softly while holding Amy's gaze.

Amy opened her mouth to respond but was interrupted by the sound of a vehicle drawing up on the gravel outside, and she quickly moved back to the window and waved to someone below. 'That's Guy now,' she said.

Pearl joined Amy at the window to see a Range Rover parked below. A tall man jumped out from the driver's side and looked straight up towards the bedroom window. Guy was dressed casually in a loose white shirt and jeans, his sleeves rolled back to his elbows exposing nut-brown forearms. Taking off his sunglasses, he smiled up at Amy, running his hands through hair the colour of a sandy beach. He opened a passenger door and offered a hand to a stout woman in her late sixties.

'And there's Babs,' said Amy, smiling down at her stepmother, who offered a regal wave before turning back to another passenger – a young man – who emerged in her wake juggling several bags and cases. 'And Simon,' Amy added. The young man stood patiently as Babs Meadows-Young appeared to admonish him, then he looked up and gave a thin smile to Amy. Meanwhile, on the other side of the vehicle, Guy was opening another door from which two other passengers emerged. 'That's my agent, Ingrid,' Amy explained, indicating a tall, stylish woman with long raven hair, power-dressed in an elegant black trouser suit with the strap of an executive laptop case slung over her shoulder. A fragile-looking blonde woman followed her out of the vehicle to be embraced by Guy. 'And Guy's sister, Sarah,' said Amy.

A heavily built man with iron-grey hair then alighted from the Range Rover, seemingly impatient as he waited for Sarah's attention while Guy continued to chat to her.

'Her husband?' asked Pearl.

Amy nodded. 'Yes, that's Toby.' She gave a wave to all the guests – which only Toby failed to reciprocate.

'Come on,' Amy said, 'I can't wait to introduce you.' She took Pearl's arm and they headed out of the room.

As Pearl and Amy were going down the staircase into the corridor, they heard a woman's strident voice booming from the hallway.

'Be careful with that case, Simon! I told you it holds a luxury perfume – Jean Patou – in a *glass* bottle.'

'I heard you the first time,' called the young man wearily.

'Babs,' said Amy, coming forward to give her step-mother a hug. Pearl hung back as Babs replied in a saccharine tone, 'Oh, so very kind of dear Guy to pick us up from the station!' She looked back as Guy entered the hallway behind her. 'If only I could have trusted Simon's driving,' she added, glancing now at Simon trailing in after her as he set down some heavy bags, 'we could have been here long before now.'

Simon heaved a sigh and pushed a pair of thick-lensed wire-framed glasses high on the bridge of his nose before running a hand through his curly black hair and picking up the bags again.

'You *can* trust my driving,' he said, trying to mask his frustration.

'Not with your condition,' Babs argued.

Simon looked at her. 'I'm not an invalid – I'm a diabetic.'

'Yes. And you could fall into a coma at the wheel.'

Simon met her gaze then looked at everyone else as he explained: 'I follow all the rules for driving, including monitoring my blood sugar regularly and keeping on top of my meds.' He pulled a pen from his top pocket then said to Babs, 'You know very well this is primed to give me the correct dose exactly when I need it – so what's the panic?'

'There's always a first,' Babs insisted. 'Better to be safe than sorry. After all,' she went on, 'my dear Amy wouldn't want to begin married life by having to arrange a funeral, would you?' She beamed at Amy, who stared apologetically at Simon. 'Thanks for looking after Babs,' she said. Simon managed a long-suffering smile. 'It's a pleasure,' he said politely.

'Looking after me?' cried Babs. 'I'm sure he's the reason my blood pressure has rocketed.' She now turned to Pearl and carefully appraised her before offering a powdered cheek to kiss. 'And how are you, Pearl, my dear? Still shucking oysters?'

Pearl smiled. 'They're still on the menu at my restaurant.'

'Fascinating,' said Ingrid, applying a fresh slick of lipstick. She wore a scarlet smile as she moved forward to introduce herself. 'Amy told me all about you – a restaurateur with a detective agency?'

'A sideline,' Pearl explained. 'Mainly local cases.'

Amy moved to Guy's side and explained. 'Pearl had some police training.'

'A cop in the midst,' announced Toby. He entered with his wife, who offered a pained look before embracing Amy. 'So good to see you.'

Guy turned to Pearl. 'You've a talent for crime?'

'For snooping,' said Babs with a pointed look. 'How's your mother, Pearl? Still a fish slapper?'

'Babs!' said Amy in embarrassment.

'It's okay.' Pearl smiled, unconcerned, before turning to explain to the other guests, 'The Fish Slappers were my mother's old dance troupe. They used to perform at the annual Whitstable Oyster Parade.'

'And memorably so,' Babs declared, 'but then Dolly always loved to make an exhibition of herself. As I recall, her costume consisted of a scallop-shelled bra and seaweed skirt.'

'Resurrected for the carnival only a few years ago,' said Pearl, failing to add that Dolly's skirt needed gusseting for the event while the scallop shells had to be replaced by a pair of oyster shells the size of dinner plates – sewn onto a flesh-coloured leotard.

'Everyone come through,' said Amy, leading the way into the dining room. Upon entering it, Babs immediately drew a breath.

'Oh, such a relief to be in elegant surroundings,' she exclaimed. 'This is going to be a wedding to remember.' She beamed again at Guy. 'And how lucky is my Amy to find such an attractive husband for herself; someone who I'm sure will take care of her in the manner she truly deserves.' She fluttered her eyelashes again, but Guy managed to escape her gaze, indicating the double doors beyond the dining table.

'Did I mention there's a games room?'

'Now you're talking,' said Toby, following Guy as he opened the doors to reveal the billiard table. 'Fancy a game later?' Guy asked Simon.

Before the young man could reply, Babs raised a hand. 'Whether he does or he doesn't, I don't want him anywhere near that table.'

'Why not?' asked Simon, wounded.

'Because clumsiness is your forte.' She stared across at

Guy. 'Hand him a cue and he'll have the baize off that in a flash.'

'I'm sure that won't be the case,' said Amy, offering Simon a warm smile which he returned.

'Actually, I play a mean game of pool,' he said in his own defence.

'Maybe,' Babs conceded. 'But billiards is a game for gentlemen.' She looked again at Guy – but it was his brother-in-law, Toby, who said under his breath, 'We may be a little short on those.'

'I'm sorry?' asked Babs, confused.

Toby ignored her question and nodded casually towards the antique card table. 'Anyone up for a few rounds of poker later?'

Before Amy could respond, Babs broke in with a warning. 'No games for you, dear,' she said. 'Nothing to cause too much excitement. We can't have you over-wrought on the big day – or me, for that matter.' She turned to Simon. 'You did remember to bring my little helpers?'

Ingrid frowned. 'Your what?'

Simon rooted in a bag and handed a packet to Babs, who announced: 'Valium, darling. I'm a slave to anxiety.'

Ingrid shrugged. 'I thought Prozac had taken over from that.'

'I don't get on with it,' said Babs, proudly.

'You never gave it a chance,' Simon muttered.

Before Babs could respond, Emma appeared at the threshold and signalled to Amy and Guy. Babs set her packet of Valium down on the table as Guy explained to the guests that Emma had taken their luggage to their rooms. He turned to Sarah and Toby. 'If you follow me, I'll show you where we're stationed in the next wing.'

Amy turned to Babs, Simon and Ingrid. 'And I'll take you up to your rooms here. Once everyone's comfortable, let's all meet back on the terrace for a drink.'

''Thought you'd never ask,' said Toby following Guy from the room.

'I could murder a gin and angostura,' said Babs.

Simon raised an admonishing finger. 'Not recommended,' he said softly, steering her towards the door.

'Medicinal!' she argued. 'A little alcohol thins the blood and certainly did no harm for Jeanne Calment.'

'Who?' asked Sarah.

'The world's oldest woman,' said Pearl.

'Indeed,' said Babs. 'A super centenarian. She was a hundred and twenty-two years old when she died and always swore by a drink every evening.' She gave Simon a sidelong look.

Simon pursed his lips and replied, 'I'm betting she didn't have your hiatus hernia.'

'You won't scare me,' said Babs. 'I have no intention of leaving this world before my time.' She frowned. 'And be *careful* with that vanity case!'

Simon gave a long-suffering sigh and clutched the case more tightly, together with the other bags, as they left the room. Pearl watched them go then looked back to see Emma emerging from the scullery with a tray of glasses and an ice bucket.

'Need some help?'

'You're here to relax and enjoy the wedding,' said Emma as she filled the bucket with ice.

'All the same,' said Pearl, 'it's difficult to do nothing when you're used to playing host.'

'I know – but you must try.' She gave Pearl a smile and took some napkins from a drawer. 'Did you enjoy your walk?'

Pearl nodded then wandered across to the window to look out. 'You're right. This place is idyllic.'

Emma said, 'It's been home to the same family for over three centuries, though the house was rebuilt in the late 1800s. Did you get to see all the grounds?'

'I only went as far as the lake,' Pearl admitted, 'then I made my way back up near the maze.' She watched Emma carefully rearranging some peonies in a glass vase on the dining table and setting Babs's pills on a smaller table near the doors to the games room, then she decided to broach something.

'I . . . thought I might have seen someone – your partner perhaps? Down near that shack by the lake?'

Emma looked back at her. 'The old pump house, you mean?' She shook her head. 'I don't think so.' Wiping her hands on her apron, she went on, 'The gardeners are off for a week and Ryan's been in Faversham all morning picking up some supplies.' Hearing a vehicle drawing up outside, she joined Pearl at the window and smiled. 'Looks like he's just got back.'

An open-topped jeep had driven up outside and a tall

man who looked to be in his early thirties was jumping down from it. Seeing Emma waving from the window, he waved back and took off the baseball cap he was wearing before nodding to Pearl, who noted he wore a brown check shirt and khaki shorts – not a flash of colour anywhere.

Emma smiled. 'I'd better give him a hand.'

Moving off, she left Pearl at the window, who watched as Emma appeared outside to join her partner and gave him a peck on the cheek. Together they began lifting shopping bags from the jeep and ferrying them towards the other wing – leaving Pearl with an unanswered question as she continued to stare out at the beautiful grounds of Mount Ephraim.

CHAPTER FIVE

L ater, after taking a shower, Pearl began to relax and feel at home – even within this grand setting. She looked through the small collection of clothes she had brought with her for the weekend. Not one for pricey fashion, her usual wardrobe consisted of vintage dresses nipped in at the waist to flatter her tall willowy frame, but considering the importance of the occasion, she had brought a pale lilac trouser suit to wear at the wedding ceremony, and for this evening she opted for an understated elegant blue dress. Weddings always presented such challenges for guests, with a need to strike a balance between making a suitable effort and not upstaging the bride. For followers of high fashion, there was also the possibility of arriving on the day wearing the same outfit as another guest, though Pearl had so far avoided such a faux pas due to her love of vintage clothes. Similarly, Dolly's own eccentric taste in clothes ensured that no one else ever wore the same outfit as her.

Pearl gave a thought to her mother as she checked her appearance in an antique mirror fixed to the wall. Perhaps if she had remained busy at the Whitstable Pearl, Dolly's words might not have left such an impression with her, raising questions about her future with McGuire. Compounded with this were further questions thrown up by Pearl's conversation with Amy, during which her old friend had described her extraordinary connection to Guy Priddey, the certainty of her feelings for him, and the natural assumption that Pearl must feel the same about McGuire. What Amy had described, however, was something quite distinct from Pearl's own relationship. Pearl and McGuire's coming together had not been a dramatic fusion of souls but a physical attraction that had grown over time into something deeper. What she felt for McGuire was complex – love, affection and mutual respect – the latter involving a fair degree of common purpose but also fuelled by an element of competition, of pitting their wits against one another as well as enjoying the satisfaction of triumphing together.

Finding McGuire had seemed to Pearl like finding a part of herself. It reminded her of a dream she sometimes had of coming across a room, in a house, which she had always known was there but had never been able to locate before. It was love but not obsession – and what Amy felt for Guy was something Pearl could only imagine – the need to be together at all times in order to feel complete, like two halves of a pantomime horse. As Pearl considered this, she reached for her travel bag and took out a small silk purse from which she selected a pair of natural pearl earrings – the first present McGuire had ever given her. Putting the earrings on, she studied her reflection in the mirror, noting how the pearls so perfectly matched the colour of her beautiful grey eyes in the pale afternoon light. Then she looked down at the engagement ring on her finger – a single diamond set in a platinum mount on a simple gold band – and turned it slightly before glancing out of the window. Watching the trees swaying in the breeze, lines from a half-forgotten poem suddenly came to her. Pearl picked up her smartphone and scrolled through search results in her browser until she found what she was looking for – wise words from the poet Khalil Gibran about the need to maintain independence within marriage:

> *Let there be spaces in your togetherness,*
> *And let the winds of the heavens dance between you.*
> *Love one another, but make not a bond of love . . .*

Pearl read the rest of the poem to herself, feeling its sentiment resonate strongly with her own hopes for her future with McGuire. On reaching its final line, she looked away from the words and out of the window once more. *'And the oak tree and the cypress grow not in each other's shadow.'* She knew she had found her reading for Amy's wedding.

After carefully transcribing the words of the poem, Pearl left her room, pausing for a moment as she considered the other rooms on the landing. Emma had explained how each bedroom had been selected for the guests. Guy, together with his sister, Sarah, and brother-in-law, Toby, were staying in the west wing with Ian Soutar, while Amy's theatre friends, Tess and James, and her agent, Ingrid, were with Pearl in the garden wing, along with Babs and her companion, Simon. The rooms of the latter two guests were on the top floor of the main house beyond the closed door at the end of the corridor. Pearl felt herself drawn towards it, recognising that, yet again, a closed door seemed almost as inviting to her as the one in her favourite painting.

She turned the handle and pushed. Unlike the pad-locked pump-house door, this one opened soundlessly to reveal a second corridor with a large bookcase filled with old volumes; Pearl thought some of them must surely be first editions. Facing the bookcase, two half-open doors revealed bedrooms. The first, decorated in a soft grey tone, was filled with the bags and vanity case that Simon had been struggling to carry for Babs. An array of make-up and cosmetics had been dumped on a dressing table. A crystal jug of water sat on Babs's bedside table next to several blister packs of pills and a romantic novel entitled *The Savage Lure*, its cover featuring a handsome young man with a falcon balanced on one arm and a buxom woman on the other.

Moving on, Pearl found the next room an orderly contrast to the first; nothing was out of place apart from Simon's jacket, which was hanging on the door of a fitted cupboard. For a second, Pearl experienced a sense of *déjà vu* linked to her dream in which she discovers a hidden room in a familiar home, but a sudden burst of laughter rang out from below, bringing her back to the moment. She looked out of the window to see Babs below, walking towards the house with Guy. Babs had changed into a long floral dress, which seemed to compete with the colourful herbaceous border, but Guy seemed relaxed, still dressed casually and uncompromisingly in a loose white muslin shirt, jeans and a pair of flip-flops. As they disappeared out of view, Pearl checked the time on her watch and realised she was late for drinks.

As she stepped out onto the garden wing's terrace, Pearl saw that Guy had exchanged Babs's company for Amy's. His fiancée stood close to his side, gazing up at him as he sipped from a champagne flute in his hand. Amy looked blissfully happy and beautiful in a dress comprised of a number of silk scarves while the gold sandals on her feet were tied with straps around her delicate ankles. Amy spotted Pearl on the terrace and welcomed her over.

'Pearl! Have you settled in?'

'Very well.'

Ingrid Davis moved forward with a smile. 'I must admit,' she began, 'I'm rather fascinated by your ... "sideline"?'

'The agency, you mean?' said Pearl. 'As I said, it's mainly local cases.'

Ingrid's arched eyebrows rose further and she toyed with a silver necklace at her throat. 'I have an image of you stalking errant husbands with a plate of oysters at the ready?'

Pearl took a champagne flute from the tray Emma offered as she replied, 'It's not only men who cheat on their spouses.'

'Quite right,' said Toby, having overheard as he returned from a walk in the grounds with his wife. 'Though it's usually we men who get the blame for everything.' He slapped his empty champagne flute onto Emma's tray and helped himself to a full one. Sarah looked pained – either from her husband's comment or the loud volume of his voice, Pearl couldn't be sure. She took a moment to study Toby. A film of perspiration covered his brow. His cheeks were ruddy, but beneath his puffy features Pearl decided a handsome man lay buried. Babs raised a finger. 'The fact that some marriages are marred by infidelity,' she began, 'does not preclude a fairy-tale ending for others.' She smiled, rather too sweetly, before concluding: 'Which is what I wish for you, dear Amy – and Guy, of course.' She took a deep breath of the countryside air, took a glass from Emma without even looking at her, and said, 'Isn't this heavenly?' She sighed before sipping her drink and surveying the grounds in front of her as the sunlight faded on the horizon.

'Yes,' said Simon before leaning close to whisper: 'but that champagne is going to play havoc with your hernia.'

Babs snapped her head to face him, her lips pursed as tight as a knitted buttonhole, and responded curtly, 'I am celebrating my dear daughter's wedding.'

Guy slipped his arm around Amy's slender waist and smiled. 'Which is not until tomorrow morning,' he said, checking his watch. 'Fifteen and a half hours from now, to be precise.'

'And I'm counting the minutes,' said Amy softly as she looked up at him.

'I'm sure you are,' commented Babs with another sweet smile. She turned back to Guy to add, 'Aren't we all?' Her eyes remained on Guy as she sipped her drink, turning from him only briefly to accept a green olive speared on a cocktail stick from Emma's tray. Still looking at Guy, Babs placed the olive between her lips and hoovered it into her mouth with a wet crunch. Emma moved on and offered a drink to Sarah, who shook her head and instead placed her empty glass on the tray. Toby accepted a refill but then leaned closer to Emma to say, 'I . . . don't s'pose there's anything stronger on offer?'

His wife gave him a reproachful look, but Emma asked, 'Would you prefer a cocktail?'

'Now you're talking.' He smiled. 'A screwdriver.' He lit a panatella cigar and blew smoke into the evening air.

Guy watched him carefully. 'Maybe you should pace yourself.' He nodded for Emma to move on while Toby ruefully watched the trail of smoke from his cigar snaking away in the breeze along with the chance of a stronger drink.

'Not stinting on the bar bill, are you, Guy?' he asked with a wry smile. 'I must admit, that's a trait that runs in the family.' Toby now eyed his wife and offered an innocent wink, but before anyone could comment further, heads turned at the sound of a car roaring up the driveway. A vintage convertible four-seater came to a halt on the gravel path, and from it a couple jumped out. Both in their thirties, they seemed to Pearl as if they stepped out of a different era. The woman wore a black cloche-style hat over her long auburn hair. Red satin trousers and a loose silk blouse hung on her slender frame. A thin trailing scarf with an Art Deco design was tied loosely at her throat, while her partner sported a long, waxed beard that perfectly matched the Edwardian style of his vintage herringbone suit. Hurrying up the steps to the terrace, the woman paused for a moment as her eyes met Amy's. She gave a guilty look before her face broke into a broad grin. '*So* sorry!' she exclaimed. 'I know we should have been back hours ago, but . . .'

'All my fault,' said her companion. 'We ended up seeing a comedy review at the Arden. I thought it'd be over far sooner.'

Amy's smile showed instant forgiveness and she kissed the pair. 'Don't worry,' she said. 'You're here now, so let me introduce you,' she turned to her other guests. 'Everyone, this is Tess Gulliver, a very talented actress, and her partner, James Jarrett.' She announced proudly, 'James is a playwright.'

'How very interesting,' beamed Babs, coming forward to eye James. 'I adore the theatre. Might I have seen any of your work?'

'Not unless you're into pub fringe,' said James wryly. 'But you might well get to see my latest before too long.' He winked while Tess explained, 'James has just finished writing an utterly brilliant play called . . . *Oblivion*. It's looking for a home in a good theatre.'

'*Oblivion*?' said Toby with a confused frown. 'Doesn't much sound like a barrel of laughs.'

Simon leaned forward and asked tentatively: 'Dystopian nightmare?'

James gave a smile. 'Of sorts. It comments on the cultural vacuum we all now face.'

Babs looked confused for a moment before enquiring, 'A . . . musical, by any chance?'

James went to reply, but someone else had just appeared on the terrace – a tall figure silhouetted against the fading light.

'Ian?' said Amy.

Voices quietened and the figure came forward. Pearl noted a taxi driving off out of the gates. Dressed formally in a smart blue suit, Ian Soutar eyed Guy's casual attire and decided to loosen his tie before setting down a small travel bag and briefcase. 'Sorry I'm so late,' he said, looking directly at Amy before addressing the other guests. 'I'm afraid I got stuck in the office. I'm just starting a new case.'

'Case?' asked Ingrid, intrigued.

Amy moved quickly to take Ian's arm, guiding him forward to join the other guests. 'For those of you who don't know, this is my old friend Ian Soutar. A barrister.'

She considered him proudly, and for a moment there was silence as everyone paused to witness Guy's reaction to the handsome man who was now on his fiancée's arm. Guy moved forward and held out his hand. 'Good to meet you,' he said warmly. The two men held eye contact in a silence that was finally broken by Emma announcing, 'The buffet supper is ready.'

'Wonderful,' sighed Ingrid. Leaning in to address Pearl, she confided, 'I could eat an orangutan.'

CHAPTER SIX

Darkness fell after the guests had enjoyed the excellent meal Emma had prepared, but the terrace was soon lit with fairy lights and a drop in temperature remedied by a patio heater. Having savoured *moules farcies* and a *plateau de fruits de mer*, Pearl recognised she might have been back at The Whitstable Pearl, although her hometown's coastline seemed even further away from this rural idyll as she gazed out at Mount Ephraim's manicured central lawn with its elegant fountain and beyond that, the white form of a cricket pavilion.

'Amazing food!' said Ingrid, sipping a cognac.

'Agreed.' James grinned and looked up at a starry sky. 'Even the weather's being kind to us.' Tess returned his smile and then addressed Amy and Guy. 'Are you two getting hitched on this terrace?'

Amy shook her head. 'In the grounds. There's a perfect setting on one of the lower terraces.' She turned to Pearl. 'Did you see it today on your walk?'

Pearl nodded and said, 'I noted where it was, but I was on the other side at the time – near the tennis court.'

'Tennis?' said James. 'Maybe we can get a game in this weekend,' he said to Tess, before turning quickly to Amy and Guy. 'If that's okay with you?'

Guy shrugged. 'Of course.' He sipped his drink as Amy said, 'We want you to enjoy your stay. And I'm only pleased you could all be here, friends and family. Old and new.'

Tess asked Ian, 'And which section do you fall into?'

'Friend,' he replied simply.

'Old flame,' said Babs knowingly. Ian threw her a glance, but she continued. 'Nothing to feel awkward about, Ian. That flame was extinguished long ago.' She sipped her drink and paused to consider something. 'I thought you might be married yourself by now. Didn't you get engaged to a young woman from Faversham?'

'I did,' he replied curtly.

'But it didn't last?' asked Babs.

Ian shook his head as though keen to shrug off more questions. Seeing his discomfort, Pearl stepped in to fill a gap in the conversation.

'Amazing that these gardens are managed only by the family and a few staff,' she said.

'Yes,' said Sarah. 'My brother and I grew up in a house of similar size. The upkeep was tremendous.'

'Not that your old man would ever have lifted a finger to help with it,' said Toby. 'Too busy living the high life.'

He glanced at Guy, who seemed unconcerned by

the comment and shrugged as he replied, 'You're right. Maybe if he had been more hands-on with our home, we'd have held on to Gravesham, but he was determined it wouldn't be left to us.' He caught his sister's eye. 'And perhaps that was a good thing.'

Toby glanced across at him. 'For you, maybe,' he said. 'But your sister got the short end of the stick.'

'We both did,' said Guy firmly. 'There's a price to be paid for waiting around for tomorrow. Much better to get on with today.'

Toby shook his head dismissively. 'Hippy nonsense. And easy enough for you to say,' he added. 'You've landed on your feet.'

'Landed?' said Guy. He shook his head. 'I played the hand I was dealt, that's all.'

Sarah stepped in. 'And won,' she commented, before addressing her husband. 'Guy's worked very hard for everything he has—'

'And I haven't?' Toby interrupted. He stared at Sarah, wounded and offended. His wife looked instantly contrite. 'That's not what I meant,' she said quickly. 'I'm sorry.'

Toby took a deep breath, and an awkward silence fell, broken finally by Tess. 'Did I mention to you that James may have a part for me in his new play?'

'That's wonderful news,' said Amy.

'As?' asked Babs.

'A woman trapped in a *ménage à trois*,' said James with a grin.

Ingrid sipped her drink. 'Intriguing.'

'If I had my time again,' began Babs wistfully, 'I'd love to be—'

'In a *ménage à trois*?' said Tess.

'On the stage,' Babs replied.

'There's one leaving in five minutes,' said Simon under his breath. Babs heard him and looked suitably affronted, but James laughed.

'The old gags are the best,' he said, winking at Simon.

'You're right, Babs,' said Amy. 'It must be a wonderful life being an actress.'

'Insecure,' commented Ian. All eyes fell on him, and he added, 'The entertainment business?'

'Tell me about it,' sighed Ingrid, wearily.

Amy shrugged. 'I don't have the confidence to act.' She glanced across at Tess. 'Let alone the talent.'

'Your talent lies elsewhere, darling,' said Ingrid, 'which is why I need to talk to you about some new commissions.' She beamed at Amy and sipped her champagne.

'You've been very successful,' Ian said to Amy. 'At everything – and in spite of everything.'

'And you,' said Guy, sitting down near Ian. 'A barrister. Defence or prosecution?'

'Defence,' Ian replied.

'Oh dear,' said Babs. Ian looked at her and she went on. 'Well, if you're going to take a job like that, you could at least prosecute the villains.'

'It's a profession – not a job,' said Simon, trying to be helpful, only to be met with a disdainful look from his employer.

'Atticus Finch is to blame,' said Amy with a smile.

'Atticus . . . ?' asked Babs, confounded.

'*To Kill a Mockingbird*,' Simon offered brightly. 'The book by Harper Lee?'

Ian explained, 'I make a point of reading it every year.'

'What on earth for?' said Toby.

'It's a great book,' said James.

Toby shrugged. 'But you know the ending.'

'Yes,' said Ian, 'but it has a useful moral code, and I don't mind being reminded of it.'

Pearl saw that Guy was carefully considering Ian before he finally asked, 'You like the idea of being preached to?'

Ian met his gaze. 'I like the idea of doing the right thing.'

'Don't we all?' said Guy.

'Defending criminals?' spluttered Babs.

'You have to be found guilty to become a criminal,' Ian said.

'And some criminals go scot-free,' said Ingrid.

'Especially with a good defence,' noted Guy.

'Perhaps,' Ian conceded. 'But I've never defended someone I knew to be guilty.'

'I should hope not,' said Amy. 'You're one of the most honourable people I know.'

Pearl noted the look that passed between them before Amy reached a hand out to Guy. He got up from his seat, bent his head towards hers and kissed her tenderly. 'I have to see about something,' he said softly, 'but I'll be right back.'

As Guy moved off, Amy stared after him, but Pearl noted Ian's gaze remained fixed on Amy. It was clear he still had feelings for her, but why he should have accepted an invitation to witness her marriage remained a mystery. Pearl sipped her drink and, in an effort to distract Ian, she commented: 'There's an element of theatre in a courtroom, isn't there?' He finally turned his attention to her, and she added, 'I once did jury service. Nothing too interesting; pickpocketing in a marketplace – or attempted theft, to be precise.'

Ian frowned. '"Attempted" would be difficult to prove?'

'The prosecution did their best,' said Pearl.

'And?' asked Amy.

'We considered the evidence, or rather the lack of evidence, very carefully,' said Pearl. 'And then found the man innocent. Not enough proof for a conviction. Very much in line with what the judge directed.'

'Job done,' said Toby, knocking back his drink.

'You'd think so,' said Pearl, 'but after the verdict, we learned that the accused had plenty of other offences to his name.' She paused. 'Pickpocketing offences.'

The other guests reflected on this.

'As I said,' Ingrid shrugged, 'lots of criminals go scot-free with a good defence.'

'Or,' said Sarah, 'if this man was known to the police and they suspected what he was up to in the marketplace, perhaps they were just trying to prevent a new offence from taking place?'

Amy considered this. 'But if the man *hadn't* committed that offence, he would have been the victim of police prejudice,' she said. 'Prejudice based on his previous offences.'

'That's possible,' said Pearl, 'but what I recognised throughout the trial was a certain . . . theatricality to the proceedings. A courtroom is very much like the stage, isn't it?'

James carefully stroked his beard then decided, 'That's very true.'

Pearl looked at Ian. 'As a barrister, you have a part to play. And I'm sure you play it well.'

'I hope so,' Ian replied modestly.

James turned to Tess and said, 'I have a feeling you'd make an excellent barrister.' He grinned but Tess shrugged. 'Except for the fact that I know nothing about law.' She allowed her partner to give her a small kiss on the lips. Pearl saw that Amy was watching the pair carefully until Guy returned to the terrace. Amy got to her feet to greet her fiancé and asked, 'Everything all right?'

'Fine.' He smiled, then said, 'It's a perfect evening.' Slipping his arm around Amy's shoulder, he gently pulled her close to him.

Ingrid, looking on, sipped her drink and sighed. 'And this wedding will make the perfect story.' She smiled at Amy. 'Your readers will be fascinated.'

At this, Amy broke away from Guy's embrace, took a deep breath and said: 'My readers won't get to hear it from me.'

Ingrid's smile remained in place as she replied. 'Well, I . . . realise you're going to take a break for a honeymoon.'

'A long break,' Amy said. 'And possibly a final one.' She looked at Guy before turning back to Ingrid, who said, 'Amy, you may well need a sabbatical, but as I told you only last week,'—she held Amy's gaze—'magazine editors are busting down my door.'

'Then you'll have to explain,' said Amy firmly.

Ingrid frowned. 'Explain—?'

'You heard what Amy said,' Guy interjected. 'Those editors will have to wait – along with your commission.' He offered a relaxed smile, which Ingrid failed to return. Instead, her mouth fell open, but no words came. Guy took a moment to compose himself before addressing the other guests: 'Amy and I were going to wait until tomorrow to announce this, but maybe now's as good a time as any.'

'Announce what?' said Ingrid, looking at Amy searchingly.

'New plans – for a new life,' said Amy, holding Guy's hand tightly. She looked up at him, urging him to go on.

'Amy won't be returning to writing,' Guy said with conviction. 'Not for some time, anyway.' His words and his look had a sense of finality about them.

'What on earth do you mean?' Ingrid sounded breathless – as though winded by shock.

'We've made plans,' said Amy. 'Together.'

'Plans?' spluttered Babs. 'What sort of plans?'

Guy replied, 'Amy and I are going to use what money we have to do something useful.'

Sarah also looked perplexed. '"Money"? You mean . . . the proceeds from the cargo?'

Guy nodded. 'It will be going to some very good causes.'

'Yes,' said Toby, lazily. He glanced at Amy. 'Wives can be costly.' He sipped his drink.

'Amy's not taking a penny from me.' Guy held Amy close as he explained, 'She's signed a prenup.'

Babs gasped. 'A what?'

Simon leaned towards her and whispered, 'He means a prenuptial agreement.'

Babs shrugged him off impatiently as she tried to absorb this news. 'But that's outrageous, unfair . . .'

'It's totally fair,' said Amy calmly. 'I don't want a penny of Guy's money – which is why I signed.'

Babs's mouth fell open once more, and Simon leaned in again to say, 'They're very common in Hollywood—'

'Shut up!' snapped his employer. Simon looked at her, stung.

After a pause, Tess gave a shrug. 'Well, for what it's worth, I congratulate you. There's no better way to show that it's the man you love – and not his money.' She tipped her head to Amy with respect and took a sip of her drink.

Ian remained silent but his expression had hardened, though Pearl couldn't be sure if this was from confusion or suspicion. James looked helpless, then asked tentatively, 'Every single penny?'

Amy nodded but Guy said, 'Most of it. We can live very simply—'

'On board a yacht?' Babs scoffed. 'Didn't someone once say that sailing's like standing in a shower ripping up fifty-pound notes?'

Amy said, 'We'll be using the boat as well as living on it.' She looked at Guy, who explained, 'We may research some more wrecks, but any profits will be put to good use.'

Babs looked unimpressed. 'Really? And just how far do you think your fortune will go in trying to solve the world's ills?'

'Quite a way,' said Guy, 'if it goes to the right people. We need to do something about climate change, the environment, the state of the oceans.'

Silence fell. Amy frowned, appearing unsure but also disappointed by the lack of positive response. 'Is Tess the only person who thinks this is a good idea?'

'No,' said Pearl boldly. 'Good luck to you. It's your lives – your money – and you're free to do what you want. I'm very pleased for you.' She smiled.

Toby turned to Guy with an undisguised sneer. 'So, the man who has everything now has "principles" too?'

'I'm still lacking one thing,' said Guy. 'A best man.' Reaching into his pocket, he took out a small jeweller's box and opened it to reveal a platinum band set with diamonds. His eyes moved immediately to Ian, who remained silent, a small muscle tensing in his jaw. For a moment, no one spoke; then Simon sprang forward.

'I'd be honoured to do it.'

Guy turned to him, smiled and finally snapped the lid shut. 'Thanks,' he said, handing the ring to Simon. 'And make sure you don't lose that.' He turned to the other guests. 'I think that's everything . . . so now we can celebrate.'

Before anyone could comment, a sudden loud crack, like the sound of gunfire, caused Babs to scream. Everyone turned to the source of the noise and saw the sky filled with a fountain of light.

'Fireworks,' said Amy with a gasp. She turned to Guy. 'You?'

'And Ryan,' Guy said. 'He's just on the other side of the ha-ha.'

'The what?' asked Ingrid.

'It's a sunken fence,' said Amy, 'a kind of ditch that's used as a boundary.'

Ingrid still looked confused, so Guy added, 'Instead of ruining a beautiful view with a fence, old estates like this used to build a ha-ha to keep cattle in one place without anything being noticed at ground level.'

Another series of fireworks whistled up into the night sky and erupted above them.

'You and your surprises,' Amy said softly to Guy. He leaned in and kissed her tenderly.

The fireworks created an explosion of colour in the sky. Sarah murmured, 'How beautiful,' but Pearl noted that her attention was focused not on the display but on Guy and Amy. Beside her, Toby heaved a heavy sigh. 'Money up in smoke.'

James slipped his arm around Tess's shoulder, mesmerised by the gold spirals shooting up into the heavens. 'A stunning performance . . . in a perfect setting . . . for a grateful audience.' He kissed Tess.

Each guest became absorbed in the kaleidoscopic display – apart from one: Ian Soutar. Pearl witnessed the bitter look on his face before he turned away and moved quickly and silently down the stone steps to the grounds. As fireworks continued to crack overhead, Pearl hurried after Ian, but once she reached the driveway she saw that he had disappeared.

On the terrace above her, the guests were still sighing and shrieking in reaction to the fireworks. Pearl looked around but couldn't tell which direction Ian had taken. She was about to remount the steps when the last rocket of the grand finale lit up the sky, exposing the surrounding gardens for a brief moment. In the far distance, Pearl was sure she had caught sight of something – a figure darting near the trees in front of the cricket pavilion across the lawn. She frowned to herself; Ian Soutar couldn't possibly have reached the pavilion in such a short space of time. It had to be someone else.

Glancing up towards the terrace, Pearl saw that the other guests remained oblivious, but before she could return to them she felt her mobile phone vibrating in her pocket. It stopped before she could answer it, but staring down at it she realised that with all the evening's distractions she had managed to miss a call from McGuire.

CHAPTER SEVEN

McGuire tossed his mobile phone on to the bed, disappointed that he hadn't reached Pearl, though he was hardly surprised as he had only just returned home after a late shift at work. He kicked off his shoes and sat down on his bed to open the window, below which flowed the Great Stour river. The night air was still warm, and the voices that carried across from the opposite bank prompted him to lie back and imagine Pearl enjoying herself with her old friend and the other wedding guests at Mount Ephraim. Pearl was a people person, and though McGuire was no misanthrope he could enjoy his own company – particularly after a day trying to track down the kind of criminals no one would wish to meet, least of all on a dark night.

He imagined what Pearl might be doing now; perhaps talking weddings – something he and Pearl had yet to do, in spite of their engagement. Things had got in the way, but the conversation would surely be had once Pearl returned home to Whitstable. The weekend would focus her attention on it, and McGuire would be prepared – after all, he wanted to be married, but most of all he wanted to be married to Pearl.

McGuire knew his profession was full of fellow officers whose marriages had failed to survive the pressure of shift work, stress and the fear that one day a spouse might simply fail to return home due to a violent incident – or even an affair. McGuire had briefly dated a few of his colleagues, but he had always resisted becoming romantically involved with them. It wasn't until his path had crossed with a duty solicitor by the name of Donna Esposito that he had decided to mix business with pleasure. Half the officers in McGuire's department had been bowled over by Donna, but it was McGuire who had won her heart – all part of a time when life had seemed to go his way, like a gambler's lucky streak.

It was Donna who had organised the trip to Venice; a week away to a city she knew well. She was a native speaker, and McGuire had been content to watch and listen, fascinated by the woman who had finally overtaken his love of work. In St Mark's Square he had asked her, 'Why don't we get married?' Not exactly a romantic proposal – and wholly unplanned – though not unexpected. Later that day, at a table in Florian's bar, Donna had thoughtfully sipped her negroni. Her smile had said it all. From then on, their time in

Venice had taken a different tone: a calm acceptance of a future together – perhaps even the prospect of a family.

Weeks later, as summer faded into autumn, that future had been erased by a single random event. McGuire had learned the news as he learned most news – from another police officer; a woman returning home from Peckham Police Station had been mown down in a car accident. McGuire closed his eyes, blotting out the image that had failed to leave him – like it was burned on to his retina – a corpse wearing the face of the woman he loved. A final goodbye . . .

His secondment to Kent had come at the right time, banishing McGuire to this outpost to deal with an over-reliance on Bourbon and gambling. But only a short while later he had found himself involved in a case with a woman called Pearl Nolan – a woman he had come to love as much, if not more, than Donna because he now recognised how easily love could slip from his grasp. It seemed right that he should have proposed to Pearl, not because he needed to be married but because he knew no other way of telling Pearl what she meant to him, how she occupied a space in his heart which he had once been sure would never again be filled.

A Latin phrase from an old war poem suddenly came to him, something about it being right and fitting to die for one's country. *Dulce et decorum est* . . . the phrase had stayed with him, perhaps because he so often tried to do the right thing – to protect others, to make things right. Perhaps he hoped that as Pearl's husband he would be able to protect her as he had been unable to protect Donna. There was no war to threaten Pearl's life and no drugged-up kids in a stolen car, but Pearl's own cases had put her in jeopardy too many times for McGuire's liking, and though she sometimes seemed to resent his need to protect her, he had never fully explained its basis, perhaps because he had never realised it until now. But McGuire recognised he had been given a second chance, and he wasn't prepared to throw it away – Pearl was too precious for that. He thought of the images he had viewed earlier of Mount Ephraim, nestled in the Swale countryside, a private estate where Pearl could enjoy the company of her friends, which was surely the reason she had missed his call. He smiled to himself, consoled by the fact that if Pearl was away from Whitstable she was out of harm's way – and he could relax. A moment later, his phone sounded.

'Sorry to ring so late,' said Pearl. 'I missed your call.' She was speaking in a hushed tone as she sauntered down to the meadow in front of the old stable block, having made an excuse to leave the guests on the terrace. The stable block was framed like a black silhouette against a moonlit sky as she made her way towards it.

McGuire ran a hand through his blonde fringe. 'I didn't mean to hassle you,' he said gently.

'You didn't.'

He smiled, relieved. 'Having fun?'

'It's . . . intriguing.'

'The house, you mean?'

'Everything,' she replied. 'It's strange, but I feel like I'm on a trail, picking up clues.'

'Clues,' echoed McGuire. 'To what?'

'I'm . . . not sure,' said Pearl. 'Yet.'

McGuire recognised something in her voice. 'Curiosity killed the cat,' he said. 'You're there for a wedding,' he reminded her.

'I know. And I'm looking forward to it, but . . .'

'But what?'

'I can't help thinking that the wedding will be only one part of this weekend.'

McGuire sat up, his curiosity piqued. 'What do you mean?'

'Something Amy's fiancé has just told us,' said Pearl. 'I can't explain right now, but it's bound to make headlines.'

'In the *Swale Gazette*?' McGuire teased.

'Guy Priddey's a wealthy man,' said Pearl. 'A lot of people will be very interested in his plans.'

'What plans?'

Pearl could hear the frown in McGuire's voice. 'I told you, I can't explain now, but I'll call tomorrow after the wedding. It's at ten thirty in the grounds here—' she broke off, then began: 'That's another thing,' but she fell silent yet again as she stared towards the lake.

'Pearl?' said McGuire, increasingly confused.

For a moment, she considered whether to tell McGuire what she thought she had seen on the bank of the lake – and later illuminated by the flash of fireworks over the old cricket pavilion – but then decided against it. Instead, it would be something to take up with Emma the next day. After all, in spite of security at the house, it was always possible that some intrepid paparazzo had managed to find a way into the grounds. If so, Pearl would ensure they'd never snap shots of the happy couple tying the knot in the wedding pavilion – photographs that could easily find a home with a celebrity magazine editor.

'Pearl,' said McGuire again, fearing she had left the line.

'I'm here,' she said finally. 'Just thinking, that's all.'

'About weddings?' he asked tentatively.

'No,' said Pearl. 'Something far more important,' she continued softly. 'About how much I miss you.'

McGuire's smile returned.

'You'll be back soon enough,' he said. 'And I'll be here,' he added gently. 'Sleep tight.'

Ending the call, McGuire pushed open his bedroom window and lay back again on the bed, listening to the River Stour outside, the sound of the fast-flowing, clear water so different to the dark, seemingly bottomless canals of Venice.

After her call, Pearl walked quickly back towards the house, eager to seek out Ian, but she paused on a path between the clipped yew hedges as she heard the murmur of voices.

'You can't imagine how bad things are,' said a woman on the other side of the tall hedge. Recognising Sarah's voice, Pearl prepared to identify herself when she heard Guy responding to his sister.

'Actually, I can,' he said stiffly. 'In fact, I imagined it on the very day you married, and I'm only surprised you've stuck it out so long.'

'He's my husband,' Sarah said with finality.

'More's the pity.'

Pearl hesitated, aware she had overheard part of a very private conversation but felt reluctant to move on, knowing that her footsteps on the bracken-covered path would reveal her presence. She remained stock still, realising that Sarah and her brother must be seated on the stone bench on the other side of the hedge.

Guy's tone softened to one of concern. 'Why didn't you listen to me, Sarah?'

'How could I?' she replied in frustration. 'You never understood what I felt for him.'

'Past tense,' Guy noted. 'Does that mean you no longer love him?'

'I've always loved him. You know that.'

'Even now?' asked Guy in hushed incredulity.

Sarah sighed. 'He's still the same man. Inside.' She paused then went on. 'But . . . perhaps if we'd had children, this wouldn't have happened. Things might have been so different.'

'They might have been far worse,' said Guy.

'No,' Sarah insisted. 'You don't understand. He blamed himself.'

'Because the problem was his,' said Guy. 'Not yours. He can't father a child and he's never been able to deal with that, Sarah.'

'But he's been so unlucky . . . all his dreams—'

'Have come to nothing,' said Guy firmly, 'because of *him*. He's always overcompensated, always tried to prove he's greater than he is, Sarah, so he set himself up to fail.' He paused. 'Toby's a failure – but he can't accept that, and neither can you. How much have we ploughed into his business exploits over the years? A small fortune wasted on his fantasies. And he drank his way through it all.'

'Do you have to be so unkind?' Sarah asked.

'Yes,' said Guy firmly, but then he softened again. 'Because I love you.'

A longer pause followed.

Guy's next words had an air of impatience. 'You don't need to put up with this.'

'With what?'

'A lazy drunk with a massive sense of entitlement.'

'That's not fair. Toby's tried.'

'Tried what?'

'To change,' Sarah replied. 'To become a better person. To give up drinking.'

'For how long?'

'It's a sickness.'

'And the abuse?'

At Sarah's silence, Guy continued. 'You don't need bruises to suffer abuse, Sarah. The scars still show. You and I should know that more than most.'

A pause followed, during which Pearl felt she must announce her presence or risk being found, but Guy spoke again.

'Is that why you married him?' he asked softly. 'Is that why you still love him? Because he reminds you of Pa?'

Peering carefully around the yew hedge, Pearl caught sight of Sarah facing away from her, towards the lake. Guy was behind her, his hand on her shoulder. 'If he never did anything else, surely that was Pa's lesson – to go our own way and never to put up with what he doled out to us.'

Sarah turned to look at him. Guy's voice softened to a whisper. 'Perhaps it isn't Toby that needs help. It's you.'

Pearl saw Guy's arm gently encircling his sister's shoulder. 'Leave him,' he continued. 'Leave him and I'll help all I can, but it has to stop now.' He paused again, then added, 'What I said tonight . . .' But he trailed off, as though conflicted, prompting Sarah to ask: 'Is it really true, Guy? You plan to give it all away – the money?'

He nodded.

'But why?' she asked, her eyes searching his face for an answer. 'Are you all right? Is the . . . pain getting worse?'

'I'm fine,' he said softly.

'That's not true,' she argued bitterly. 'You'll never be "fine" again.'

'I'm okay,' Guy insisted. 'And I'm in love.'

Sarah looked up at him again as though realising something. 'You mean . . . this is her idea – Amy's?'

'It's *my* idea,' said Guy firmly. 'But Amy agreed to it – another reason why I love her.'

'But you can't,' Sarah hissed. 'It isn't fair. First Pa – now you? How could you do this to me?'

Guy seemed torn by this, but he rallied and took his sister's shoulders. 'Leave him,' he said. 'Leave Toby and I'll help you – but I won't go on financing his abuse.'

Sarah continued to look up at him, but Guy failed to waver. Finally, as if unable to bear her brother's resolve any longer, Sarah turned on her heels and moved off quickly, leaving Guy staring after her until his phone suddenly sounded. After a moment, Pearl realised the voice on the other end had brought him back to the present.

'Amy,' he began, putting his hand to his brow in an effort to concentrate. 'No . . . no, everything's fine – and everything *will* be fine,' he said firmly. 'Tomorrow.' He paused then whispered, 'I love you too.' Then he ended the call and silence followed. Pearl heard his footsteps moving off into the distance. When she was sure he had disappeared, she rounded the hedge and stared at the empty stone bench before she moved off herself – to the house.

Minutes later, as Pearl was mounting the steps to the garden wing, she caught sight of a figure sitting at a table near the tea terrace, and she headed across. Against the night sky the topiary figures appeared like a surreal dreamscape; a sailing boat, an elephant, birds, an aeroplane. As Pearl approached, the figure spoke. 'Nice and peaceful, isn't it?' Tess turned and smiled slowly. 'James has turned in already,' she explained. 'Must have been all the excitement, fireworks – and the drink, of course.' As she looked away, her smile faded. 'Just what he needs to help with the restless nights.'

'Restless?' said Pearl, joining her at the table.

'He's been working hard to finish edits of his play. As I said, it's very good,' she added quickly, 'but perhaps not good enough – or someone would have picked it up by now.' She began gently tapping her fingernails on the table.

'And you would be starring in it?' Pearl ventured.

Tess looked back at Pearl and summoned another smile. 'Unless, of course, James managed to cast a bigger name.' She gave a casual shrug. 'I would understand. I'm not exactly suffering at the moment – for money – or acclaim. A recent stint in Dubai paid handsomely.' She paused, then asked, 'Have you been?'

Pearl shook her head.

'Oh, you must go,' Tess insisted. 'I'm sure you've seen photos of the archipelago – the famous islands – all artificial, of course? And culture is imported. Concerts, theatre, the Bard. It was a gruelling Shakespeare schedule, so I needed some R & R afterwards. Took myself off to Thailand.' She stared towards the topiary silhouettes. 'I've got rather used to sunnier climes.'

'And . . . is that where you met Amy and Guy?'

Tess nodded. 'A breath of fresh air. Phuket is full of expats, backpackers and kids on gap years. By comparison, Amy and Guy were . . . stable . . . like part of the landscape.' She smiled, this time to herself. 'We had so much fun; sailing out to the islands, watching the moon rise above the cliffs, diving, eating breakfast on the deck of Guy's yacht – boiled eggs served in precious porcelain egg cups. Magical times.' She took a deep breath. 'The aroma of lemongrass and coriander takes me right back.'

Pearl nodded towards the hedge around her. 'Lavender doesn't quite hit the spot?'

Tess gave a little laugh. 'No. But now I have James to distract me,' she said. 'We're an item. I'm hoping to be his muse.'

'But . . . he needs an angel for his play?' Pearl asked tentatively. 'That's what they're called, isn't it? Someone who invests in a theatre production?'

'Yes,' said Tess. 'But it seems dear Guy won't be able to oblige. Shame,' she shrugged. 'But then, this weekend is about a wedding, not a play.' She finished her drink and sighed before checking her watch and getting to her feet.

'Is Guy okay?'

At Pearl's question, Tess turned. 'In . . . what way?'

'His health?'

'But of course,' said Tess. 'What a strange question. The man's a machine.' She gave a slow smile, hitched the long chain of her evening bag across her shoulder and moved off towards the house.

Soon after, Pearl got up and sauntered across the terrace to look out towards the lawn. Somewhere between the fountain and the cricket pavilion lay the ha-ha where Ryan had ignited the fireworks for the evening's display. They had illuminated what Pearl felt sure had been a figure near the pavilion. It was now late, almost midnight, and she didn't want to worry Amy on her wedding day, but tomorrow she would find a moment to talk to Emma about what she had seen. Moving back along the terrace, she saw lights still shining in the games room and wondered if anyone was playing a game of cards or billiards. Then she saw the figure of Babs at the window. For a moment, Pearl considered moving on to the house, but she stopped as she heard Amy's voice and decided to investigate. Neither woman appeared to notice Pearl as she moved closer. Instead, looking preoccupied, Amy turned away from Babs and headed to another window. Babs's voice rose as she followed her. 'Well, it can't be true,' she said stiffly. 'He was surely just saying that for the benefit of his sister and her charmless husband.'

'It *is* true,' said Amy. 'I signed a prenup. But it really doesn't matter because Guy's giving away most of what he has.'

Babs looked shocked and took a moment to summon her thoughts. 'Then why on earth are you going ahead with this marriage?'

'Why do you think?' said Amy.

'Love?' Babs scoffed. 'I promise you, love won't take care of you in your old age. And I hope to heavens you never find yourself alone – like me.' She turned quickly away from Amy and headed to the window but missed sight of Pearl, who stepped back into the darkness.

'You're *not* alone,' said Amy wearily. 'You have me and . . .' She found herself suddenly lost for words. 'And Simon,' she said finally.

'But for how much longer?' asked Babs, turning back to her.

Amy frowned. 'What do you mean?'

Babs paused before admitting, 'I'm . . . not sure I'll be able to afford him much longer. I'm struggling, Amy.'

It was Amy's turn to sound shocked. 'But you have plenty of money. Daddy's legacy, from the sale of the business?'

Babs sighed heavily. 'I'm afraid I . . . made a few unwise investments.'

'With Daddy's money?' Amy looked away to try and assimilate this news. 'But . . . that was everything he ever worked for—'

'You don't understand,' said Babs. 'I needed more. Things are so expensive these days. And the new shares seemed like a sound move. I was . . . misled.'

Amy stared at her, still in shock. 'Why didn't you tell me?'

'I didn't want to burden you with this. You were away,

busy working, as usual. And . . . I was so pleased about the news of your engagement.'

'I bet,' said Amy. 'For all the wrong reasons.'

Babs gaped as Amy went on. 'Were you really pleased for me or simply relieved that I might be marrying a rich man?' She began to pace the room. 'All that talk earlier about family support? You were just preparing the way. How long was it going to take before you asked Guy for money – or me?'

'Amy—'

'I can't believe you would do this.' She stopped pacing and turned back to Babs, looking both sad and disappointed, and said fiercely: 'You really *are* a Stepmonster.' With that, she turned on her heels and walked out.

Once the door had closed after Amy, Pearl saw Babs sit down on the sofa in the games room, trying to make sense of what she had just heard. For a few moments, Babs seemed to struggle with her thoughts, then she opened her handbag and took from it a miniature bottle of gin. She unscrewed the top, put the bottle to her lips and tilted back her head as she took a slug. A wince and a hiccup followed, after which Babs screwed the top back on to the bottle and replaced it in her bag. Then she took a deep breath and raised her palms to her temples before pushing her lilac grey hair back from her face. In the next instant, she froze, as if catching sight of something outside. Pearl caught her breath and moved quickly back from the window, expecting the worst, but Babs simply got to her feet and walked slowly and steadily out of the room leaving Pearl relieved – but with plenty to ponder.

Pearl entered the garden wing and tiptoed to the upper landing. For a moment she stood in front of the two doors leading to Amy's master bedroom, her hand raised to knock and perhaps comfort her friend after the contretemps with Babs – or at least try to raise her spirits for the day ahead – but her instincts told her to leave things until the morning and allow a new day to act as a fresh page in Amy's life – one she would now share with the soulmate she had been so lucky to find. Pearl moved on, seeing a light beneath Tess and James's bedroom door and hearing the soft strains of music, a song by Dusty Springfield and the Pet Shop Boys, coming from the direction of Simon's room along the corridor. Another light was visible beneath Ingrid's door. Pearl moved closer to it and heard Ingrid talking to someone on the phone. 'I'm here right now,' she said, 'and I'm telling you I can't get through to her.' She paused, then: 'Yes, maybe you're right. Maybe there *is* only one way to change her mind.' After another pause, Ingrid said, 'I'll call again tomorrow.'

Silence fell, and Pearl moved quickly along the corridor and entered her own room. She stood transfixed for a moment at the sight of the moon, framed by one of her windows, hanging like a silver sixpence in a starlit sky. She poured herself a glass of water from the jug on her bedside table, but she had taken only a few sips before she heard a door closing in the corridor. Curious, Pearl looked out but found no one there. She returned to her room, drew the curtains slightly before she undressed and slipped into bed. For a time, Pearl stared at the mirror on the wall reflecting back part of the starlit sky before her eyes finally closed and she slipped into a deep and dreamless sleep.

CHAPTER EIGHT

Pearl woke abruptly. For a few moments she simply lay back with her eyes wide open as she tried to recognise her unfamiliar surroundings. The day was entering through a gap in the curtains, slender fingers of sunlight stealing across the coverlet of her bed. Reaching for her phone on the bedside table, Pearl saw, with shock, that it was almost nine o'clock. She sat up quickly and put a hand to her brow, feeling as though a dull weight was pushing her back down. Too much champagne, or the countryside air, had surely caused her to fall into such an unexpectedly deep sleep. She gathered her thoughts, grabbed her phone and dialled a number.

'Amy?' she began, 'I'm so sorry, but I've overslept.'

'It's okay,' said Amy, her tone polite but expectant. 'Did you manage to find a reading?"

'Yes,' said Pearl, relieved that at least she had managed the one favour asked of her.

'That's brilliant. Thank you,' said Amy warmly.

'And don't worry about oversleeping. There's still plenty of time, just join us when you're ready.'

The line went dead, and Pearl threw back the curtains to reveal a gloriously sunny day – perfect for a wedding ceremony in the pavilion on the terrace below Pearl's window.

A cool shower dissolved Pearl's headache, and she changed into her outfit and applied some lipstick. Checking her transcription of the verse from Gibran, she quickly headed out of her room, pausing at the top of the stairs as she remembered Dolly's gift for Amy. The painting was still in Pearl's room. For a second she wondered whether to take it downstairs with her, but, as wedding presents were usually opened after the ceremony, she hesitated. Dolly's reminder of the old rhyme troubled her once again: *'Something old, something new, something borrowed, something blue.'* These were items a bride was meant to receive to stave off bad luck. Just as Pearl turned back to her room to fetch the painting, she heard the tolling of a bell. The old clock tower was sounding ten. Leaving Dolly's gift in her room, Pearl hurried downstairs.

Heads turned as Pearl entered the dining room to find Babs and Simon seated with Ingrid and James at the dining table. Emma, busy near the Aga, gave Pearl a warm smile. 'Sleep well?'

'Too well,' said Pearl.

'I've just made some coffee,' said Emma. 'What would you like for breakfast?'

Pearl shook her head. 'I'm fine—' She broke off at the sight of Babs pacing up and down.

Simon sighed. 'Will you please come and sit down?'

'Yes.' James frowned as he stroked his beard. 'You're making me nervous – and I'm not even getting married.'

'I can't sit down,' said Babs tersely. She turned to Simon. 'If I do, my outfit will crease, and there isn't enough time for you to press it for me!' She stared fretfully down at her buttercup-yellow suit.

Ingrid gave Babs a cursory glance. 'It's an acceptable look for linen.'

'Not for me,' said Babs determinedly. 'I don't plan to attend Amy's wedding looking as though I've just slept in my wedding suit.'

'Actually, I think all eyes will be on the bride,' said Ingrid.

'Maybe,' Babs conceded. 'Nevertheless, there will be photographs taken and they may even find their way into the press.' The thought seemed to increase her anxiety. 'Perhaps I should change into something else?'

'If you have an alternative, that might be a good idea,' said Simon calmly. 'After all, I've got my own role to perform today.' He smiled proudly and produced the jeweller's box from his breast pocket, opening it to check the ring was still there.

'Wasps,' said James.

Puzzled by this apparent non-sequitur, Babs turned to face him, but Ingrid stifled a smile. 'He's right,' she said.

'They love yellow. Why don't you take one of your "little helpers" instead?' Babs stared down at her wedding suit, her mouth open in shock, while Pearl took advantage of the silence to ask, 'Has anyone seen Amy?'

'In the sitting room,' said Emma.

James called across the room, 'Tess is helping her to get ready.'

Pearl nodded and moved for the door. Emma stepped forward with a pot of coffee, saying, 'Guy and the other guests will be leaving from the west wing. Ryan is going to call me to let me know when they're in place at the pavilion, and then Amy and everyone else can make their way down.'

Pearl thanked her and left the kitchen, heading along the corridor to the sitting room, where she found the door slightly ajar. She heard voices as she approached.

'Are you sure?' Amy was asking.

'But of course,' came Tess's reply. 'I wouldn't have said it otherwise.'

Pearl tapped on the door and announced herself. 'Can I come in?'

'Please do!' called Tess.

Pearl opened the door as Tess said, 'Would you like to tell Amy how beautiful she looks?'

Amy turned around slowly, and Pearl saw that she was wearing a simple ivory dress. A halo of tiny satin lilies sat like a crown on her bobbed hair.

'I'm not sure I want to wear this veil,' she said,

indicating the soft net fabric in her hand. 'Do you think I need to?'

Pearl found herself momentarily silenced as she took in how truly stunning Amy looked – in spite of her anxiety.

'Then don't wear it,' Pearl replied softly before stepping forward. 'You really do look beautiful, Amy.'

'Do I?' Amy smiled and looked back at Tess. 'I'm sorry,' she said. 'I've been as much of a drama queen this morning as Babs.'

'You're allowed to be,' said Tess. 'It's your wedding day.'

Pearl smiled. 'Tess is right.'

'Yes,' said Amy, as if realising this for the first time. 'But there's been so much to do, and I admit I had a . . . disagreement with Babs last night.' She looked back at Pearl. 'Perhaps more than a disagreement,' she admitted. 'I should have found some self-control. After all, I know what she's like.'

'Well,' said Tess, 'whatever it was about, forget it – for twenty-four hours, at least.'

'Yes, I must,' said Amy. 'There are more important things to worry about. I haven't even checked the pavilion today. The florist was there all morning, dressing it.'

'And I'm sure she's done a perfect job,' said Tess.

'All the same,' said Amy, 'Emma has her hands full with the wedding breakfast and I'm not sure Ryan has an eye for flower arranging. And then there's the celebrant.' She frowned. 'I think she's here already.'

'Don't worry,' said Pearl, taking control. 'I'll go and check. And I'm sorry I'm so late down this morning or I could have helped you more – but I slept like a log.'

'It's okay,' said Amy managing a smile. 'Are you sure you don't mind?'

Pearl shook her head. 'Of course not. I'll see you there.'

Minutes later, Pearl made her way down to the lower terrace. The lake was visible as she descended a flight of stone steps to see a row of white chairs, decorated with satin bows, arranged in front of the wedding pavilion. The pale ivory blossom of Japanese wisteria crept across an old stone wall while the entrance to the area was framed by garlands of white roses. As Pearl approached, she saw a man dressed in a smart suit talking to a woman, but it wasn't until she drew closer that she recognised Ryan, looking vaguely uncomfortable out of his work clothes. Seeing Pearl, he moved to speak but was interrupted by his mobile phone.

'Sorry,' he said. 'It's Emma, so I'd best answer.' As he turned away to take the call, the woman stepped forward with a smile to introduce herself.

'Anne Armstrong, I'm the celebrant for today's happy occasion. And you are?'

Before Pearl could answer, Ryan ended his brief call and turned to face them.

'Something wrong?' asked Pearl.

'I hope not,' he replied. 'Emma says everyone's ready in the west wing – apart from Guy.'

Anne's smile faded, but Ryan said, 'I'm sure it's nothing to be worried about, but, well, he does like springing surprises.' He looked at Pearl. 'The fireworks last night?'

'Yes,' Pearl agreed. 'Has anyone tried calling him?'

'His sister and Emma. No reply,' said Ryan. 'Emma's checked his suite but he's not there either. She doesn't want to worry Amy, but . . .'

The celebrant frowned and checked her watch. 'Cutting it fine?'

'He must be in the grounds,' said Ryan, looking around.

'Let's check,' said Pearl. She gathered her thoughts. 'Will you stay here?' she asked Anne. 'I'm not too familiar with the grounds,' she said to Ryan, 'but I did a circuit around the lake yesterday and then back up to the house via the maze.'

Ryan nodded. 'Do the same now,' he said. 'I'll take the terrace and water gardens. He can't be far.' He managed a tense smile before moving off while Pearl headed down towards the lake. Once again, her gaze fell on the old blue shack that Emma had confirmed to Pearl was a pump house. Heading quickly towards it, Pearl called out Guy's name and listened carefully; she heard nothing but the soft rustle of trees in the gentle morning breeze. She moved up the bank and called out again, imagining that if Guy had taken a walk in the arboretum he would surely hear her, but again there was no response.

As Pearl continued along the lakeside, she recalled the figure she had thought she had seen in this very spot the day before, and she suddenly remembered that Babs Meadows-Young was wearing yellow this morning. There again, Babs had been present during the firework display when Pearl thought she had seen someone else near the cricket pavilion. Was it possible she had imagined both instances – a trick of the light? Even if she had, what she clearly hadn't imagined was the fact that, with only minutes to spare before his wedding ceremony, Amy's fiancé had gone missing.

Moving swiftly on, Pearl was about to call Guy's name once more when a noise filled the air – the raucous sound of rooks circling high up among the bank of tall oaks. Staring up towards the birds, she asked herself – as she had the day before – whether the creatures were driving her from their territory or perhaps warning her of something else. From their vantage point, they were surely alert to all imminent danger.

Pearl became aware that her beautiful satin pumps were now damp with the morning dew. A cold breeze ran through her long dark hair as she headed on, down towards the wooden bridge. Once she crossed it, she would be only minutes away from the house – but what would she say to Amy? Perhaps Guy had been found by Ryan or had returned to the house by now; but if so, why had no one called her to let her know? She took her phone from her pocket and found no messages or missed calls.

Halfway across the bridge, Pearl hesitated, staring across towards the Miz Maze and its tall plants swaying in the breeze. Might Guy have entered it for some quiet contemplation? She considered calling Emma, but instead she listened to the soft trickle of water entering the lake beneath the bridge, trying to focus her thoughts.

Leaning forward, she concentrated and allowed the pastoral scene to calm her mind, which still seemed dull from heavy sleep. There had been so much to absorb since her arrival yesterday and so much tension beneath the surface of what purported to be a happy occasion. Guy's announcement last night and Amy's refusal to consider continuing with her career had provoked the altercation with Babs and the family tensions between Sarah and her brother. Added to the mix was Tess and James's disappointment at a dead end in their search for funding for a new theatre production, while Ian Soutar's presence, in the midst of everything, seemed like a spectre from the past arriving to haunt the future. Moreover, Guy's extraordinary suggestion for Ian to be the best man for this wedding seemed to add salt to the wound of Ian's broken relationship with Amy.

All of this Pearl had yet to process, but the immediate problem was finding Guy. Could he have run out on his bride – jilted her on this most perfect day? Pearl inhaled deeply and prepared to move on when the same breath caught in her throat. Once more she thought she smelled the remnants of skunk cabbage, but she could see no sign of the strange yellow blossoms on the banks. Something else was floating wide on the surface of the water below the bridge – a man's hand, nut-brown among water lilies . . .

CHAPTER NINE

'Only you could go to a wedding and find a dead body,' said Dolly to Pearl on the other end of her phone. Dolly stirred a teaspoonful of honey into a mug of herbal tea, sat down on the daybed in her conservatory and was about to take a sip when Pearl replied, 'There *was* no wedding. I've told you, it was Guy's body I found.'

Dolly allowed the full weight of this information to settle before she gave out a loud sigh. 'Poor Amy,' she said. 'And he drowned, you say?'

'We don't know yet,' said Pearl.

Dolly frowned at this. 'But you just said you found him in the lake. Had he been swimming?'

'No,' said Pearl, 'he was fully dressed and wearing the same clothes that he was wearing last night.' She checked the time on her smartphone. 'We won't have a firm cause of death until the police perform an autopsy.'

'Police?' said Dolly, shocked. 'Surely it was an accident?'

'As I said,' Pearl reminded her, 'we don't yet know.' She added anxiously, 'Please don't say anything to Charlie yet. Not until we do know more?'

Dolly felt torn at this request but agreed. 'Okay. But we've been here before, Pearl. Come home,' she said firmly, 'and bring Amy with you.'

'I can't,' said Pearl with frustration. She raked a hand through her long dark hair. 'No one is allowed to leave Mount Ephraim.'

'You mean . . . you're all under house arrest?'

'Not exactly. But the local police have made it clear they want us to remain here – within a short radius, anyway. For now.'

Dolly's outrage was palpable. 'They're interfering with your civil liberties, Pearl. Tell them to talk to McGuire!'

'There's no point,' Pearl explained. 'This isn't Canterbury – it's Swale.'

'It's what?' said Dolly, straining to hear on the line.

'Swale,' said Pearl, louder. 'A completely different district with a police force over which McGuire has no authority.'

Dolly groaned. 'Well, have you talked to him?'

'Not yet. But I left a voicemail message for him earlier and I really should clear the line because he may be trying to get through.' She checked her smartphone again and found no missed calls, though a text had just arrived for her from Emma. It read, *The police would like another word*.

'Pearl?' said Dolly.

'I have to go.'

'Well, be careful,' Dolly warned – before realising her daughter had already hung up.

Pearl opened the door to the sitting room on the ground floor and found its elegant interior transformed. A chestnut table which displayed a vase of peonies yesterday was now stacked with papers and a tape machine. A woman in her mid-forties sat on one side of the table gesturing for Pearl to join her.

'I'm Detective Inspector Jane Bowell,' she said brusquely as Pearl sat down. 'You gave a statement to Sergeant Falconer here,' she went on, nodding to a younger woman who took her own seat at the table. 'I'd like to go over a few things with you.'

Pearl observed DI Bowell, who offered a tight smile before focusing her attention on the notes before her. She looked to be the same age as Pearl, a lean woman with a fine bone structure and long dark hair pinned up into a pleat.

The physical features the two women shared allowed Pearl to imagine that she might be looking at herself, having climbed to the detective's rank after continuing with her own police training. But while observing DI Bowell, she also questioned whether she would have been comfortable having to wear the mask of police professionalism – the necessary blinkers to human suffering – which enabled officers to get on stoically with their job. Perhaps, thought Pearl, it was a mask this detective had assumed for far too long, judging by the tension in DI Bowell's voice as she asked, without looking up, 'You are a friend of Miss Young?'

Pearl nodded. 'Yes.'

'A guest of hers this weekend.'

Pearl nodded again.

'And you found Mr Priddey's body in the lake this morning. Shortly after ten o'clock?'

'That's right,' said Pearl. 'The bell on the estate clock tower had sounded a short while before.'

'And what made you go in search of Mr Priddey?'

Pearl collected her thoughts. 'I heard from Ryan, who works here, that Guy hadn't been seen that morning, so we decided to make a search of the grounds.'

'On your suggestion?' Bowell held Pearl's look.

'Yes,' said Pearl. 'I didn't know what else we could do in the circumstances. I didn't want to return to the house to tell Amy the bad news.'

'That Mr Priddey was dead?'

'That he was missing,' clarified Pearl. 'At that point I had no idea he was dead.'

'But it was you who found the body.'

'You know that from my statement.'

DI Bowell folded her hands and studied Pearl carefully before asking: 'Was there any particular reason you chose to search near the lake?'

'What do you mean?' asked Pearl with suspicion.

Bowell indicated the view from the windows. 'There are several acres of grounds to choose from.'

'Ten to be precise,' said Pearl. She paused as she looked out of the windows and saw a line of uniformed police officers conducting a careful search of Mount Ephraim's grounds. She looked back at the investigating officer. 'Was Guy murdered?'

DI Bowell remained silent for a moment before replying, 'Why don't I ask the questions, Miss Nolan?' She repeated, 'Why the lake?'

Pearl said nothing as she continued to watch the officers beyond the window. DI Bowell asked once more: 'The lake, Ms Nolan?'

As the officers moved out of view, Pearl gave Bowell her attention once more.

'I took a walk near the lake yesterday,' she explained. 'It's the only part of the gardens I'm really familiar with – the lake, the wood above it and—'

'The wooden bridge?' said Bowell.

Pearl nodded. 'I crossed it yesterday on my way back up to the house.'

'And when you did that again this morning,' said Bowell, 'you found Mr Priddey's body.'

Pearl held the detective's gaze and said finally: 'I thought I saw someone yesterday, near the old pump house by the lake.'

DI Bowell's eyes narrowed. 'Who?'

Pearl shook her head. 'I don't know. I couldn't be sure there was anyone there. I just saw a movement,' she went on, 'a flash of colour – yellow – disappearing into the trees on the bank. I followed but I didn't find anyone.'

'And today,' said Bowell, 'you chose the same route.'

'I told you,' said Pearl. 'It's the only route I'm familiar with.' She paused then decided to follow her own train of thought, recalling: 'It struck me yesterday that there was an atmosphere . . .'

Bowell looked askance. 'What kind of "atmosphere"?'

'It's difficult to explain,' said Pearl. 'There are some tall trees nearby, high up on the bank near the bridge – a rookery. As I approached, the birds made a terrible din – strange cries – as though they were protecting nests.'

'At this time of year?'

Pearl shook her head, confused. 'I don't know.'

The detective shared a look with Sergeant Falconer then asked, 'And what did you do when you found the body?'

'I called Emma Clarke. She's in charge of accommodation and catering here, but some years ago she used to work for me.'

'Doing what?' Bowell tipped her head to one side.

'She started as a kitchen hand then became a commis chef in my restaurant – the Whitstable Pearl.'

The detective leaned back in her chair and carefully considered Pearl. 'You're a busy lady, Miss Nolan. I hear you have a private investigation company too?'

Pearl nodded quickly but tried to steer the interview back to her main concern at that moment. 'How's Amy?' she asked. 'I haven't seen her since this morning. After I found Guy's body, I stayed with it until Ryan returned – then your officers arrived and I gave my statement straight away.' She nodded towards Sergeant Falconer but DI Bowell said nothing as she toyed with the pen in her hand.

Pearl continued. 'I . . . presume you're interviewing everyone. Everyone here, I mean?'

'We're investigating Mr Priddey's death,' said Bowell simply.

'And you haven't once used the word accident,' said Pearl.

At this, Bowell sat forward in her chair. 'The person you thought you saw yesterday – can you give me a description?'

Pearl shook her head. 'I told you, it was just a glimpse and I could have been mistaken, but later I thought I saw someone – on the lawn in front of the cricket pavilion.'

Bowell leaned back again. 'Go on.'

'It was just momentarily – a firework had exploded. It briefly lit up the whole area.'

'And you mentioned this to who?'

Pearl shook her head. 'No one.'

Bowell frowned. 'Why not?'

Pearl met the detective's gaze. 'Because I wasn't sure.'

Bowell shared another look with Falconer then said, 'Twice in one day you think you saw someone in these grounds. Wouldn't you be inclined to think you *weren't* mistaken, given that possible second sighting? And why would you not mention this last night, as soon as it happened?

'It . . . was an awkward time.'

'Awkward?' echoed Bowell.

'We'd just heard some news from Guy and Amy, about their plans.'

Bowell frowned. 'What news?'

Pearl hesitated, but, recognising that other guests would be explaining their own version of events, she now gave her own.

'Amy explained she was giving up writing to help Guy with some causes. He said he was going to use his fortune for that.'

'What causes?'

'I don't have the details.'

'What was "awkward" about this?'

Pearl gave a shrug. 'It seemed to have repercussions for others.'

'For whom?'

Pearl paused. 'I think you should ask the other guests.'

'I'm asking you, Ms Nolan.'

Pearl heaved a sigh. 'For anyone expecting to benefit from the proceeds of Guy's auction.' She paused. 'Or from Amy's work.'

DI Bowell made a brief note of this and said, 'Mr Priddey's sister is here.'

'And her husband,' said Pearl, before adding, 'and Amy's agent and her stepmother.'

Without looking up, Bowell asked: 'And Mr Soutar?'

'An old friend of Amy's.'

'A good friend?'

Pearl hesitated. 'Good enough to be invited to the

wedding,' she said, recalling Ian's reaction last night before the firework display.

Bowell considered this, then: 'And Ms Gulliver?'

'A friend of Amy and Guy's. I believe they met in Thailand.'

'Where Mr Priddey raised a cargo of porcelain?'

'That's right,' said Pearl. 'Tess's partner, James Jarrett, is a playwright.'

'And Ms Gulliver is an actress.'

Pearl nodded. 'I believe they'd like to stage a play together.'

Bowell looked up. 'For which they need funds?'

After a pause, Pearl nodded again.

'And you, Ms Nolan – what's your place in all this?'

'I told you – I'm an old school friend of Amy's.'

A silence settled between the two before Pearl noticed two figures walking past the window.

'Can I go now?' she asked impatiently.

A moment passed before DI Bowell nodded. As Pearl got to her feet, Bowell added: 'I've explained that all the guests are to remain here until our preliminary investigation is over – until Forensics have finished their work. I'm sure you'll understand why.' She added pointedly, 'As a private investigator?'

Pearl ignored the cynicism in the detective's tone and left the room.

Once she was in the hallway, Pearl took a moment to reflect on the interview with DI Bowell before heading out. Staring down from the terrace, she caught sight of the two people she had seen from the sitting-room window, now walking slowly in the meadow near the stable block, and she hurried after them.

'Amy?' At the sound of Pearl's voice, Amy turned and waited for Pearl to reach her. Sarah stood close by, watching as Pearl embraced her friend.

'I'm so sorry,' said Pearl gently, aware that Amy was trembling beneath her touch. As though silenced by grief, neither Amy nor Sarah seemed able to speak for a few moments. Finally, Amy looked to Sarah, whose pale blue eyes looked raw from weeping, and took her hand as she whispered, 'I feel like we're trapped in some kind of waking nightmare. On this day, of all days, Guy is dead?' She framed the words as a question, perhaps in the hope that Pearl might explain to both women that it was all a mistake – that Guy was still alive and waiting in the grounds below for Amy to join him and exchange their marriage vows.

Pearl knew it was no mistake and looked away, feeling helpless.

'You found my brother,' said Sarah. 'How?'

'I was crossing the bridge at the far end of the lake.' Pearl shook her head. 'I don't know any more.' Then she asked, 'Have you . . . given statements to the police?'

The two women nodded slowly. 'Everyone has,' said Sarah.

'What will happen now, Pearl?' asked Amy, helplessly. 'What am I meant to do?' Her voice rose in panic.

'Nothing,' said Pearl, trying to calm her. 'We just have to stay here—'

'But for how long?' It was another voice that had spoken. Looking up, Pearl saw Toby standing near the stable block. He made his way urgently towards them. 'Did the police tell you?'

Pearl shook her head. 'Well, they surely can't keep us here against our will,' Toby insisted. 'They must need a warrant—'

Sarah tried to interrupt. 'Toby—'

'We have rights!' he continued. 'We're not prisoners. They can't do this.'

'Be quiet,' said Amy impulsively before suddenly appearing contrite. 'Please?' She looked imploringly at him. Sarah suddenly reached out and held Amy tight. Pearl could see the two women were finding comfort in their shared grief, but she also noted the look of exclusion on Toby's face before he shook his head and turned smartly on his heels.

'I'm so sorry,' whispered Sarah to Amy as Toby headed back to the house. 'He's upset too, but . . . he finds it hard to deal with his feelings.'

Amy nodded slowly. Detaching from their embrace, she stared out across the meadow as though trying to draw strength from it. 'This place has always been a beautiful sanctuary for me,' she said. 'It must have been the same for the Belgian refugees who were billeted here in the Second World War. They planted snowdrops on this bank – a sign of hope in the depths of winter?'

Then she frowned as though confused. 'But all the while they were homeless, stateless . . . That's how I feel right now without Guy.'

Pearl spoke softly and reached out to lay a hand on each of the women's shoulders. 'I'm so sorry,' she said. 'I feel for you both.'

The grieving women nodded to acknowledge Pearl's words, then linked arms before heading back to the house.

Pearl remained in the meadow, recalling how, only the day before, Amy had confided in her about being alone for much of her life but never lonely. Pearl had identified with her, but she now knew it was impossible to imagine her own future without McGuire, and she understood how Amy must feel to have lost the man she had truly loved – just as they were about to embark on a future together. The shock of discovering Guy's body that morning had sent a surge of adrenaline through Pearl's system, but it was waning, and she now began to feel as drained as she had felt on waking that day. The fatigue was unfamiliar to Pearl, who was always primed with energy to tackle anything she needed to do – both at the restaurant and for her agency clients.

Staring across the gardens, she wondered if Mount Ephraim was capable of casting an enchantment on those who spent time here. Emma had said something about the estate being a separate world – a parallel universe – far removed even from the busy dual carriageway which, at this very moment, was still ferrying others to and from London. Pearl took a deep breath and started to make her way back up the path to the garden wing.

She paused at the stone bench, reminded that Guy Priddey and his sister had sat here the night before, discussing Sarah's marriage to Toby. *A lazy drunk with a massive sense of entitlement* was how Guy had described him. Pearl could only imagine how Toby might have reacted to that had he been aware of it – though Pearl was sure Sarah would never have told him. Guy's comments about Toby's drinking and his allegations of physical and mental abuse had gone unchallenged by Sarah, which convinced Pearl they must have been true. Nevertheless, Sarah had seemed keen to defend her husband to Guy, summoning reasons to mitigate Toby's abuse; his alcoholism being one. *A sickness*', she had said, though Guy had dismissed this justification, his tolerance of his brother-in-law having apparently worn thin. His words continued to echo in Pearl's mind as clearly as though he was still seated on the bench, relaying them to Sarah: *'Leave him, and I'll help you – but I won't go on financing his abuse.'*

Guy had appeared to be showing 'tough love', and 'love' it no doubt was; he had assured his sister he would help her, albeit only if she ended her marriage. Guy's support was conditional – and Sarah had shown no willingness to agree to her brother's conditions. Instead, she had walked away, dissatisfied and disappointed with all that he had put to her, including confirmation of the surprise he had sprung on them all – his plan to give away his fortune.

Babs had conveyed her own disappointment to Amy in another conversation that Pearl had overheard. And it was only when questioned by DI Jane Bowell that Pearl had recognised what a disappointment Guy's decision must also have been to Tess and James and their hopes for their play. But then, as Pearl had learned yesterday, Guy was known to enjoy springing surprises – something Ryan had mentioned only that morning. Perhaps Guy had encouraged Amy to take pleasure in surprising people too, though her admission to Ingrid about giving up her career had provoked shock rather than surprise. Pearl now wondered who Ingrid might have been talking to on the phone in her room the night before. From what Pearl had overheard, it may well have been someone involved in a proposed deal for media coverage of Amy's marriage to Guy. But now Pearl remembered Ingrid's last words: something about there being *only one way to change her mind*.

Pearl changed her mind, and instead of returning to the house she made her way down the slope towards the lower terrace. The lake was now sectioned off with police tape, but the wedding pavilion remained decorated, reminding Pearl how a day that had begun filled with hope was now marred by tragedy. A row of vacant seating still awaited guests. White roses remained entwined above the pavilion's entrance, but they had begun to wilt in a chilly breeze, petals strewn across the terrace. A few spots of rain splattered against a stone plaque engraved with the entwined initials of long-departed family members for whom Mount Ephraim had been home. Without a bride and groom on this day, the pavilion's perfect setting seemed almost tomb-like.

Pearl shivered and turned away, walking over to the balustrade where she stared down towards the lake. The steps from the terrace had been taped off and the wooden bridge was covered by a white tent. Beyond it, two uniformed officers stood guard over the investigations as forensics officers in white boiler suits headed up the path beyond the Motto Gate. It was only now that Pearl remembered the Gibran verse she had selected and painstakingly transcribed for Amy's wedding ceremony; one line in particular stayed with her:

'Let the winds of heaven dance between you.'

Words that would always be true even if they remained unread at a wedding that would never take place.

matters; after their first case, concerning the death of a Whitstable fisherman, several other homicides had followed – all involving Pearl to some extent. McGuire had never fully explained his relationship with Pearl to any of his fellow officers – especially Welch – and neither had he formally declared her as an informant. This meant that using any local knowledge from Pearl had to be handled carefully because associations between officers and informants were strictly regulated and monitored – at least in theory.

A close personal relationship between a local private eye, like Pearl, and a senior officer involved in the investigation of a serious crime could easily come under scrutiny from McGuire's superiors, and if that ever happened Welch would finally have enough rope to hang McGuire – metaphorically speaking, at least. Well-trained police officers were apt to look down on private investigators, not least because PIs were often former officers who had left the force under a cloud. Sometimes they managed to gain too much of a hold over a Senior Investigating Officer – as Pearl had done with McGuire – though not in the usual way. Since proposing to Pearl, McGuire had allowed himself to hope that marriage would help to smooth out any conflicting interests between his relationship and his job. Certainly things would be easier if Pearl confined herself to working in her restaurant, but McGuire now knew he couldn't persuade her to give up the agency – she was determined to keep going with Nolan's and seemed impervious to the dangers she exposed herself to in her cases. Pearl resisted all attempts to persuade her to leave crime solving to McGuire.

It was gone midday when McGuire finally made his way back to his office and closed the door behind him. He hoped to enjoy some quiet afforded by this space, disturbed only by the low rumble of traffic passing by his window on the road beneath the Roman city walls. Built as a defence against invasion, the old stone walls had been maintained throughout the centuries, though they had failed to protect the city from Wat Tyler's army during the Peasants' Revolt of 1381. These days, just over half the original circuit still survived, with the city's police station now standing guard outside a section close to Watling Street – which was also the name of the ancient route first used by the Ancient Britons between Canterbury and St Albans. For a moment, McGuire stared beyond the wall to the spires of the cathedral still looming in the dull rain. The morning had begun promisingly before slate-grey clouds had gathered and he hoped that didn't set the scene for the rest of his day.

He turned the rod on a set of Venetian blinds, closing them partially as a small cloud of dust settled on the air. Taking his phone from his pocket, McGuire began to retrieve his calls: the first from a sergeant reporting back on a house-to-house enquiry, another from his landlord replying to him about a plumbing problem – but the last was from Pearl. McGuire sat down at his desk to listen to Pearl's message, concerned by her tone. She sounded agitated as she tried to relay a series of facts as quickly as possible, staccato phrases that seemed to make little sense. The discovery of a dead body, belonging to Guy Priddey, in the lake at Mount Ephraim – the same lake she had been describing to McGuire just the day before – and only shortly after her arrival. The message came to an abrupt end with two words: 'Call me?' An inflection in her tone indicated it wasn't an order but a plea for help.

McGuire rang immediately. As he waited for his call to connect, he checked his watch, aware that he had a Health and Safety course to attend in a few minutes. 'Come on . . .' he murmured urgently. Finally the call connected – but to Pearl's own voicemail. McGuire waited for the recorded message to end then left one of his own: 'Pearl, it's me,' he said. 'What the hell's going on? Call me as soon as you get this. Please.'

Ending the call, he waited for a minute, willing Pearl to call – but his phone remained silent. McGuire raked his fingers through his blonde hair and tried to think. Finally, he picked up his office phone and dialled. He spoke quickly. 'Get me the number for Swale Police, will you?'

At exactly the same time, Pearl was sitting at the dining table in the garden wing at Mount Ephraim, her smartphone on charge in her room. Several guests were with Pearl, but nobody spoke. Toby drummed his fingers insistently on the table's surface, making a sound that resembled a horse galloping on firm ground.

'Do you have to do that?' said Babs finally. 'My nerves are shot to shreds as it is.'

Toby glowered at being admonished in this way, but before he had a chance to respond, the door opened and Emma entered. Heads turned in anticipation of news of their host. Pearl asked, 'How is she?'

'Resting,' said Emma gently. 'She seems a little calmer.'

'Thank goodness for that,' sighed Babs. She turned to Sarah beside her. 'I suppose there's a chance she may even doze off if I give her one of my little helpers.'

Tess turned to her. 'You actually think it's a good idea for Amy to take your own prescription drugs?'

'It's a light tranquilliser,' said Babs.

Simon nodded. 'Babs is right. I'm sure it won't do Amy any harm.' He smiled in an effort to appease.

'Then maybe we could all do with one,' suggested Toby, as he stared at Sarah dabbing her eyes with a handkerchief.

Babs frowned, but Emma asked: 'Can I get anything for anyone?'

'I wouldn't mind something to eat,' said Toby. As heads turned to him, he reacted defensively. 'What?' he asked innocently. 'I'm famished. I haven't eaten since breakfast. Are we expected to starve as well as being held captive?'

'No one's being held captive,' said Ian, springing to his feet.

'No?' said Toby. 'Then what else d'you call this? The police have taken over the estate, they're calling the shots, telling us we can't go home?'

'They made a request for us not to leave,' said James. He looked at Tess beside him as he added, 'And we've all agreed not to do so, haven't we?'

Tess nodded. 'Yes.'

Toby frowned. 'Why?'

Sarah looked pained. 'Because Guy's dead and they need to find out what happened.' She put a hand to her brow then hung her head low.

'That's right, Sarah,' said Babs, giving Toby an evil look, which he ignored. He turned to his wife and asked, 'Well, surely they can do that without keeping us all here?'

Nobody spoke for a moment until Simon suggested, 'Unless . . . they think one of us had something to do with it?' He offered an innocent look, but Babs thundered a harsh response. 'Don't be stupid!'

'It's not stupid,' said Ian, turning from the window to face everyone.

'What isn't?' asked James tentatively.

Ian looked at him. 'The idea that one of us might . . . know what happened?' His question seemed to hang in the air until Sarah abruptly frowned, stood up and said, 'Stop it!'

'Yes,' Toby agreed. 'It was clearly an accident.' Then: 'Wasn't it?' He turned to Pearl. 'You should know, you found him.'

Pearl took her time before replying. 'All I know,' she began, 'is that the police have a job to do and they want us to stay put – for now.'

The door opened, and Ingrid burst into the room.

'My God,' she said, pointing back to the door. 'That inspector's a piece of work. She just put me through the third degree!'

'You're not alone in that,' said James, getting to his feet.

Ingrid turned to Emma. 'Could I please have a coffee?'

Emma nodded and returned to the kitchen while Ingrid sat down and leaned forward across the table. 'Who was it that told the police I was "distraught" about Amy giving up writing?' She looked at everyone in turn.

Babs shrugged. 'It's true, you were,' she said, unabashed.

Ingrid's scarlet lips tightened. '*Et tu, Brute?*'

'I don't think you have anything to fear,' said Ian.

'How do *you* know?' Ingrid demanded.

'The police just need to establish the facts,' said Pearl. 'That means going over everything that happened last night.'

Emma brought a plate of game pie and artichoke to Toby. 'At last,' he said, sitting down at the table. Sarah shook her head slowly. 'How can you possibly eat at a time like this?' Toby glanced at her as he unwrapped his cutlery from the napkin in his hand. 'I know you're upset,' he said. 'Guy was your brother and it's only understandable you're going to miss him, but—'

'You'll miss him too, surely?' interrupted Simon.

Toby seemed brought up short by the comment, but he responded, 'Of course. After a fashion. Anyone got a pill for that too?' With that, he began tucking into his food.

Pearl considered the general mood and took a deep breath. 'Look,' she began, 'it's clear we're all going to be here for a while, at least until the police have finished their investigation, so perhaps we should agree to make more of an effort – for Amy's sake?'

Silence fell, then Tess spoke first. 'You're right.'

'Yes,' said Babs. 'Poor Amy.' She held out a flapping hand to Simon, who read her need and handed her a tissue. She blew her nose, sounding like a high-pitched bugle.

Tess sighed. 'This is like a bad dream.'

'I'll second that,' said James.

Toby looked up from his food. 'One thing's for sure,' he began, 'we'll have plenty of time to kill, so'— He looked at James and Ian—'anyone up for a game of snooker after this?'

Ian's lips narrowed. Without saying a word, he suddenly exited the room. Pearl decided to follow him.

Outside the sitting room, Pearl saw the front door of the garden wing closing after Ian. She quickly followed, and once out of the front door she saw Ian leaning across the terrace balustrade. Coming up beside him, she spoke softly. 'I'm sorry,' she said. 'Everyone's upset. Some people just have a bad way of showing it.'

After a moment, Ian gave a nod. 'Maybe.' He looked back up to the house. 'At least he's honest.' Pearl noted the anguish in his expression before he moved quickly down the steps to the path below. Again, she followed after him. 'Ian?'

He stopped abruptly in his tracks and allowed Pearl to catch up with him.

'What is it?' he asked wearily.

Pearl took a deep breath. 'I just need to ask you something.'

He met her gaze then nodded again. 'Go on.'

Pearl began carefully. 'Guy was meant to be spending last night in the west wing – with Sarah and Toby . . . and you. Did you see him any time after the fireworks?'

Ian shook his head. 'No.'

'But you left before the fireworks had ended. Why?'

Ian frowned. 'Because I'd had enough for one night.'

'Of Guy?'

'No,' he replied firmly. 'I had work to do on my case.' He met her gaze. Pearl considered him before asking, 'Why did you come here, Ian?'

He shrugged. 'Why else?' he asked. 'For Amy.' He looked away to the house and said softly, 'She's the only reason I'm here.'

Pearl paused then posed another question. 'Did you happen to hear anything last night, while you were . . . working on your case?'

Ian nodded. 'Yes. Toby, arguing. I could hardly miss

it – the man has a voice like a foghorn. And you've seen yourself, subtlety's hardly a strong point.'

'Who was he arguing with?'

'Who else?' said Ian. 'That wretched wife of his.'

'You heard Sarah?'

'No, but . . . it was pretty obvious who he was talking to.'

'Why?' asked Pearl. 'What did you hear?'

Ian took a moment to think and nodded slowly as he tried to recall. 'He was saying . . . he didn't know why he'd come . . . and that he didn't have to put up with this any longer, and . . . he was . . . sick of surprises. Then—' He broke off and Pearl noted his dark eyes narrowing as he stared beyond her, as though trying to remember something.

'What?' asked Pearl.

'He said, "*maybe I have a surprise too*".' Ian looked back at Pearl. She paused to take this in, but the moment was broken by Emma calling out to her.

Emma was standing on the terrace, indicating the upper floor. 'Your phone,' she said. 'I just heard it ringing in your room.'

Pearl hurried into the house and raced up the stairs to her bedroom. Her smartphone was no longer ringing, but as she unplugged it from its charger she noted several missed calls from McGuire. Just as she was about to call him, the phone began ringing once more. She answered it quickly.

'Are you okay?' asked McGuire, concerned.

Pearl caught her breath. 'I'm sorry,' she began, 'I forgot to put my phone on charge last night . . . but you got my message?'

'Yes,' said McGuire. 'And I've been in touch with Swale Police. I've got a contact there.'

'And?'

McGuire paused before delivering his reply.

'Looks like they have a murder investigation on their hands.'

CHAPTER ELEVEN

That evening, it took Pearl only ten minutes to walk to The Red Lion pub on a public footpath that carved its way across the Mount Ephraim estate, passing through orchards as the last of the day's sun streamed through the fields. A few locals turned their heads as Pearl entered, but, after giving a nod to the bartender, who was busy serving, Pearl made her way straight to the pub's secluded garden. It was filled with empty tables, and she chose one that was largely concealed by an apple tree and sheltered by a gazebo, just in case any of DI Bowell's officers were still in the vicinity. Pearl could certainly say she hadn't gone far; across the high fence that formed the pub garden's boundary, the rural landscape was still visible, the orchards of Mount Ephraim stretching almost to the horizon.

A few minutes later, car tyres sounded on the gravel of the car park. An engine stopped and McGuire appeared in the garden. Pearl sprang to her feet and lost herself in his embrace. McGuire kissed her tenderly, his hands gently framing her face as his eyes scanned hers.

'You okay?'

Pearl nodded and sat down again at the table. McGuire joined her, and the bartender approached and took their drink orders. McGuire declined the food menu.

'Are you sure?' Pearl asked, concerned, but McGuire shook his head. 'When I get back,' he said, not wanting to be distracted. As the bartender moved off, Pearl looked back at McGuire.

'What did you find out?'

'Some facts from the initial medical report.'

Pearl waited for him to continue.

'Priddey drowned.'

Pearl shook her head in confusion. 'But you said—'

'It's complicated.' McGuire produced a notebook from his pocket, opened it and handed Pearl a folded sheet of paper that had been tucked inside. Pearl skimmed it.

'Oxycodone?' she asked, staring back at him.

'It's a painkiller.' McGuire explained. 'It seems Priddey's been using the stuff for some time.'

'Why?'

'Did you know he served in the US Navy?'

Pearl nodded. 'Amy mentioned he'd left after failing a medical. Do you know why?'

McGuire nodded. 'He suffered a couple of diving accidents. He may have underestimated their seriousness, but they were bad enough to cause decompression sickness.'

'Decompression . . .' Pearl looked away as she tried to make sense of this. 'You mean, the bends?' she said. 'That's how I know it. It happens when you come up from a dive too quickly?'

McGuire nodded. 'Divers breathe compressed air containing nitrogen. At higher pressure under water, the gas goes into the body's tissues. It doesn't cause problems when you're down in the water, but if you rise too quickly the nitrogen forms bubbles in the body, and that can lead to all kinds of tissue and nerve damage.'

'Yes,' said Pearl. 'And paralysis or death if the bubbles form in the brain?'

'That's right,' said McGuire. 'Nitrogen narcosis can also happen on the kind of deep dives Priddey was used to, and if he suffered from that his judgement may have been impaired, and he may have played down some incidents, believing he was okay.' He looked at Pearl and went on. 'He may even have ignored warnings not to dive again until cleared by a doctor, or he could have continued diving outside the dive table recommendations used by the US Navy.'

Pearl took a moment to register this. 'He was certainly still diving when he was working on bringing up that cargo.' She paused. 'But there's medical treatment available for the bends, isn't there?'

McGuire checked his notebook. 'Something called a hyperbaric chamber gives recompression treatment, but it has to be used soon after diving. Left untreated, decompression sickness can cause necrosis, which can damage areas of bone in the body. Joints collapse and become painful—'

'But . . . Guy seemed fit.'

'Maybe the painkillers were helping give that impression.'

The bartender reappeared to bring a glass of wine for Pearl and a beer for McGuire. Pearl waited until McGuire had paid for the drinks and the bartender had moved off before she said softly, 'Amy didn't mention any of this to me.'

McGuire gave a shrug. 'I'm not surprised.' He sipped his beer and explained, 'If you think about it, Priddey must have needed investment to raise that cargo. He wouldn't have wanted it known that his health was compromised in any way.' He set down his beer and Pearl studied him. 'Why do Swale Police believe this might be murder? And what's it got to do with oxycodone?'

McGuire met her look. 'Toxicology reports have been ordered.'

'You mean, Guy was poisoned?'

McGuire leaned closer and held Pearl's look. 'I don't know. I need more details, but something's not right. Priddey died in the early hours of the morning – no later than 2 a.m. – but no one seems to know why he was in the grounds so late at night. His bed hadn't been slept in, and Swale Police reports show he returned to his room some time before midnight when he took his medication.'

Pearl took this in.

'What're you thinking?' asked McGuire.

'I'd just gone up to my room last night when I heard a door close in the corridor. But that was before midnight.'

McGuire shrugged. 'Could have been someone going to the bathroom.'

Pearl nodded. 'Yes. And Guy was in the west wing. But he went to the lake – why?' She paused to think. 'I was standing on a wooden bridge when I found his body. A course of bricks acts like a dam but there are a few missing bricks in the centre where spring water enters the lake. Guy's body was wedged there. It's an odd place to choose if you're planning to drown someone – or yourself.' She looked at McGuire. 'Any forensics?'

McGuire shook his head. 'The area was contaminated – you were there and the gardens were full of visitors only a few days ago – as well as the wedding guests all yesterday. Seems you all took a turn around them, including down to the lake.'

'Yes, but for some reason Guy also went there – after taking his medication.'

McGuire shrugged. 'I don't know why – yet. Swale CID are still waiting for a full autopsy. It seems from tests done so far that he would have been very unstable on his feet.'

'So, he fell into the water . . .'

'And found it impossible to get out.'

Pearl looked up at McGuire. 'You mean he tried?'

'Residue was found under his fingernails – mud, lakeside plants.'

'Skunk cabbage,' murmured Pearl. McGuire looked at her and she went on. 'I thought I smelt it yesterday even though it's late in the season. It gives off a strong odour, like rotting meat. Dead flesh . . .' She trailed off. 'Maybe it was just a premonition of what was to come.'

McGuire failed to comment and pocketed his notebook.

Pearl went on. 'Bowell's team and forensics have been all over the area – and the house. They set up an incident room in the garden wing where I'm staying. Presumably they haven't found anything suspicious in any of the guests' rooms or belongings, or there would have been an arrest?'

McGuire gave a nod. 'I'm sure.' He finished his beer. Pearl thought again. 'It's possible there was an intruder,' she said. 'Someone who came into the gardens yesterday? The gates were open for much of the time to allow guests to arrive. Someone could have hidden out—' She broke off, then: 'I thought I saw someone.'

McGuire looked at her. 'When?'

'When I was on the phone to you, describing the lake. I went to the old pump house I told you about, and as I was checking it out I felt there was someone there – among the trees on the bank.'

'Who?' asked McGuire, holding her gaze.

Pearl shook her head in frustration. 'I don't know. But I told Bowell about this and how, last night during a firework display, I thought I saw someone moving across the lawn near to the cricket pavilion. I'm not sure she took me seriously.'

'Did you tell anyone else?'

Pearl shook her head.

'Why not?'

'Because I wasn't completely sure. I never thought for a moment anyone could be in danger.'

'With an intruder in the grounds?' said McGuire. 'You said the gardens were closed to visitors at the moment.'

'They are. But there's a public footpath running through the estate so it's impossible to keep everyone out.' She took a deep breath. 'I planned to talk to Emma about it, but ... events took their own course.' She looked down and McGuire considered her before he laid his hand gently on her cheek.

'I want you to come home, Pearl.' She looked up at him as he went on. 'I talked to Dolly and she agrees.'

Pearl frowned and shook her head. 'I can't,' she said quickly. 'Bowell wants all the guests to remain at Mount Ephraim.'

'I'm sure she does,' said McGuire. 'That makes things more convenient for her investigation but you're still free to go.'

'She could arrest me.'

'Unlikely,' said McGuire. 'She has no reason to suspect you.'

'But I found the body.'

'Pearl—'

'Look, if I were to leave, it would only encourage everyone else to do the same. Toby's already complaining about being held captive.'

'Toby?'

'Lawson. Guy's brother-in-law.' She paused, summoning resolve. 'If Guy really was murdered, I owe it to Amy to find out who did it.'

McGuire shook his head. 'That's not your job.'

'But it's my responsibility,' said Pearl firmly. 'I've known Amy since we were at school. This was meant to be her wedding weekend.'

'And that wedding is not going to happen,' said McGuire gently. 'So, come home and let the police do their work.'

Pearl saw McGuire's conviction but once again shook her head. 'I can't,' she said again. 'I found Guy's body. And now I need to find out who killed him.'

McGuire took a deep breath, looked away towards the surrounding countryside and exhaled deeply. He then turned back to Pearl and held her hand tightly in his own. 'Nothing I say is going to change your mind, is it?'

Looking at him, Pearl shook her head slowly.

'Right,' said McGuire softly. 'Then at least work with me.' He held her look as he went on. 'I'll find out all I can, but you have to promise me you won't take any unnecessary risks.'

Pearl nodded. 'I promise. But can you really find out more? Time and cause of death?'

'I can try,' said McGuire. 'But if Bowell finds out I'm interfering in her case, she could close down my contact at Swale.'

Pearl continued to look at him and McGuire took the opportunity to move closer until his lips finally met hers. As they kissed, Pearl considered how easy it would be to do what McGuire wanted: to return to Whitstable and allow DI Bowell to complete her investigation – without Pearl. But as they broke apart, she knew how she would feel if she were to lose him, as Guy had been lost to Amy. She rested her cheek against his shoulder, and for a moment neither spoke. Then McGuire said softly, 'I'll drive you back before you're missed. You can tell me more as we go.'

CHAPTER TWELVE

McGuire parked up along Mount Ephraim's boundary wall. As he killed his engine, he took a moment to consider all that Pearl had just told him.

'So,' he began. 'Eight guests in all?'

'Nine – including me.'

McGuire gave a smile. 'I think I'm safe in discounting you as a suspect. But from what you say, Toby Lawson seems the one person who's not about to mourn Guy Priddey.'

Pearl seemed troubled by this assumption. 'Maybe. But if Toby was going to kill Guy, why argue with him in front of everyone and point out their bad relationship?'

McGuire considered this then asked: 'What about his wife?'

Pearl looked away. 'Yes,' she said thoughtfully. 'Sarah was certainly upset about Guy's plans to give away his fortune – but enough to murder him?' She shook her head. 'Guy may have upset her with his opinion of Toby, but he and Sarah were still siblings, and she now seems genuinely heartbroken by Guy's death.'

'What about the others?'

Pearl heaved a sigh. 'I suspect Babs Meadows-Young will be mourning the loss of access to Guy's money. From what she said last night to Amy she's made some bad investments, and she has a companion on whom she seems curiously dependent – though she abuses Simon as much as she did her former husband. They're like an old married couple, always bickering.' She looked back at McGuire and saw him smile.

'Do old married couples always bicker?' he asked.

'I don't know,' said Pearl. 'But maybe one day we'll get a chance to find out.' She went on. 'Tess is an old friend of Amy and Guy. They met in Thailand, but her new partner is looking for a backer for his play, an "angel", so . . .'

'Perhaps they thought this weekend might lead to that?' asked McGuire.

'Why wouldn't they?' said Pearl. 'This was meant to be a happy occasion, everyone in a positive mood. James seems an attractive, intelligent man, and writers are always meant to have an insight into people's characters, aren't they? I'm sure, given the chance, he may well have tried to charm Guy.'

'Or Amy?'

Pearl shrugged. 'The news of them both giving away a fortune to good causes must have been a bombshell – to James, at least – and especially if Tess had raised his hopes about the prospects for his play.' She looked towards Mount Ephraim and thought for a moment. 'Amy's agent, Ingrid, made it clear last night that she had been chasing up commissions for Amy, perhaps to write about her marriage or even her life with Guy, until—' She broke off.

'Until what?' McGuire prompted.

'Until she learned that Amy was planning on giving up writing. I heard Ingrid on the phone to someone last night. She was saying how she would try something to get Amy to change her mind.'

'Try what?'

'I wish I knew.'

'All right,' said McGuire. 'So that leaves . . .'

'Ian,' said Pearl. 'I was surprised Amy had invited him to the wedding. I was even more surprised that he came. They were once in love – or so I thought – but things didn't work out, though I'm not sure why.'

'But she still invited him,' said McGuire, thoughtful.

'Yes,' Pearl agreed. 'It's curious. Ian was engaged at one point to a local girl, Kate Parsons, but that didn't last either. If he and Kate had stayed together, I could have understood why Amy would invite him – but as a single guy, and a former boyfriend?'

McGuire considered this. 'He also accepted the invitation.'

'Yes,' said Pearl, 'and extraordinarily, last night Guy actually offered him the chance of becoming his best man.' She looked at McGuire, who said knowingly, 'Nothing like rubbing salt into the wound. One-upmanship on Priddey's part?'

Pearl shrugged. 'Or maybe he thought Ian was the best man for the role? In any case, Simon took over, so Ian was off the hook.'

McGuire looked doubtful, but Pearl went on. 'Ian's a nice guy.' She frowned. 'Perhaps too nice. He's a defence barrister.'

'Criminal law?'

Pearl nodded.

McGuire considered this. 'So he knows the ropes.' He gave Pearl a significant look.

'No,' said Pearl. 'I can't imagine that Ian Soutar came here with the intention of killing Guy.'

'Maybe he didn't *intend* to,' said McGuire. 'Maybe it wasn't premeditated.'

'Maybe,' said Pearl. 'But that could be the case for anyone.'

McGuire looked up, thoughtful. 'So that leaves'—he looked back at Pearl—'the couple taking care of the place.'

'Emma Clarke,' said Pearl. 'But I know Emma. She once worked for me, and I trust her implicitly.'

'And her partner?'

'I've no reason to doubt her choice in Ryan.'

McGuire paused before responding. 'I wasn't actually referring to Emma and Ryan.'

Pearl read his look. 'You . . . surely can't mean Amy?'

McGuire said nothing as Pearl stared at him. 'But you

can't,' she repeated. 'Amy was totally besotted with Guy. She still is. You didn't hear what she had to say to me the other day – her feelings for him. She couldn't have invented that.'

McGuire spoke calmly. 'Presumably, she had the most to gain from his death.'

Pearl shook her head. 'No,' she said emphatically. 'They weren't yet married, remember? And she'd already signed a prenuptial agreement and supported Guy's plans for giving away his fortune. They were doing this together – planning to live modestly, dedicating themselves to what they believe in. In fact,' she concluded, 'Amy had the most to *lose* – a future with the man she loved.'

At this, McGuire turned from Pearl and stared through the windscreen at the gates of Mount Ephraim. 'Pearl, this killer—'

'May not be someone at the house,' she insisted. 'Like I said, there could have been an intruder.'

McGuire looked back at her. 'Which is why I don't want you to take any risks.' He leaned towards her once more, kissing her long and hard as though willing her to change her mind. But when they finally broke apart, Pearl placed her hand on the passenger door and opened it quickly.

'Pearl,' said McGuire.

Staring back at him, she saw her partner's torn expression. 'Please be careful.'

Pearl nodded then got out of the car and walked a few steps to the gates. The light had faded and the trees on the driveway were looming black against the sky. Pearl turned back again and gave a last smile for McGuire before the headlights of his car switched on and he drove slowly away from her along the empty country road. Pearl looked up at the tall wrought-iron gates and walked through them, making her way along the driveway to the house, while recognising how alone she felt in that moment.

Entering the garden wing, Pearl soon found the other guests had retired to their rooms. The ground floor was empty, the Aga pushing out heat into the darkness. She closed the kitchen door behind her and was just about to head towards the grand wooden staircase when she hesitated. Glancing back down the corridor, she considered a door beneath the stairs. She tried it but was unsurprised to find it locked. Taking a step back into the main hallway, Pearl stared in the direction of the terrace, still wondering what might be on the other side of the door beneath the staircase – perhaps it was simply cupboard space on the same level as the corridor, or maybe there were steps leading down to a basement. If the latter, those stairs would surely give access to what Emma had explained was once the old kitchen. Pearl stepped quietly back to the front door and left the wing. Once outside, she took the short flight of stone steps down to the path and made her way to the concealed porch beneath the terrace.

Entering the area, she peered once more through the dusty glass door-panels but saw only darkness and cobwebs on the other side. The door was still locked, but now she realised that any stairs leading from the door beneath the garden wing's staircase could well lead straight down to the same basement area – and provide a concealed exit into the grounds from the garden wing. She paused, wondering whether the basement area itself was connected in any way to the west wing where Ian, Sarah and Toby were still staying, but it was at that moment she heard footsteps on the terrace above.

Pearl froze, her body tense as she remained stock still while hearing someone descending the stone steps. A moment later, she ducked further into the cover provided by the dark porch as she heard the footsteps approaching on the gravel driveway, then passing by and finally receding into the distance. After waiting a few more moments, she emerged from her hiding place and glanced searchingly around in the darkness. Pearl finally sighted a dark figure silhouetted by moonlight moving quickly across the front lawn to disappear behind an old redwood tree. Pearl followed, keeping her body close to a yew hedge so as not to be seen. Suddenly, she realised her path was obstructed as the land before her gave way into a wide ditch. It was the ha-ha that gaped before her. Over a metre deep at this spot, it prevented Pearl from moving on. She surveyed its path across the lawn, noting how it began just after a pair of ancient rusting gates. She quickly made her way to them and crossed through the gates and on to lawn – only to find she was now alone. Frustrated, she stared around, her gaze finally fixing on the Miz Maze. She set off towards it.

Rising in the darkness, the tall plants in the maze swayed in the night air, but Pearl continued on beyond the old Motto Gate that was creaking on its hinges and made her way towards the wooden bridge by the lake. The police forensics tent had now disappeared. The officers had completed their work. As she headed down, she noticed, for the first time, that below the tennis court a small stone bench was inset into two curved buttresses that helped to support the outer walls of the lower terrace. She moved on but paused at the sight of the bridge and studied the entry of water into the lake from the meadow – at the foot of which flowed a spring. Looking down, Pearl discovered an area of scorched earth – a spot perhaps used by gardeners to burn old vegetation – but the sound of running water drew her back to the bridge. There, staring down into the depths, she saw in her mind's eye Guy's face staring up at her – but only as a momentary flash. Reflecting on what McGuire had told her, she wondered what Guy could have been doing here, coming to this spot shortly after taking his medication – oxycodone – the painkiller he had come to rely on for so long. Had his medication been tampered with? If so, how? And who would have known of Guy's need for it in the first place? Certainly his sister, thought Pearl. She suddenly remembered the conversation she had overheard and Sarah's questions to Guy: *'Are you okay?'* she had asked, and, *'Is the pain getting worse?'* to which Guy had replied that he was fine.

'You'll never be "fine" again,' Sarah had said bitterly.

'I'm okay,' he insisted. *'And I'm in love.'*

Sarah had surely known of her brother's condition, so it was likely her husband, Toby, would have known too. Tess – who had travelled with the couple on their sailing trips in Thailand – would have also known, though she had dismissed Pearl's questions on the night before the wedding, perhaps from loyalty. It was possible that Tess shared the secret with her new partner, James. Amy, in turn, may have confided in Babs, who could well have told Simon. Ingrid might also have been aware of Guy's health problems, in which case, perhaps the only guest not to have known about them would have been Ian Soutar – and Pearl, until now.

Pearl was still considering this as the bell in the old clock tower began to chime the hour, but she was suddenly distracted by another high-pitched sound – a woman's voice – not a scream but a sharp exclamation – a voice raised in anger rather than distress, and only for a moment. Pearl listened for it again but heard only the steady trickle of spring water into the lake. Following the direction of the woman's cry, Pearl rushed up the slope, emerging on the pitch before the old cricket pavilion, its structure appearing almost spectral in the moonlight. Pearl hesitated then hurried quickly across the field.

Standing on the pavilion's veranda, Pearl stared through the dusty windows to see old scoreboards and trophies stored on shelves near the doors. She stepped back onto the pitch outside, looked up quickly and noted that the clock on the pavilion's roof showed the time as 11.05. Then she heard a sound in the bushes nearby. At the side of the pavilion, a large badger halted in its tracks at the sight of Pearl, then bustled its way into undergrowth at the rear of the pavilion. Pearl waited a moment then followed, to find only some gardening equipment: an old upturned rake, a wheelbarrow and a heavy lawn roller. About to give up, she had just begun to move off when she caught sight of something – a small piece of fabric snagged on a twig. Pearl reached out and freed it – and saw it was wool, bright yellow in colour.

Perhaps she had not been mistaken after all.

CHAPTER THIRTEEN

'I can't believe Guy's death could be anything other than a terrible accident,' said Amy the next morning. She was seated on the edge of her bed and seemed dwarfed by her surroundings, looking almost childlike to Pearl as her fingers toyed nervously with the handkerchief in her hands. In spite of her suntan, she appeared drained – empty of the vitality and passion she had displayed, in this same room, only days before.

'The investigating officer, DI Bowell,' said Pearl, 'she's explained to you—'

'Yes,' said Amy curtly. 'She told me about a . . . problem with Guy's medication? Maybe they mean some kind of overdose. But if they're right about that, it must have been a mistake.' There was firm conviction in the look she gave Pearl.

'Is that likely?' asked Pearl.

It took a moment before Amy admitted, 'Guy often took his painkiller with alcohol. He carried a hip flask of brandy. I warned him about mixing the two . . .'

'But he'd been taking the oxycodone for some time.'

'That's true.'

'And he'd never had a problem – until now?'

Amy shook her head, then got up and gave her attention to the view beyond the bedroom window.

Pearl waited before offering a suggestion. 'There is another possibility,' she said in a sombre tone. Amy looked back sharply and shook her head. 'No,' she said firmly. 'Guy didn't kill himself.'

'I'm sure he didn't,' said Pearl, remembering the look of love that had passed from Guy to his fiancée just two nights prior on the terrace below. Amy frowned. 'Then . . . are you asking me to believe he was murdered?'

Pearl spoke softly. 'I'm asking you to consider that, yes.' She paused. 'Is there anyone you might have reason to suspect—'

Amy broke in quickly. 'Are you seriously suggesting we invited someone here who could be capable of murder? The answer is no, Pearl. You are all just . . . friends . . . family.'

Pearl took a deep breath. 'All the same,' she pressed on, 'Guy and Toby were hardly the best of friends.'

'Well, that's true,' Amy conceded. 'They didn't get on – but that was because of Sarah. Guy was always very protective of her and, as Toby said himself, she got a raw deal from Frank – their father. He left them both with very little – but they did inherit some money from their mother. Guy used his to carve out a life for himself.' She paused. 'And Sarah married Toby.'

'Who has a drink problem.'

Amy nodded. 'I think he gambles too. Often the two go together. He seems to like an adrenaline rush and takes things to the wire. I don't think he can help himself. Maybe that's why his business ventures have all come to nothing.'

'And Guy feared for Sarah?'

Amy nodded again. 'When we came back from Thailand, he went to visit her. She had told him Toby had been trying hard not to drink and that he was doing well. But Guy noticed she had bruises. Cuts to her arms. She said she'd been playing with one of her cats – they're like surrogate children – and she told Guy the cat had scratched her. Guy didn't believe her. He told me he always knew when she was lying.'

Pearl took a deep breath and braced herself to pose another difficult question.

'I have to ask you, Amy,' she began, 'about Guy's finances. Was he really telling the truth?'

'About our plans?' asked Amy. 'Of course he was. Guy was never really into money for its own sake. For him, a challenge was everything. And once he had decided to do something – like raising that cargo – nothing could stop him or change his mind. The auction may have proved how valuable the cargo was, and how well he had done in bringing up so much of it safely, but the millions it raised meant nothing in the bigger picture to him. It was all just . . . figures on a balance sheet.' She paused. 'Guy already had what he wanted.'

'You?'

Amy gave a sad smile and shook her head. 'His freedom,' she said finally. 'He had created a good life for himself – his home was his boat, the *Tranquil C*.' She reached out and picked up a book from her bedside table, a collection of short stories by Ernest Hemingway. Tucked inside it were a few photos, which she passed to Pearl. They showed a large schooner with Guy at the helm and Amy at his side.

'He never wanted a luxury home ashore,' she explained. 'A "land station", as he called it. Instead, he wanted to live in the world and be constantly reminded of that – not in a series of rooms, however beautiful.' She looked around. 'I can't help thinking,' she began, 'if only I hadn't decided to take up the invitation to come here, he might still be with me.' Her eyes filled with tears. Pearl handed back the photos, which Amy carefully replaced inside the book before setting it back on the bedside table.

'Are you saying,' said Pearl gently, 'that there was no financial motive for anyone to murder Guy?'

Amy dabbed at her eyes with a handkerchief then held Pearl's look and shook her head. 'Not since he'd made his decision about the money. He was starting up a charitable foundation,' she said. 'Virtually everything from the cargo auction was tied up in that, so with his death those funds will now be distributed to the causes.'

She paused. 'I signed the prenuptial agreement, so I won't benefit from anything Guy left.'

Pearl took a moment to take this in. 'And what do you remember of last night?' she asked softly.

Amy thought for a moment. 'Well, after the firework display, Guy went with Ryan to make sure everything was safe.'

'At the ha-ha,' said Pearl. 'That's where Ryan set off the display?'

'Yes, I think so. I had a chat with Emma, then I went to speak to Babs in the games room. She said she wanted to talk to me about something.'

'And . . . you said you had fallen out?'

Amy nodded. 'To be honest, she was shocked by Guy's plans.'

'Shocked?'

'Concerned – for me – but I told her there was no need.'

Pearl decided against telling Amy that she had overheard this conversation, wanting to hear her friend's account. Amy continued: 'Then I went up to bed. I'd called Guy a little earlier, one last time on his mobile, just to say goodnight.' Her face crumpled at the thought. 'It was such a stupid thing for us not to spend the night together. Tradition,' she said. 'Nonsense. Because if we hadn't observed that, we'd have been together, instead of Guy being in the west wing.'

'In the groom's suite?'

Amy nodded. 'Alone.' She left a weighted pause, then

JULIE WASSMER

added, 'like I am now. Those were the last words we had.'
Her voice had dropped to a whisper. 'A hurried goodbye.
And yesterday morning I got ready. Emma cooked
breakfast here, then went to the west wing and did the
same for Sarah and Toby.'

'And Ian?'

'I . . . suppose so,' stammered Amy. 'She didn't
mention him.' She frowned. 'But it was Sarah who told
Emma she hadn't seen Guy in the morning, and I believe
Emma then tried to call Ryan. He was with the celebrant
– and you?'

Pearl nodded then thought for a moment. 'Amy, since
you've been here, have you seen anyone in the gardens?'

'Like who?'

'Anyone other than us?'

'You think someone could have come here?'

'It's possible,' said Pearl. 'The gates are left open when
guests are expected.'

'Yes,' said Amy. 'But no one would have had access to
Guy's room in the west wing – or to his medication. Only
Emma, and perhaps Ryan, have spare keys to the rooms.'

Pearl looked over at the antique wardrobe, then produced something from her pocket. 'Have you any clothes
made from this material?' Pearl held up a small transpar-
ent plastic bag containing a piece of the fabric she had
found snagged near the cricket pavilion the night before.

'What is it?' Amy asked, puzzled.

'Some yellow wool.'

Amy shook her head. 'I never wear yellow,' she said.

'Babs once told me it did nothing for my complexion and that put me off wearing it for life.'

Pearl considered this for a moment. 'Babs's wedding outfit was yellow,' she reminded her.

'That's true,' Amy agreed. 'And it's one of her favourite colours; but her wedding suit is linen, not wool.' She handed the bag back to Pearl. 'Is . . . this important?'

'No,' said Pearl. 'At least, not yet.'

She slipped the plastic bag into her pocket. Amy held Pearl's look. 'Look, I know we have to remain here,' she said. 'The police—'

'Want us to stay put for now,' said Pearl, 'which will help.'

'Help them?' asked Amy.

'Help me,' said Pearl. In the pause that followed, Amy seemed to comprehend something. 'You're going to do that,' she said, 'find out what happened to Guy?'

Pearl nodded slowly. 'Of course.'

Amy gave an exhalation, as though a heavy load had just been taken from her shoulders. Her eyes searched Pearl's. 'Whatever happened,' she began, 'however terrible it may be, I need to know. Nothing could be worse than getting the news of Guy's death.' She reached for Pearl's hands and held them tightly in her own. 'Promise me you'll find out, Pearl? You'll do this for me?' Pearl nodded once more. 'I promise.'

On leaving Amy's room, Pearl headed downstairs, trying to absorb all she had just heard, when she noticed someone leaving the kitchen. Emma was just about to close the door behind her when she caught sight of Pearl on the stairs and paused in her tracks.

'Pearl—' she began. But before she could go on, Pearl asked, 'Can I have a word?'

Emma looked torn, but as she stared back at the kitchen behind her she seemed to recognise there was no escape. Resigned, she nodded.

CHAPTER FOURTEEN

Emma opened the door to the apartment she shared with her partner and allowed Pearl to enter before her. 'Ryan's doing some work in one of the orchards,' she explained, 'so we won't be disturbed here.' She invited Pearl to take a seat at a large pine kitchen table then moved to the sink to fill a kettle, leaving Pearl to glance around the open-plan living space. It was tidy, with few personal possessions on display, although a red sofa was scattered with what looked like handmade cushions decorated with multi-coloured pom-poms. A few stained-glass panels hung at the window allowing sunlight to stream through them, creating patterns that danced on the wall. A heart-shaped photo frame showed Emma and Ryan smiling for the camera in Mount Ephraim's grounds. Pearl eyed an oak breadboard on the table, shaped like a rabbit. Emma joined Pearl at the table and said, 'All Ryan's handiwork. He did it with a jigsaw in his workshop one afternoon. Must have been a bit bored.'

Pearl gave a smile and nodded towards the photo. 'Have you been together long?'

'Three years,' said Emma. 'We met here at the house. This apartment comes with the job. Our own little world.' She remained silent until the kettle boiled, sending a plume of steam up a kitchen window pane.

'Would you like some tea?'

Pearl nodded. 'Thanks.' She watched Emma prepare two mugs of tea which she brought to the table with some cake.

'Lemon drizzle,' she explained. 'My own recipe.'

After handing Pearl a slice, she sat down and suddenly took on a grave expression as she waited for Pearl's first question. 'You wanted to talk to me?'

Pearl nodded. 'I take it you've been in touch with the owners of the house?'

Emma frowned. 'Yes, of course, but communication's difficult,' she explained. 'They're on a cruise ship right now but they'll be docking in Sydney in a few days' time when they're due to meet relatives.'

'So they're not returning straight away?'

Emma shook her head. 'But that doesn't mean they're not as shocked about this as we are. I'm keeping them updated and I believe they're helping the police with enquiries as best as they can from so far away.'

Pearl took something from her pocket and placed it on the table. Emma looked at her. 'What's this?'

'A piece of yellow fabric. Does it look at all familiar? Perhaps it's from an article of clothing – belonging to you or Ryan?'

Emma picked up the plastic bag and eyed the piece of woollen material inside. She shook her head. 'Where did you get this?'

'In the grounds last night,' said Pearl. 'Near the cricket pavilion. I heard a woman's voice. When I got there, she was gone. But I found this.'

Emma looked surprised. 'Have you told the police?' she asked as she handed the packet back. Pearl nodded. 'I gave some of it to a uniformed officer this morning.'

'Some?'

'I kept this small piece so I could ask some questions of my own.' She eyed Emma, who hastily picked up her mug and sipped her tea.

'What is it?' asked Pearl.

'The whole thing,' said Emma, 'Guy's death . . . it's terrible, but . . . it's like Ryan and I have been dragged back into reality.' She stared at Pearl. 'Being here, for so long, has made us feel safe, cocooned, as though nothing bad could ever happen again.'

'Again?' said Pearl.

Emma looked uneasy at Pearl's question then gave a heavy sigh.

'Ryan and I haven't had things too easy. Before I came here, after I'd left The Whitstable Pearl, it felt like . . . like I was in exile. Moving from place to place. Never really settling. Never really feeling at home, as though I truly belonged.'

'Emma—'

'It's my fault, Pearl. I just felt restless, as though I didn't really deserve any peace.' She looked away. 'Perhaps I was trying to compensate – for what had happened at school.' She frowned and went on. 'I never really explained to you – or to anyone else – only Ryan, but I was bullied at school. I know I should have told someone, but I felt too ashamed. Too . . . weak. It went on for some time. Stupid remarks, taunts about my clothes. My long, fair plaits. My schoolbooks went missing, messages were put in my desk. I couldn't tell my mum. She had enough to worry about when Dad left us.'

Emma paused. 'It was hard to make sense of why he'd left. I thought maybe it was my fault he'd gone, so maybe I needed to be punished. That's how I made sense of it all at the time. But one day, I couldn't stand it any more. I fought back. And for the first time, I saw fear in the eyes of my bullies. That gave me hope that, if I learned how to be strong, it could stop.'

She looked at Pearl. 'Of course, I wasn't strong; it was just an act – but it worked. And after that, I felt like I could do anything. So I started playing truant. Making everyone else scared of me, even teachers. I got suspended from school – then expelled.' She paused. 'Then you took me on, and . . . suddenly I felt like I could finally be the person I was meant to be. I looked up to you, Pearl. For a while I even wanted to be you.' She smiled. 'But I knew I couldn't. There's only one Pearl Nolan. So I went off.'

'Travelling.'

Emma nodded. 'I had to *learn* to be me. Somewhere else. A long way away. And when I knew who I was'—she looked around for a moment—'I came here – and met Ryan. He'd had problems too.'

'What kind of problems?'

Pearl saw Emma struggling with indecision before she finally confided: 'He'd been in a gang. Got involved with drugs.' She looked pained. 'Heroin.'

Pearl sighed.

'I know. It was such a waste of life, and it caused him loads of problems, but I suppose it was his own way of escaping. Ryan had a tough childhood. He left home at fifteen and was on the streets for a while.'

Pearl looked away. Emma went on. 'But then he got some work with a gardener, and a place to stay. It wasn't easy, but he got clean and he's never looked back.'

Pearl stared again at the photo of Emma and Ryan, recognising how close together they were standing on the stone bridge by the Japanese rock garden – the spot where so many couples had stood to pose for photos on their wedding day – and where Emma and Ryan might one day do the same. Pearl reached for Emma's hand. 'I'm pleased you found each other,' she said sincerely. 'Kindred spirits?' A moment of understanding passed between the two women.

Pearl took a deep breath and prepared to change the subject. 'Guy's room,' she began, 'in the west wing.'

'It's a suite,' said Emma, 'named after the original owner, Sir Edwyn Dawes, who built the house. It's actually our bridal suite.'

'But you said it's often occupied by the groom on the night before a wedding?'

Emma nodded. 'That's right. And the bride joins the groom there for the wedding night.'

Pearl looked thoughtful. 'But the suite hadn't been slept in on the night Guy died?'

'No,' Emma confirmed. 'Guy's things were all there: his clothes and wedding suit, his toiletries in the bathroom.'

'Did you notice a hip flask?'

Emma nodded. 'That was on the bedside table – until the police took it away. Together with some pills.'

'And did you notice what they were?'

Emma shook her head. 'I wouldn't know, Pearl. I just happened to see them beside the hip flask yesterday morning.' She paused, then ventured: 'Have . . . have they got something to do with Guy's death?'

'I'm not sure,' said Pearl, guardedly, 'but that medication may have played a part.'

Emma looked confused. 'It doesn't make sense,' she said slowly, 'that Guy should want to kill himself just before his wedding. It was obvious how much he loved Amy. Anyone could see that. They had everything.'

'Yes,' Pearl agreed. 'And they had each other.'

Emma's expression grew pained at her use of the past tense. 'In any case,' she continued, 'if he had planned to kill himself with an overdose, why would he then go to the lake? You found his body under the wooden bridge, didn't you?'

Pearl nodded. 'And I think he must have entered the water on the meadow side, just before the brick dam. The spring water flows over the bricks in the centre but it's not deep enough for Guy's body to have flowed through into the lake.'

Emma frowned. 'You mean, his body was trapped under the bridge?'

Pearl gave a nod. 'I might even have missed seeing it,' she said, 'but I was looking down at the plants. There was an odour . . .'

Emma turned her head away.

'I'm sorry,' said Pearl, aware she needed to change tack. 'Tell me what happened. You prepared breakfast for the guests in the garden wing?'

'Yes. But Amy didn't want any. Nerves, she said, so I fixed breakfast for everyone else – except Tess, who was helping Amy to get ready. She just had some toast and coffee in Amy's room. Everyone else ate in the garden wing downstairs, apart from you.'

'Yes,' said Pearl, thoughtfully, 'I don't know why I slept so deeply. Perhaps it was the champagne the night before – and I'm certainly not used to the quiet here. What happened then?'

'I went across to the west wing to make breakfast for Mr and Mrs Lawson, and I took it to their room.'

'And Mr Soutar – Ian?'

'He'd already told me the night before not to bother with breakfast for him.'

'Oh?' Pearl frowned. 'Not even tea or coffee?'

Emma shook her head. 'The rooms in the west wing have tea and coffee provided because they're all B & B status.'

Pearl considered this. 'So, you didn't see either Ian or Guy in the morning?'

Emma shook her head. 'No. But then I had so much to do I didn't really think too much about it. Everything seemed to be under control until Sarah, Mrs Lawson, said she'd tried Guy's mobile several times and he hadn't answered. That's when I called Ryan.'

Pearl nodded. 'And I was there with him and the celebrant at the wedding pavilion. We then went looking for him in the gardens.'

'Mrs Lawson was still getting ready, so she asked me to check Guy's room. I knocked on the door but there was no reply.'

Pearl thought for a moment. 'You have a spare key?'

Emma nodded. 'But there was no need to use it,' she said quickly, 'because I was in the main house at the time, preparing settings for the wedding breakfast – the meal after the ceremony.'

'The main house?' said Pearl.

'Yes, there are two doors to the Sir Edwyn Suite – one is on the lower landing of the west wing, but the other leads onto a landing in the main house. That door is always locked for B & B guests – except for weddings because there's always so much prep to do, and it's easier for the bride and groom to gain access to the main house that way, rather than walking over from the other wing.'

'So,' said Pearl, 'both wings actually connect via the main house? From the Sir Edwyn Suite through that second door . . .'

'And from the garden wing through the upper corridor,' Emma said.' Would you like me to show you?'

Pearl quickly finished her tea. 'Yes, please.'

Minutes later, Pearl stood with Emma between the white columns of the main entrance to the house while Emma fumbled for the key. After she opened the heavy front door, she allowed Pearl to enter first. Once inside, Pearl took a sharp intake of breath at the sight of the grand hall before her with its marble tiled floor and sweeping cantilevered staircase. As though she had never tired of seeing this spectacular entrance, Emma stopped in her tracks and gazed up to where sunlight flooded down from a glass lantern roof. A display of white delphiniums and hydrangeas was positioned at the foot of the staircase, still tied with an ivory satin bow – another reminder of a wedding that would never take place.

Emma gestured for Pearl to take the stairs. As she climbed them, Pearl took note of the framed portraits which lined the walls of the galleried landing. One in particular, featuring a dark-haired man in an Elizabethan ruff collar, was perfectly positioned between two marble columns – and two closed doors. Emma noted Pearl's interest and pointed to the area, saying, 'That door on the left leads into the Sir Edwyn Suite.'

'And the one on the right?'

Emma moved to the door and indicated for Pearl to open it. As she did so, Pearl was reminded of her recurring dream, and she found herself facing the familiar upper corridor of the garden wing and the large bookcase filled with antique volumes facing two bedroom doors. At that precise moment, one of the doors suddenly opened and a young man emerged to offer an innocent smile.

'Hi there,' said Simon Mullen. 'Everything OK?'

CHAPTER FIFTEEN

Pearl strolled through Mount Ephraim's grounds as the heady scent of rose blossom filled the warm air. 'Thanks for agreeing to talk to me.' She smiled. Beside her, Simon gave a nod. 'It's a pleasure,' he replied in his Irish lilt. 'Well, not in these circumstances, I mean. We really should be celebrating a wedding.' He turned away in the direction of the wedding pavilion then back to Pearl.

'I know,' she said gravely, noting that by now the chairs had all been packed away and the white roses that had decorated the pavilion had disappeared. She leaned against the balustrade and took a moment to study Simon. He seemed an amiable young man with a fair complexion but ruddy cheeks. His blue eyes were as much a contrast to his black hair as Pearl's moonstone grey eyes were to her own raven curls.

'What part of Ireland are you from?' she asked, curious.

'Donegal,' Simon replied, 'though I haven't been back

for a while.' He smiled at Pearl, who asked, 'Amy mentioned you're a trained nurse?'

Simon nodded. 'I am, but I really don't need the qualification in my job. I think Babs just feels more confident that I've had some medical training.'

'In your job as her carer?'

'Companion,' Simon corrected her. 'It's a live-in position. I have a small studio flat in her home.'

'In Whitstable?'

'Babs lives in Seasalter now, a little further up the coast from you – where the fine folk live.' He smiled then quickly checked himself. 'Sorry, I didn't mean—'

Pearl shook her head. 'It's okay,' she said, understanding very well how the beach-front homes of west Whitstable were becoming increasingly sought after – and by the likes of Babs Meadows-Young.

'But as a matter of fact,' said Simon, 'I much prefer downtown Whitstable. It reminds me in some ways of home; I come from a small coastal community – oysters were always on the menu.' He smiled again.

'Then you must come to the Whitstable Pearl one day and try some of ours.'

Simon nodded. 'Thanks for the invitation. I will – when this episode is all over.'

'Sadly, it won't be over for some,' said Pearl. Simon looked at her as she clarified, 'Certainly not for Amy.'

'Of course,' said Simon soberly.

'And,' Pearl added, 'for whoever might be responsible for Guy's death.'

Simon looked back at her in alarm. 'Do the police really suspect foul play?' He frowned. 'I . . . thought it was some kind of overdose?'

'Why would you think that?'

'Well, Babs told me she'd heard it from someone – I can't remember who. She said that was the impression given by all the questions being asked by the police?'

He had framed this last sentence as a question, and Pearl felt the need to respond to it as such. 'I don't think the police have the autopsy results yet.'

Simon took this in as Pearl considered him. She asked, 'Did you know that the bedroom corridor in the garden wing leads directly into the main house?'

Simon shook his head. 'Not until you appeared there this afternoon,' he said. 'And you'd have given me a fair fright if it had been the middle of the night.'

Pearl went on. 'Emma said that the door has been unlocked since we all arrived.'

Simon shrugged. 'I wouldn't know about that. I'm not in the habit of trying closed doors.' He offered another smile and Pearl returned it as she considered how unalike they were in that respect.

Simon said, 'I'm . . . guessing you're helping with the police investigation?'

'Aren't we all?'

'Sure, but then not all of us are private detectives. And you had some police training yourself?'

'A long time ago.'

'Can I ask why you gave it up?'

Pearl paused. 'The uniform didn't suit me.' Her smile remained in place, disarming Simon, who said, 'I reckon the local police must think themselves lucky to have someone like you – on the inside, as it were. After all, they only came on the scene after you found Guy's body – but you were here from the start.'

'Yes,' said Pearl, thoughtfully, recognising that Simon had just made a good point. For all the forensic evidence available to DI Bowell and her team, Pearl had been able to observe far more during the time she had been at Mount Ephraim. If only DI Bowell realised that too, then Guy Priddey's death might not remain a mystery for much longer. Simon considered Pearl again before asking, 'I'm guessing you have some ideas about what might have happened?'

Pearl realised Simon had taken control of the conversation; his habit of finishing statements with a questioning intonation wasn't just a characteristic of his Irish heritage; it also provoked more responses from Pearl than she intended to give. When she failed to reply, Simon went on. 'I didn't choose the room I'm in,' he said plainly. 'It was chosen for me – as was Babs's room. We may be further along the corridor from the rest of you in our wing, but . . . I honestly had no idea we were so close to the main house – or that it leads through into the room Guy was using.'

'The Sir Edwyn Suite,' said Pearl. 'It's just across the landing of the main house.'

'So you say,' said Simon, 'but I wouldn't have known

that until today. I've hardly had a minute to myself since Babs and I arrived – and if she wasn't taking a nap right now, you can bet she'd be finding me something to do. You may have noticed, Babs is quite . . .' He paused as though searching for an appropriate adjective.

'Demanding?' said Pearl.

Simon met Pearl's gaze. 'She has needs,' he said. 'And I'm there to satisfy them.' He suddenly smiled. 'And not in that way,' he warned. 'If you hadn't already guessed, Babs isn't my type. I'm gay,' he announced proudly.

Pearl returned his smile and resolved not to be taken off course again.

'The night before last,' she began, 'after you went up to your room—'

'Babs came up after me,' Simon explained quickly. 'I heard her coming along the corridor – she's not exactly light on her feet.'

'But it was definitely Babs?'

Simon gave a nod. 'She called out to me, wanted to make sure I woke her up early for the wedding. She was fretting about her suit getting creased and said it might need pressing. I told her the creases would fall out overnight.'

'Yes,' said Pearl, 'I remember her being concerned about that.'

Simon heaved a sigh. 'Babs is very good at finding concerns. She's a worrywart. If there's nothing for her to fret about, she'll find something to fill the vacuum.'

Pearl reached into her pocket. 'Does she have any clothing with her made of this material?' She showed him the small plastic bag containing the fragment of yellow fabric. Simon eyed it – then Pearl. 'Have you asked her?' he said, dodging the question.

'No,' said Pearl plainly. 'I wanted to ask you.'

Simon frowned, looking vaguely disgruntled. 'I'm . . . not sure. I don't think so; I helped her to pack, but—' He paused then suddenly moved closer. 'Look, one thing I can tell you is I turned in quite early and managed to fall straight to sleep. But something woke me. I thought it was just that old clock that chimes the hour? It was making its usual din when I woke, and I didn't notice the time because it was already chiming. But I got up and went to the bathroom, and after I came back to bed I was just dropping off again when the door to my room opened.'

'Opened?'

'Slightly.'

'Are you sure?'

Simon nodded. 'Positive.'

'And?'

'And nothing.' He shrugged. 'I thought someone might be there but no one came in, so I just assumed I hadn't closed it properly and a draught from the corridor must have caused it to open.'

Pearl let this sink in. 'A draught?'

'Yes,' said Simon. 'It's quite possible the latch wasn't properly in the keep?'

For a moment Pearl considered this, about to enquire whether Simon had told DI Bowell about it, when a voice pierced the silence.

'Simon?'

He turned quickly to see Babs standing at a distance, a scowl on her face. 'I've been looking for you,' she said, before stomping across and upbraiding him. 'Why don't you take your mobile with you when you disappear like this?'

Simon took a deep breath, but Pearl answered for him. 'My fault,' she said quickly. 'We were chatting.'

'Chatting?' echoed Babs, clearly dissatisfied.

'Is anything wrong, Babs?' Simon asked with concern.

'My anti-inflammatories,' she said, peevishly. 'I nearly missed taking them – and you know I shouldn't have them on an empty stomach, but I've managed to swallow a few with a bit of lunch.'

Simon gave her a smile and said calmly, 'You don't need me to give them to you, Babs.'

'But I need you to keep track!' she whined. 'I can't think straight. I . . . can't find anything at the moment, it's . . . all too upsetting.' Her face puckered like a resentful child. Simon looked back at Pearl and said wearily, 'Okay, let's go, Babs. I'll find whatever you're missing and then we'll get you a nice cup of tea, how about that?'

'And a piece of cake?' asked Babs hopefully.

Simon smiled. 'Why not?'

Pearl watched the pair as they headed off together towards the upper terrace – an odd couple in a strange symbiotic relationship – but she was thinking less about Babs and Simon than the image of a bedroom door slowly opening in the middle of the night. With that thought still in mind, she turned and found herself coming face to face with DI Bowell.

CHAPTER SIXTEEN

'You say you followed someone here last night?'

DI Bowell had asked this question while examining the thorns and brambles on the undergrowth at the rear of the cricket pavilion. Then she turned back to Pearl, who replied, 'I can't say for sure the person came here. I lost sight of whoever it was behind the trees on the other side of the ha-ha, so I went down to the maze, and then the bridge.' Pearl frowned. 'I take it you found the patch of scorched earth on the meadow close to where the spring flows? Your forensics team was able to take a proper look before the rain came yesterday?'

Bowell looked stonily at Pearl, ignoring her questions and asking one of her own. 'Why did you come here to the pavilion when you say you lost sight of this person?'

Pearl took a deep breath to calm herself. 'Because I heard something when I was down near the maze,' she said. 'It seemed to come from this direction. A woman's voice – a cry. It was quite loud.'

'A scream?'

Pearl shook her head. 'No, more like a sudden outburst of . . . anger, or maybe exasperation? I don't know. But I came here and found that material snagged on the thorn. It suggested to me that I hadn't been mistaken about what I had heard – or perhaps what I thought I saw on the night of the firework display.' She looked at Bowell; the DI remained silent, so she went on. 'So far, no one seems to be able to tell me anything about that fabric.'

Bowell frowned. 'You've been questioning the other guests?'

Pearl answered carefully. 'I've asked some questions, yes.'

'It might be more constructive for this investigation if you didn't,' said Bowell bluntly.

'Why?' asked Pearl. 'I thought you'd welcome some information.'

'Information is one thing,' said Bowell, 'conducting some kind of parallel investigation by which you prime possible suspects regarding evidence is not only unhelpful, it's obstructive.' She held Pearl's gaze.

'"Suspects"?' said Pearl, picking up on the word. 'So this *is* now a murder investigation?'

'*Possible* suspects,' Bowell clarified.

'So,' said Pearl, 'even though your own line of questioning has suggested to everyone here that Guy's medication had something to do with his death, and even though I've explained to you that an intruder may have been in the grounds on the night of his death, and that I was aware of someone leaving the house last night and perhaps coming to this very spot, where I found a piece of snagged clothing, which I informed your officers about, you still want me to—'

'Back off, Miss Nolan,' said Bowell. 'I expect you to keep me fully informed of anything that might have a bearing on this case, but if I find you're interfering, I'll have no hesitation in taking steps against you for obstructing my investigation. Is that understood?'

Pearl took another deep breath, this time to stifle her own anger. How could she possibly mention what Simon had told her now? She looked away to the house and thought again of the proximity of Simon's room to the galleried landing of the main house, then she suddenly became distracted by the sight of Ian Soutar framed in the gap in the yew hedge. Looking back at Bowell, Pearl replied, 'Perfectly.'

Satisfied with Pearl's response, Bowell moved off. Pearl watched her go, and after a moment she moved across the lawn and joined Ian. He looked troubled and said, 'Don't worry. You're not the only one she's giving a hard time to.'

'You too?'

Ian took a step forward and sat down on a wooden bench. He asked: 'Have you seen Amy?'

Pearl nodded and sat next to him. 'It's so hard to know what to say,' she began, 'but she knows we're here for her.'

Ian looked thoughtful, then blurted out, 'What you asked me before? I lied. I didn't want to come here at all.' He looked down. 'After all, why would I?'

Pearl read the sadness in his eyes as he passed a hand through his dark brown hair. 'Then why did you?' she asked.

'Why else?' he said. He stared towards the fountain on the lawn. 'Sometimes we look beyond the facts only to what we want to see. I've learned that in my job. It's so much easier to believe my clients than to simply recognise that, guilty or not, they are all entitled to a good defence – and we are all innocent until proven guilty.' He paused. 'Amy and I have kept in touch throughout the years,' he went on. 'I was always pleased about that.'

'And you were very close,' said Pearl.

'Until we finally broke up,' he qualified. 'Her choice, not mine.'

'It was quite a while ago,' said Pearl. 'But you managed to remain friends.'

Ian remained silent. Pearl prompted him. 'You got engaged yourself – to Kate—'

'As I said,' Ian broke in, 'that didn't work out.' He looked at Pearl and gave a heavy sigh. 'Maybe there comes a time for all of us when we know how it feels to have our hearts broken – and also to break another's heart?'

His words struck a chord for Pearl, but she kept silent and allowed him to continue.

'I wasn't ready to move on after Amy,' he said. 'It

wasn't just a case of missing her. It was like . . . part of me had disappeared. So I tried very hard to replace her.'

'With someone else,' said Pearl softly.

Ian paused then nodded slowly. 'We all expect to get married one day,' he said, 'to settle down – like sediment in a jar. Build a home, have a family, stay in one place – be happy ever after? You must have had the same expectations, Pearl.'

'I did,' she admitted. 'But . . . sometimes life gets in the way. I had my son to bring up, so maybe in some ways I'm living my life back to front.' She managed a smile. 'Maybe you're doing the same. You're a good man, Ian. Kind. A hard worker. A good barrister. You'll find someone.'

'Perhaps I already have,' he said. 'Perhaps . . . there's never been anyone else.'

Pearl's smile faded. 'Amy.'

Ian looked away, increasingly troubled. 'I've been a fool, Pearl. I actually allowed myself to think there was another reason for her to want me here this weekend.'

Pearl frowned. 'You mean . . . other than to see her get married?'

He jerked his head back to her. 'And why would I want to witness that?' He seemed to struggle with the thought and rubbed his brow. 'When she emailed me from Bangkok, making it clear she had something important to tell me, that she was returning here to England, I couldn't help but think . . .' He trailed off and Pearl remembered the email she had received from Amy

– almost the very same wording – perhaps copied and pasted between all the emails sent to all the guests; but, seeing Ian's discomfort, she couldn't find the heart to say so to him.

'You hoped it was something other than news of her wedding to Guy?'

'Of course,' said Ian. 'I allowed myself to ignore the facts – the most important being that if we were meant to be together she would never have broken up with me when she did.' He paused. 'She had moved on. She thought I had too – but in truth I had only moved forward: with a career, my life in London . . . but my heart had always remained here. I realised I had been waiting for Amy to return. To come home.'

'To you,' said Pearl.

Ian nodded slowly. 'Even when I got her invitation, I still couldn't help wondering whether things might change once I arrived. Like I say, I've been a fool.'

'No,' said Pearl. 'Maybe we're all blinded by love. And maybe we're meant to be.' Pearl allowed her thoughts to drift briefly back to her own first love – a relationship that had blossomed one summer and faded by autumn, but a love never to be forgotten as it had provided her with her beloved son. She frowned in thought. 'It must have been very difficult for you having to suffer Guy's offer of becoming his best man.'

Ian gave a shrug. 'By that time,' he said, 'I could see how much she loved him. I'd heard about their plans together. I already knew there was no hope.'

Pearl looked away, towards the house. 'So you slipped quietly away from the terrace.'

'That's right. I told you, I came up to my room.'

Pearl glanced over at the tall hedge by the pathway, remembering the conversation she had overheard between Guy and Sarah, when he had voiced his concerns about the problems in her marriage, and how he would only help Sarah to leave Toby – not to stay with him. Pearl thought for a moment then asked, 'Where were you yesterday morning? Emma mentioned you had told her not to bother making breakfast for you?'

'I hardly ever eat breakfast,' said Ian getting to his feet, 'and I knew I wouldn't have much appetite for what was to come.' He turned and met Pearl's gaze. 'I stayed up late the night before, trying to distract myself with some work.'

'You mentioned that, yes.'

'I slept for a bit then got up early and went for a walk.'

'Where to?'

Unable to conceal his irritation, Ian turned away and said, 'I told the police all this.'

'But the police aren't likely to tell me,' said Pearl, with a smile that put him at ease.

He replied wearily, 'Just across the lawn here.'

'To the cricket pavilion?'

Ian looked uneasy but gave a quick nod. Pearl continued. 'And did you happen to see anyone?'

At this, Ian blinked a few times then looked away. 'No,' he said finally. 'No one at all. I was alone.'

Pearl held Ian's gaze for another moment, but then her phone sounded. She pulled it from her pocket and saw a text had just arrived from McGuire. Five words only, it read:

I need to see you.

CHAPTER SEVENTEEN

It was gone 7 p.m. before McGuire was able to leave the station. He parked near a country pub called The Three Horseshoes and walked several hundred metres until he found the public footpath Pearl had mentioned in her response to his earlier text. If he had been driving, he might have missed the entrance – a break in the manor wall just before a lodge that he assumed had once belonged to a gatekeeper. It looked like the kind of house a child might draw; a small stone dwelling set within a country garden which wrapped around it, with a line of washing swaying in the warm breeze. Its latticed windows looked out onto the valley and the fields through which a wide footpath carved its course. McGuire set off on the path just as the setting sun shed a warm glow across the countryside. The detective wasn't one for scenery, but something about this place, set off the road and away from all passing traffic, seemed like a secluded Shangri-La – or perhaps, he now thought to himself, he was simply allowing himself to respond to the environment because he was about to see Pearl . . .

These days, most of McGuire's time was spent viewing landscapes through the windscreen of his car. In London, that had been a bonus because a vehicle acted not only as transport but as a shield or carapace – modern-day armour against whatever the city aimed at him, especially in the course of his work. A few years ago, however, Whitstable had cast its own spell on him, as Pearl had done, compelling him to stay. To McGuire, Whitstable and Pearl were now intrinsically linked, and he had come to realise that the woman he had fallen in love with truly personified the town. Whitstable was only an hour's drive from south London, but, as with the landscape he was now walking through, he recognised it was also a world of its own – a one-off with an independent spirit, like Pearl herself. Somehow, in the face of a constantly changing world, Pearl, her restaurant, and the town which held her in such affection and esteem, remained unchanged and steadfast in nature. That sense of permanence held its own attraction for McGuire.

Strolling on along the footpath, he took a deep breath of fresh air and glanced around him. He was unable to identify any of the trees he saw apart from a few tall oaks, but he noted fruit ripening on the branches of orchard trees, and he welcomed the sense of calm and quiet, broken only by the song from birds wheeling in the sky above. He could almost feel his pulse beginning to slow;

nevertheless, he couldn't help but remain concerned by Pearl's insistence on staying at Mount Ephraim after finding Guy Priddey's body – and offering what he knew Swale Police would only consider as interference in this case.

McGuire knew DI Jane Bowell only by reputation: a tough, former-uniformed copper who had worked her way up the ranks to occupy her CID position much in the same way that McGuire had at the Met in London. It was a route McGuire knew Pearl would have wanted to take herself, if only she hadn't chosen another role – as a single mum. There was something to be said for letting go of the past, especially if it was getting in the way of the present. McGuire knew that more than most, and so he had allowed himself to loosen the ties that still connected him to Donna, in order to connect to Pearl. He only wished Pearl felt the same about revisiting her old ambitions, but as he walked on along the country footpath he allowed himself to consider that it wasn't simply old ambitions that kept Pearl tied to crime solving; her nature prevented her from allowing any mystery to remain unsolved. McGuire had to concede that it was this part of Pearl's character, together with her perseverance and a natural sense of justice, that would have made her just as good a police detective as Bowell – or himself. But it also made Pearl an invaluable asset with McGuire's own cases, and he now saw as clearly as the footpath before him that he had a responsibility to help Pearl find a killer who had robbed her friend of the man she loved.

McGuire remembered an old saying – something about angels whispering to a man when he is out walking – and he allowed himself to consider whether Priddey's murder could have been committed to prevent a marriage taking place. From what Pearl had told him so far, none of Priddey's associates – or even close members of his family – had welcomed his new financial plans, but Pearl had also mentioned a possible intruder in the grounds, which added a new dimension to the case. There again, it wasn't too difficult for anyone to find their way on to the estate, as he had just discovered himself.

McGuire's professional experience had taught him that in murder investigations female victims were usually killed by a partner or a family member while the chief suspect in the murder of an adult male was most likely to be a friend or social acquaintance. Priddey, however, was no ordinary male victim; he was an attractive and wealthy individual with a high profile acquired from his success in raising a precious cargo. He also appeared to have had undisclosed health problems for which he had been self-medicating for many years. His death might have been deemed a tragic accident following an unintentional overdose, had it not been complicated by the detailed facts of the autopsy – which, thanks to McGuire's contact at Swale Police, he now possessed. McGuire needed to brief Pearl, but he also needed to see her, to be with her, if only for a short time, and so he quickened his pace, taking an incline towards the house, which he could now see before him in the distance. As he strode on, a figure stepped out from the fields and confronted him.

'If you're heading to Mount Ephraim, the gardens are closed.'

McGuire considered the man before him. Appearing to be in his early thirties, he wore heavy-duty jeans, a tartan shirt and workmen's boots, but his face was partially hidden by the shade of the lowering sun. McGuire reached into his pocket and took out a leather wallet containing his warrant card. The man leaned forward, checked the details, then gave a nod and a faint smile, signalling a détente. Replacing his ID in his jacket pocket, McGuire asked, 'And you are?'

'Ryan Robson. I work here. My partner, Emma—'

'Looks after the accommodation and catering.'

Ryan nodded slowly. 'That's right.' His eyes narrowed slightly as he stared at McGuire. 'I . . . thought the police had finished here for now.'

'For now?' echoed McGuire.

'With the grounds,' said Ryan. 'They were all over the place, fingertip searches.'

Having shown his warrant card, McGuire felt reluctant to have to admit that he wasn't in fact part of the team investigating Priddey's death. Instead, he simply said, 'I'm here to meet Miss Nolan.'

At this, Ryan nodded and jerked his head away from the fields. 'She'll be up at the house,' he said. 'Is she expecting you?'

McGuire nodded then paused before asking, 'Have you worked here long?'

'Little over three years,' said Ryan. He frowned, troubled. 'It's been a perfect place to be – until now.'

McGuire glanced over at the orchards then back at Ryan. 'I know you'll have given a statement, but have you had a chance to think about things since then?'

'Think about what?' asked Ryan with some suspicion.

McGuire paused. 'Sometimes it takes a while before . . . before something seemingly unimportant takes on some significance. Something unusual. Something you might have forgotten about but then remember.'

'About yesterday morning, you mean? When Guy went missing?'

'Or the night before.'

Ryan looked away and took a deep breath. 'Emma was looking after the guests,' he began. 'There was a meal on the terrace. She looked after everything – apart from the fireworks.'

'There was a display,' said McGuire. Ryan nodded. 'Guy asked me to help with that, so I set it all up – in the ha-ha.'

'The ditch?'

Ryan nodded. 'I asked if he wouldn't prefer to wait until the wedding night – after the ceremony? That's the usual time for a display.' He went on. 'But Guy said he was known for his surprises and . . . if he did things when everyone else did, they wouldn't be much of a surprise.' He managed a smile then stared down the path, adding, 'He was a nice fella.' He looked back again at McGuire.

'So I've heard.'

The two men considered one another for a moment before McGuire indicated the footpath. 'Do many people use this?'

'You mean, do they get into the gardens without paying?' He shook his head. 'There's a ticket office ahead, just after the car park. If it's unstaffed, I'm never far away.'

McGuire nodded. 'Thanks.' He set off again, but Ryan spoke. 'Inspector?'

McGuire turned back.

'I hope you find who did this.'

CHAPTER EIGHTEEN

McGuire passed the car park and ticket office Ryan had mentioned. As the gardens were closed to the public, the office remained unstaffed, so McGuire followed the instructions Pearl had given him and walked straight on to find her standing by a paddock near some estate buildings. She was leaning across the paddock rail giving her attention to a strong chestnut cob mare and a group of ponies that looked like they might have escaped from a local gymkhana. McGuire ignored the animals and simply watched Pearl spotlighted by the last golden rays of a dying day. When he moved towards her, she turned at the sound of his footsteps on the gravel path and smiled. 'You made it,' she said softly.

McGuire took her in his arms and held her close, feeling the tensions of his day fading away. His lips brushed hers before they separated, and he then took note of the buildings behind her, one of which had a clock tower set in it. Pearl followed McGuire's gaze and saw the old clock showed it was almost seven-forty-five. 'That will start sounding soon,' she warned. 'It's a loud chime, so be prepared.'

McGuire threw a glance around the grounds. 'Where are the other guests?'

'Up at the house.' Pearl explained. 'Amy's still in her room, but when I left Tess and James were talking to her, trying to tempt her out. Ian was taking a walk in the gardens with Sarah.'

'And her husband?'

'In the games room. Did I mention there's a billiard table? He's potting balls and drinking brandy to kill time.' She gave McGuire a look, then added, 'And Ingrid was working on her laptop in the sitting room.'

'And the others?'

'The last time I looked, Simon was ministering to Babs Meadows-Young on the tea terrace. Emma had just served them a snack.'

'That's the cook?'

Pearl looked at him and tipped her head to one side. 'Strange that so many women are described as "cooks" while men seem to get the "chef" title,' she said. 'As a matter of fact, having tasted Emma's food, she could teach me a thing or two these days.'

McGuire looked back towards the path. 'I just met her partner on the way here – checking who I was.'

Pearl frowned. 'And you told him?'

'I flashed him my warrant card and said I was here to

see you. Hopefully he'll just assume I'm part of Bowell's team.'

Pearl looked thoughtful. 'I talked to Emma this morning.'

'About?'

'You first,' said Pearl. 'You said you've got some information?'

McGuire took his tablet from his pocket. 'Autopsy results – though there are still some missing details.'

Pearl came closer and McGuire went on. 'But it's been confirmed that Priddey took a dose of oxycodone on the night he died.'

'An overdose?' Pearl asked tentatively.

McGuire grimaced. 'It's complex,' he said. 'Oxycodone is highly addictive. In fact, there's a real crisis right now caused by the misuse of opioids – painkilling drugs like this.' He checked his tablet. 'Last year alone, seventy thousand users died from them in the States.' He looked at Pearl, who asked, 'Guy would have been taking the stuff long enough to become addicted?'

'For sure,' McGuire replied. 'But because of that it would have taken a large overdose to kill him. And that wouldn't have been practical for a killer because Guy would have noticed it.'

'So, what are you saying?'

'Something else was involved.'

'Alcohol?' said Pearl. 'He'd been drinking that night and Amy told me herself that she'd warned him about mixing the two.'

McGuire shook his head. 'Seems there was something else – but I'm not yet sure what it is.'

McGuire put his notebook away and Pearl considered what she had just learned. 'So,' she began, 'if the killer was aware that Guy took a regular dose of oxycodone every day, and possibly with alcohol . . .' She looked at McGuire, who finished her sentence: 'He could well have been spiked.'

'His hip flask?' said Pearl. 'That was found by his bedside.'

'But he drowned.'

'Under the effects of drugs?' Pearl frowned. 'But why would he have gone to the lake if he was feeling those effects?'

McGuire shrugged. 'Because he wasn't feeling them when he left for the lake?'

Pearl fell silent.

'What're you thinking?' asked McGuire.

'Babs,' said Pearl. 'She seems to travel with a portable medicine chest. She probably doesn't need all of her medication – I think she's a hypochondriac.'

'Bowell's team would have checked what medication she has with their initial search.'

Pearl gave a nod. 'True.' She thought again. 'She seems to rely on Simon to administer everything she needs. He was a nurse, though I'm not sure why he gave it up.'

'I'll try and find out.' McGuire held Pearl's look as he leaned back against the paddock fence. 'Method.

Motive. Opportunity. If you're putting this Meadows-Young woman in the frame, where's her opportunity, and what would be her motive?'

'I told you,' said Pearl. 'She was outraged when she heard about Guy and Amy's plans for his money. She's managed to build up a close relationship with Amy, and she must have been hoping Amy's marriage to Guy might get her out of financial trouble.'

'Opportunity?'

'Simon said he heard her coming upstairs to her room the night before last and she called out to him – something about her outfit. I'd overheard some of her conversation with Amy in the games room and I can vouch for the fact that she left shortly after that – and went upstairs. That would have been around eleven-forty—' Pearl broke off and looked at McGuire. 'Earlier today, Simon told me he'd been woken by something that night.'

'By what?'

'He wasn't sure.' Pearl looked beyond McGuire to the clock tower behind him. 'He thought it might have been that clock. He said it was already chiming so he didn't register the hour, but he went to the bathroom, returned to bed . . . then something curious happened – his bedroom door opened.'

'You mean someone opened it?'

'That's what he thought. But there was no one there, so he just assumed it had fallen open due to a draught.'

McGuire considered this. 'What are you thinking?'

'There are no windows in that corridor,' Pearl explained,

'just a large bookcase and only two bedrooms off it – his and the one Babs is occupying next door.'

'So, it could have been Babs?'

Pearl shrugged. 'It's possible. She could have passed by his room and then opened the door to the main house. I learned this morning from Emma that the corridor outside their rooms leads on to a galleried landing in the main house.' Pearl reached into her pocket for a map of the house and showed it to McGuire. 'The door that leads into the main house was unlocked on the night of Guy's murder, and the galleried landing leads directly across to a door to the suite Guy was staying in. That door *also* remained unlocked.'

'So, it's possible,' said McGuire, 'that anyone from your wing could have entered the main house from this door close to Simon's room – around midnight? You said yourself you heard a door closing shortly after you went to your room.'

Pearl nodded. 'That's true, but someone staying in the west wing could have done the same,' she said. 'For now, it's all hypothetical. There's still a chance that Simon simply failed to close his bedroom door properly and it fell open.'

McGuire reflected on this. 'Have you told Bowell about this?'

'Not yet.' She slipped her map back into her pocket.

'Why not?'

'Typical copper,' she said. 'Earlier she warned me not to interfere – or to question the other guests.'

As she eyed him, McGuire responded. 'She's not "typical".'

'No?' said Pearl. 'If it was your case, would you have told me any different?'

'It's not my case,' said McGuire. 'And it's not yours either. I hear you when you say Amy's your friend, but . . .' He held Pearl's gaze. 'She's still a potential suspect.'

Pearl stepped away from him and turned back to face the cob and ponies in the paddock. 'Please don't say that again.'

'It's true. You know as well as I do what the official stats show: most victims are murdered by those close to them.'

'I know,' Pearl agreed with frustration. 'And there are also crimes of passion, and everyone could see those two were in love. You also don't need to tell me how money and greed play their own part in murder cases. But Guy said himself – he told us all – that Amy doesn't stand to inherit a thing; so why on earth would she murder him?'

McGuire paused. 'There could be a loophole,' he said. 'Some way of her profiting in spite of this charitable foundation?'

Pearl looked at him. 'Has Bowell looked into Priddey's finances?'

'I'm sure she's doing that, but with the kind of fortune Guy amassed it won't just be a case of assessing his accounts. His financial affairs will be complex.'

'Well,' said Pearl, taking a deep breath, 'we still have to consider that a guest staying in the west wing took the same route that night.'

McGuire turned to her. 'Or a member of staff? That guy I met on the way in, Ryan, he said the last time he saw Priddey alive was just after the firework display, but he also said that Priddey was one for "surprises"?'

'Yes,' said Pearl. 'And his new plans for the money were certainly surprising.'

McGuire pointed at her. '*If* Priddey had actually planned to go ahead with them.'

Pearl shook her head. 'There was no reason not to believe him,' she said. 'Amy confirmed it all. And I believe her.'

'Because she's an old friend?' McGuire moved closer. 'When was the last time you actually saw one another?'

Pearl replied guardedly. 'Not for a while. But . . . she's always kept in touch.'

'And invited you to her wedding.'

'Why shouldn't she?' asked Pearl defensively, but McGuire's look put her under pressure and she turned away to reorganise her thoughts. 'Look,' she began, turning back to face him. 'Sometimes you meet someone at a certain time in your life and'—her eyes scanned McGuire's face—'that person stays with you. You know they'll always be a part of your life . . . because of what you shared together . . . and because at that particular time you happened to be looking for something – and they helped you to find it.' She continued to hold McGuire's gaze and spoke very softly. 'You know what I'm talking about?'

McGuire nodded slowly, knowing full well. As the last of the daylight began to fade, he leaned forward to kiss her. His lips met hers, and Pearl suddenly forgot what she had been trying to explain; she knew only that McGuire understood.

A moment later, the bell on the old clock tower began chiming. Pearl and McGuire broke their embrace and then smiled at one another – but Pearl's smile soon began to fade.

'What is it?' asked McGuire.

'Something Ian Soutar said today,' she began. 'He opened up about his relationship with Amy.'

McGuire frowned. 'I thought that was over.'

'Amy must have thought the same to have invited him here, but . . . he came because he thought there was still a chance for them.'

'You mean, he still has feelings for her?'

Pearl nodded. 'He loved her. And maybe that kind of love never dies.'

McGuire felt conflicted. He turned away, but Pearl went on. 'He said he thought he'd moved on but in fact he'd just moved forward – with his life, his job. He even got engaged, to a young woman called Kate Parsons, but it didn't work out.' She looked at McGuire. 'Maybe Amy was the reason why.'

A silence fell. McGuire felt that the ties that still connected him to a ghost were being loosened once more. He gave his attention again to Pearl.

'Are you saying that he killed Priddey out of jealousy?'

Pearl searched his features for an answer then finally shook her head. 'No. No, I . . .' she trailed off as a thought came to her. 'I need to call Mum,' she said, 'and ask her to do something for me.'

'To do what?' asked McGuire, confused.

'I can't explain now,' said Pearl, 'but I'll let you know when it's done. You'd better get back. And I need to return to the house. It's supper time and a good opportunity for me to ask a few more questions.'

McGuire heaved a heavy sigh, confident that Pearl would never agree to obey Bowell's dictum and leave this case to the police. He also saw that Pearl still seemed preoccupied. There was something on her mind, but it was something she wasn't going to trust him with at this point in time – only Dolly. He leaned forward and kissed her once more, wishing she could walk with him back through the fields along the footpath to the road so he could take her away from this place, which, for all its beauty, still filled him with fear for what might yet happen.

'Go on,' she said finally. 'I'll call you in a while, I promise.'

McGuire turned and began heading away from the stable block. Once he was on the path again, he turned back, but Pearl had vanished.

CHAPTER NINETEEN

On her way back to the house after leaving McGuire, Pearl came across an old oak tree fenced off from the public by a wooden railing. A box attached to the trunk confirmed the reason why: it was a lightning protection system to minimise the risk of damage from a strike – a reminder of ever-present danger even in such a bucolic setting. Nevertheless, the oriental stone bridge appeared in the distance like something from a fairy tale. Pearl could hear the water trickling down the series of rock pools – its flow maintained by the pump in the old lakeside shack. A two-hundred-metre walk up the slope adjacent to the Japanese rock garden would bring her back to the house, but Pearl's mind was still racing, and instead she headed down towards the lake, retracing the route she had taken on her first day on the estate.

Nearing the lake, she saw a cloud of dragonflies hovering above the surface of the water. A small flock of mallards glided away to disappear among the leaves of devil's rhubarb on the bank. She stopped in her tracks and considered that for all the natural beauty of Mount Ephraim's gardens, there seemed to be an element of theatre about it, as though it comprised the sets of a play – all marked on the map Emma had given to her on her first day. She took the map from her pocket once more. In the fading light it was impossible to read properly, so she switched on her phone and used it as a torch. She studied the various features on the map; the rock garden, the Miz Maze, the arboretum, the rose and tea terraces, topiary garden, water garden, stable block, and the lake itself with the wedding pavilion on the terrace above it – a stage that had been carefully set for a marriage that had never taken place.

Moving on towards the pump house, Pearl heard the whirring of the generator inside. Reminded of her first day at Mount Ephraim, she stared towards the false acacia tree, its leaves still vivid as they shivered in the evening breeze. Had she really seen someone that afternoon? And, if so, had that figure been spying on her, vanishing in the undergrowth as soon as Pearl had turned to face the lake? If she had not been mistaken, who could the figure have been? She continued on, retracing her steps until she heard, once more, a trickle of water – this time, spring water from the meadow flowing beneath the wooden bridge under which she had found Guy Priddey's body. She quickly dialled Dolly's number, crossing the bridge as she heard the call connect. But it did so only to her mother's voicemail, Dolly's voice sounding a strident 'hello' before ordering callers to leave a message. Pearl frowned in frustration but did precisely that. 'It's me,' she said, urgency in her voice. 'I need you to do something for me, so I'll try you again soon.'

Ending the call, she stepped into the meadow and stared up in the direction of the Miz Maze.

From a distance, the tall plants still seemed vibrant in the glowing evening light – a Catherine wheel of colour – tempting Pearl to investigate. Making her way up the incline to this mysterious feature, she paused at its entrance before stepping onto the maze's path, where she found herself immediately dwarfed, enveloped by the towering rudbeckia and joe-pye weed. Pearl felt sure she could easily find her way out of the maze at the top of the slope, but while she was within it she hoped she might experience some of the calm clarity that medieval monks had sought during meditational prayer circuits in mazes such as this. Perhaps, she thought, the Miz Maze might even unlock the puzzle of what had really happened on the night of Guy Priddey's death.

Stepping further into the maze, Pearl heard the soft flapping of tiny wings – a bird or perhaps a pipistrelle in flight on the evening breeze. A fox shrieked, a cry that segued into the distant noise of a tractor engine approaching and then receding on the road beyond the estate, and then melded into the sudden rustle of the plants that framed the maze. Or was it? She stopped in her tracks and listened carefully. She had not been mistaken.

Somewhere within the maze she had heard something – and could still hear it – the sound of footsteps, light but unmistakable.

Pearl's heartbeat quickened. She thought to call out, but instead she moved on as quickly and silently as possible, following the circular path until she confronted a wall of vegetation before her. Forced to retrace her steps, she took another path, listening carefully all the while. She moved on faster this time, feeling her pulse beginning to race with the rhythm of footsteps close by. Her throat became dry as she continued in a small circle, trying to remind herself that she was heading up the incline towards the main house – and safety. Then doubts crept in again: she was in danger, or was she? Perhaps her imagination had been running away with her yet again. Perhaps she had allowed it to do so ever since she had arrived: the smell of decay in the lake, the odour of skunk cabbage that would surely have long evaporated with the early flowering of the blossoms, her mind playing tricks on her every day that she had been here on the estate. But then, her discovery of Guy's body had been no mistake, and neither were the final autopsy results or the yellow fabric caught on the shrub behind the old pavilion . . .

Darkness was beginning to fall like a shroud. The tall-stemmed plants appeared to be closing in on Pearl. She tried to hurry on but found herself trapped yet again, tricked into trusting another blocked path. Again she turned, but this time she caught sight of a shadow darting past ahead of her. A chill ran through her. Another

illusion? McGuire's words echoed for her: *'Be careful.'*
Dolly's too: *'Come home. And bring Amy with you!'* Pearl bit
her lip. Summoning resolve, she moved on, in search of the
shadow, hearing no warnings – only footsteps – moving
quickly away, treading another orbit. Pearl followed but
found herself facing two distinct paths. Which one to
take? Listening carefully, she could hear nothing.

She ducked behind the tall rudbeckia and waited –
but not for long. A few moments passed before a shadow
reappeared, moving towards her, then away. As it
receded, Pearl found her courage and reached to grab
the shadow from behind. A cry of terror rang out. The
figure struggled in Pearl's grasp, kicking backwards with
one foot while losing balance with the other. Dragged
forward with such force, Pearl almost lost her grip, but
in an involuntary reaction her hold tightened, fingers
clutching at clothing in her hands. A hood came away,
long fair hair tumbling out of a yellow woollen jacket.
A woman stared up at Pearl, fear written on her face.

'You . . .' said Pearl, breathless.

The woman remained silent, still trying to catch her
breath. More footsteps were heard – this time running to
where Pearl held the woman in her grasp. Tess and James
appeared out of the darkness, joining Pearl in the maze.
Ian caught up with them in the next instant.

'Who is she?' asked Tess.

Pearl said nothing but looked at Ian. He stared,
defeated, then finally spoke.

'Her name is Kate.'

CHAPTER TWENTY

'Kate Parsons?' said Dolly into the cordless phone in her hand. 'What on earth was she up to following you into that maze?'

'I'm not sure she did follow me,' said Pearl, her voice lowered into her own smartphone as she stared out of her bedroom window and explained what had happened the night before.

Dolly frowned at this. She found a spot for herself on the daybed in her conservatory that wasn't occupied by her familiar, Mojo the cat.

'What do you mean?'

'Well,' said Pearl, 'I'm sure I was the one who followed Kate into the maze, without realising.'

'Explain,' Dolly ordered.

'I was making my way back up to the house,' Pearl began, 'and I went to take a look at the maze. It's really magnificent, especially at this time of year. The rudbeckia is almost seven feet tall—'

Dolly cut in. 'I don't care about the plants, Pearl, just get to the point!'

Pearl sighed. 'What I'm trying to explain is that Kate must have been close by, in the same area, which isn't too far from the ha-ha.'

'The what?' asked Dolly.

'It's a ditch, about a metre deep, separating the cricket pitch from the central lawn in front of the main house. Did you know Capability Brown was very keen on ha-has?'

'The point!' Dolly exploded in frustration.

Pearl continued. 'If Kate heard me approaching, she may well have ducked into the maze just as I was coming up from the lake. Then I entered and—'

'She heard you but couldn't escape?'

'Exactly,' said Pearl. 'So *I* followed *her*.'

'And then?'

'Then the police were called. By Emma.'

'Oh dear.'

'Kate was trespassing, after all,' said Pearl, 'and Emma has a responsibility to the owners while they're away.'

'But why had she gone there?'

'Why else?' said Pearl. 'To see Ian.'

'You mean . . . she *knew* he was there – at the house?'

'I believe so,' said Pearl, reaching out to pick up the wedding invitation lying on her dressing table. 'Just a short while before the incident in the maze, I called you.' Pearl's eyes scanned the invitation's aerial photograph of Mount Ephraim nestled in its stunning grounds.

'I remember,' said Dolly. 'I got the message when I got home. I'd been down to the beach to pick up some shells for my new painting.'

'Well,' said Pearl. 'I was going to ask you to do a bit of detective work for me.' Pearl turned the invitation over in her hand.

'On Kate?' asked Dolly, suspicious.

'Doesn't she have a relative who works in Faversham as a wedding planner?'

'Her aunt Sylvia,' said Dolly.

'And aren't wedding planners sometimes put in charge of sending out invitations?'

'I believe they are,' said Dolly, with an enlightened smile. 'Like the lovely one that came for you?'

Pearl also smiled as she noted the name Thompson's of Faversham on the back. 'It's perfectly possible that if Sylvia sent those cards out for Amy . . .'

'Word would have reached Kate about Ian having been invited to the wedding?'

'Exactly,' said Pearl. She put down the invitation and went to look out of one of her bedroom windows. 'I'd been talking to Ian earlier yesterday – about Amy. I'm sure he's never really got over her. He even admitted that he'd only accepted Amy's wedding invitation because he thought – or rather, hoped – that there might be some other reason for her wanting him there.'

Dolly paused to consider this. 'He must have it bad,' she said finally.

'Yes,' Pearl agreed, 'but having realised he was wrong,

perhaps he consoled himself with the thought that he might now at least be able to move on.'

'Only that wasn't to be,' said Dolly, 'with a murder having taken place.'

'That's right. He's stuck here with the rest of us – and Amy. But,' she went on, 'though we only talked for a short while, something he said stayed with me.'

'And what was that?'

'He said we all reach an age when we know what it's like to have your heart broken . . . but also to break another heart.'

'Mmmm,' Dolly mused. 'Very perceptive – for a man. It's true we usually only remember our own heartbreak.' She paused. 'But what was so important about that?'

'Well,' said Pearl, 'I think he was reflecting on his broken engagement with Kate Parsons – and perhaps he was doing so because the two had recently been in contact.'

Pearl stared out of her window beyond the terraces to the lake. 'On the first day I came here, I had a feeling there was someone else in the grounds. Later that night, I was sure I saw someone near the cricket pavilion. It was after Ian had slipped away from the terrace during the firework display, but he couldn't have got that far so quickly. Then, the other evening, I heard someone leaving the house. I saw a figure moving across the front lawn. I lost them – but I *found* a small piece of fabric snagged on a branch. No one owned up to knowing anything about it. Now I'm sure it matches the yellow jacket Kate was wearing last night.'

'Proof she had been there *before* last night?'

'Not conclusive – but I'm sure she did come here, and that she met with Ian,' said Pearl. 'I could see that from the look on Ian's face last night – he wasn't shocked to see her, more . . . disappointed.'

Dolly considered this as she reached out to stroke Mojo, who warned her off with a gentle nip. 'But why would they be meeting in secret like that?'

'Perhaps she gave him no choice?'

Dolly frowned at this. 'You mean she was stalking him?'

Pearl turned away from the window and suddenly realised something.

'Maybe it wasn't Ian she was stalking,' she said. 'Maybe Kate was more interested in—'

'Amy,' said Dolly. 'Sometimes a rival for a man's affection can be a fascinating subject for a woman.'

'Yes,' Pearl agreed. 'Kate and Ian got together only *after* Amy went abroad.'

'So they would never have met?'

'That's right,' said Pearl, 'but Kate would have been well aware of Amy's magazine features, and she could have followed the course of her life from them.'

'Perhaps,' said Dolly, 'she might even have hoped that there was still some chance of a reunion with Ian. She's an attractive woman but she's still on her own, you know.'

Pearl reflected on this. 'And Ian's still single too,' she said, 'but then he hoped to be reunited with Amy . . .'

Dolly reminded her, 'All just theory.'

'True,' said Pearl, 'but I've got little else to go on at the moment.' She heaved a sigh and then asked, 'How are things at the restaurant?'

'We're surviving without you,' said Dolly. 'And I haven't breathed a word to Charlie, but surely it won't be long before the papers get hold of this. Maybe you should call Charlie and explain—'

'No,' said Pearl firmly. 'He'll only worry, and I may not be here much longer.' She felt conflicted, though, as she admitted, 'Something tells me the local police are much further on than I am with all this, although the forensics team must have been hampered by the rain that fell the morning after Guy Priddey's death.

'These first few days of a murder investigation are crucial because witnesses' recollections are all still fresh in the mind,' she went on. 'Plus, the killer may not have had enough time to plot a good alibi—'

'Or make a getaway,' said Dolly.

'So far,' said Pearl, 'we're all still here.'

'But now one more has been added to the mix.'

'Kate,' said Pearl, weighed down by all of the weekend's events.

A knock sounded suddenly at her door. 'I have to go, Mum.'

'Pearl?'

Another knock. Feeling torn, Pearl said to Dolly, 'I'll ring later!' and ended the call. She now opened her door – and found Emma there, looking apologetic.

'The police?' asked Pearl.

Emma nodded.

Pearl exited the garden wing to find DI Jane Bowell standing near a police car on the gravel driveway. Inside the car, Sergeant Falconer was sitting patiently at the wheel. Pearl hurried down the steps to Bowell.

'Are you . . . planning to take me to the station?'

Bowell turned to Pearl but took her time replying. 'I don't think that will be necessary,' she said finally, 'but I would like to talk to you – informally.' She gave Pearl a look then walked slowly onto the central lawn. Pearl got the message and followed. At the fountain, Bowell said, 'I thought you'd like to know, Kathryn Parsons is under arrest.' She paused. 'Together with Ian Soutar.'

'Have they been charged with anything?'

'Cautioned,' said Bowell.

'I'm sure,' said Pearl. 'But has Kate explained what she was doing here?'

Bowell ignored Pearl's question and said only, 'She's asked to see a solicitor before she makes a full statement.'

Pearl considered this then looked at Bowell. 'And presumably you took note of the jacket she was wearing? Yellow wool.'

Bowell held Pearl's gaze but gave nothing away, so Pearl went on. 'For what it's worth, I don't think Kate had anything to do with the murder of Guy Priddey.'

Bowell looked unimpressed but asked, 'And why is that?'

'She has no reason to kill him – no motive.'

Bowell sat down on the fountain's edge and crossed her arms against her chest.

'Then what was she doing here?'

Pearl shrugged. 'I don't know, and I don't want to speculate.' She held Bowell's look. 'It might incriminate her.'

'And Ian Soutar?' said Bowell. 'You live in Whitstable. You know these people.' Her eyes narrowed. 'I understand those two once had a close relationship?'

'They were engaged,' said Pearl finally. 'Some time ago – before Ian moved to London.'

Bowell looked away from Pearl and focused on a tree on the lawn. Staring up into its branches, she asked, 'Do you happen to know what this is?'

Pearl frowned. 'I think it's a false acacia. There's another one down by the lake.'

Bowell studied the gnarled branches and hollow spaces within the trunk. 'This one seems to have holly growing on it.'

'Yes,' said Pearl. 'It's a very old tree and holly takes advantage of any place in which to grow. Birds eat the berries and spread the seeds.' She moved closer to note where the holly was growing. 'This looks like it's entangled. Maybe the holly will put stress on this tree . . . but it's always possible the acacia will kill the holly. Or they could grow together for many years.' She gave a slow smile and looked up into the branches. 'Trees are amazing – they're actually social. Like us. Forest trees take care of each other; they can nourish the stump of a felled tree for hundreds of years after it's been cut down, feeding it nutrients to keep it alive. They share food, they exchange information about threats to their survival and . . . they need each other.' She glanced around at the trees on the central lawn then back at Bowell. 'They're a community, like us. That's how they survive.'

Bowell studied Pearl then looked away to the house, asking, 'What was Kate Parsons doing here last night?'

Pearl shook her head slowly. 'I'm sure she'll explain in due course – when her solicitor arrives.'

Bowell got up from the edge of the fountain and considered Pearl. 'You've been talking to the housekeeper,' she said, 'about access to the victim's suite?'

Pearl nodded. 'Emma isn't just a "housekeeper" – she's a friend.'

'Part of your "community"?'

Pearl nodded slowly. For a moment, neither woman spoke, then Bowell slipped her hand into her pocket and handed Pearl a business card.

'Tell me straight away if you learn anything more.' She continued to hold Pearl's look then sauntered slowly back to the car and got into the passenger seat.

Pearl watched the car turn on the gravel before finally moving off along the serpentine driveway and out onto the road.

CHAPTER TWENTY-ONE

That evening, Ingrid leaned in beside Amy at the dinner table on the candlelit terrace. 'I'm glad you managed to eat something,' she said. 'You must keep your strength up.'

'She's right,' said Babs, seated on the other side of Amy. 'I know how you must feel, my darling, but we are all here to support you.' As she offered Amy a sweet smile, Pearl noted scarlet lipstick smeared on Babs's incisor.

'We're here because we're all suspects in a murder case,' said Toby, a full glass of claret in his hand. Sitting next to him, Sarah eyed her spouse sharply, but Toby merely took another sip of wine. 'What?' he asked, unconcerned. 'It's true, isn't it?'

'If it is,' said Babs, 'now that the police have made an arrest, surely it won't be long before we're all free to go?'

Amy suddenly looked up. 'Ian hasn't been arrested for any crime,' she insisted, 'only for questioning.' She turned to Pearl for confirmation. 'That's right, isn't it?'

Pearl gave a firm nod. 'As far as I know.' She looked to the other guests as she explained. 'And the police caution is just a warning that the person being interviewed has a right to silence. They don't have to answer questions put to them, but if they find themselves in court giving an account which conflicts with what was said to the police earlier, the court may be less likely to believe that person. That's why it's good to have a solicitor present to offer some advice.'

'This woman,' said Ingrid.

'Kate Parsons,' said Pearl.

'She was engaged to Ian?'

'Some time ago.'

James frowned. 'Well, what was she doing here?'

Pearl shook her head. 'I don't know – for sure.'

Tess picked up on Pearl's tone. 'But you have an idea?'

Pearl framed her words carefully this time. 'I'm sure the police will get to the bottom of this.'

Sarah sprang to her feet and moved to the balustrade. 'Meanwhile, my brother is dead.' She stared out in the direction of the lake. 'Drowned . . .' Her voice trailed off and a deathly silence fell, broken only by Amy asking softly: 'What was Guy doing at the lake at that time of night? And why have the police been asking me so many questions about his medication?'

Ingrid looked from Amy to Simon. 'Have they said anything to you? You're a trained nurse, aren't you?'

All eyes turned to Simon. He gave a small shrug before replying. 'I'm qualified, yes, but I stopped working as a nurse some time ago.' He went to sip his drink but stopped when Toby asked bluntly: 'Why?'

Simon's glass remained poised at his lips.

Tess turned to Toby. 'What's it got to do with you?' she asked wearily, clearly irritated by his tone.

'I'll tell you,' said Toby. 'It strikes me that if my brother-in-law was murdered, and his medication had something to do with it, then someone with medical knowledge would be *just* the person to ask.' He fixed his gaze on Simon once more.

'Nonsense!' said Babs. 'Simon is my companion. My trusted employee.'

Simon gave her a grateful smile. 'Thank you,' he said proudly.

James turned to Pearl. 'Well, what I fail to understand is what the woman was doing there, in that maze, when the place is meant to be off bounds.'

Before Pearl could reply, Ingrid spoke. 'Come to think of it,' she began, turning directly to Pearl. 'What were *you* doing there?' She fixed Pearl with a look. Troubled, Amy spoke quickly. 'You don't have to answer that.'

'But I'd like to,' said Pearl. 'I was on my way back up to the house after meeting someone near the stable block.'

Sarah turned to Pearl. '"Someone"?'

'DCI Mike McGuire.'

Amy frowned. 'Of course,' she said softly. 'You must be missing him.' She looked pained at the thought. 'I'm so sorry, Pearl. You should have brought him to the house.'

Babs looked confused. 'Am I missing something?'

Amy explained. 'Pearl's engaged.'

'To a cop?' asked Ingrid.

'Well, well,' said James. 'A gumshoe and a uniform.'

'He's CID,' Pearl explained.

'Then why isn't he on this case?' asked Tess.

'Wrong district,' Pearl replied.

'Shame,' said Babs.

Toby got to his feet. 'I need a refill,' he commented to Emma, who was passing.

'Me too,' sighed Ingrid, handing Emma her empty glass.

Tess looked at Pearl. 'So, what now?'

Before Pearl could respond, Sarah spoke. 'Presumably the police will need time to question Ian and . . .'

'Kate,' said Pearl.

'And no doubt those two will be as obstructive as possible,' said Toby. 'All you have to do these days is give the old "no comment" routine.'

'How do you know that?' asked Pearl.

Toby grabbed the full wine glass Emma handed to him and took a large gulp of claret. 'I watch TV,' he said unashamedly.

Simon spoke up. 'Mr Soutar will know his rights.' Babs shot him a look and Simon shrugged. 'He's a barrister, right?'

Amy shook her head. 'Ian wouldn't have had anything to do with Guy's death. But Kate—' She stopped herself and asked instead, 'Did she try to harm you, Pearl?'

'Toby and I can do that,' said Sarah, suddenly finding resolve.

'What?' asked Toby.

Tess got to her feet. 'Why don't you have another drink?' she said dismissively.

Toby stared at her. 'And why don't you join me in one – you might not be so uptight.'

Tess turned quickly to face him, but she restrained herself from responding. Instead, it was James who spoke up. 'Now look here—' he began firmly.

'Calm down, Shakespeare,' said Toby wearily. 'You might like to show off in front of your girlfriend, but don't try and write lines for me.' James sprang to his feet, but it was Tess who spoke. 'Ignore him.'

'Yes,' said Toby, unconcerned. 'It's all a bit of a waste of time now, isn't it? The great benefactor is no longer with us. The money's all been given away.' He threw out his arms in an expansive gesture, but Sarah's voice broke in.

'Toby, please—'

'It's true, my darling,' he said, casually. 'Unless, of course, dear Guy was lying?' He turned slowly to face Amy, who said nothing – so he retrained his gaze on James and Tess. 'It would seem the game's up for you two, isn't it? Must be hard work, scratching around trying to find someone to prop up your play.' He glanced from James to Tess. 'Trying to find a suitable role for . . . Dame Tess? There's always *pantomime* dame?' He smiled and raised his glass to his lips, but James drew back his

Pearl shook her head. 'No.'

'Well,' said Toby. 'One thing's for sure. We won't be going anywhere soon.' He took another gulp of his claret while Ingrid accepted a fresh glass of white wine from Emma. 'Local police are always inept.'

'Why d'you say that?' asked Pearl.

Ingrid eyed her. 'If they weren't, they would surely have found out by now what happened to Guy. But instead—' she broke off as Amy pressed a handkerchief to her eyes. 'Oh, I'm sorry, Amy,' she said gently, taking her client's hand. 'When all this is over you must come and stay with me in London.'

'Nonsense!' said Babs. 'Amy's coming with me to Seasalter.' She leaned closer as she purred: 'The sea air will do you the world of good.'

'It hardly passes for "sea",' said Toby. 'It's an estuary.'

Babs looked affronted but Ingrid remained unimpressed. 'He's right. Not exactly the Med.'

'Maybe,' said Babs with a pinched look, 'but it will always be Amy's home. And at times like this, there's only one place to be – with family.' She offered a simpering smile. Tess also turned to Amy. 'You know you'll be very welcome with us in Brighton.'

Amy met her gaze then looked at James, who nodded. 'Of course,' he said.

At this, Amy seemed overwhelmed. 'Thank you. All of you. But . . .' she broke off for a moment. 'I simply can't think ahead right now. I can't even plan Guy's funeral . . .' She looked up, helpless.

fist. Sarah screamed a warning and quickly took hold of James's arm, preventing him from landing a blow. Tess gave a quick shake of her head and James got the message. Looking back at Toby, James recovered some dignity, straightened his jacket and strode away from the terrace to disappear into the grounds.

CHAPTER TWENTY-TWO

Some time later, after the guests had dispersed from the terrace, Pearl took the flight of stone steps into the grounds with the intention of checking her phone. She had not gone far before she caught sight of someone standing near the Japanese rock garden. For a moment, James Jarrett looked to Pearl much like a figure in an Edwardian painting, until the sound of her footsteps caused him to spring to life, taking his hands from his pockets and turning to face her as she approached. She offered a smile. 'I thought you might have gone back to the house.'

James shook his head. 'I needed some time to cool down,' he explained. His hand moved to stroke his beard, as if for comfort, before he looked back at Pearl. 'You must think me a lout for losing my temper like that.'

Seeing James looking genuinely troubled, Pearl replied, 'Toby was being deliberately provocative.'

'All the more reason why I shouldn't have risen to his bait.' He sighed. 'It was a good thing Sarah stepped in when she did, or . . .'

'Or what?'

'It was pretty obvious what would have happened.' James shrugged. 'I would have shut him up – once and for all.' He looked at Pearl. 'That's not to say I'm a violent person. I have a long fuse, but when I blow – I blow.' He paused. 'He shouldn't have insulted Tess like that.' He took a step away from Pearl and turned to view the oriental bridge, his voice lowering as he went on. 'You know this was meant to be a fun weekend away for us both? A celebration.'

'The wedding?'

'Of course. Everyone loves a wedding, don't they?' he said with a note of irony.

Pearl considered this, then asked, 'Was there any truth in Toby's suggestion?'

James turned back to her. 'That I would have liked Guy Priddey to back my play? Of course. Why on earth would I *not* want someone with Guy's kind of wealth to invest in a worthwhile project like this? I may not have convinced the right people so far, but I still have confidence in my work.'

'And this play in particular?'

James gave a determined nod. 'It's my best. I put my heart into it. Tess will tell you; it deserves an audience.'

'As does Tess?'

James smiled. 'She really is the most gifted actress – but

she also works hard at her craft. To bring her characters to life, she pays incredible attention to detail, in every aspect of the roles she takes – especially wardrobe – right down to the kind of footwear they might choose. Tess says she only comes to fully inhabit a role when she walks around in a character's shoes – literally. Tess and I make a good team.'

Pearl considered this. 'But you never got a chance to properly discuss your play with Guy?'

'How could I?' said James in frustration. 'It certainly wasn't the right time on the eve of his wedding, and you know what happened after that.'

'Tell me about it,' Pearl said. 'The play, I mean. You mentioned it's based on a *ménage à trois*?'

James gave a sudden smile. 'A fascinating dynamic, don't you think? The triad. The eternal triangle. And three, of course, is a very special number.'

Pearl noted how animated he had suddenly become. 'Special?'

'Yes, of course. In storytelling the power of three is always there – even in fairy tales: three little pigs, three bears, Snow White's evil stepmother returns three times to kill her. And after spinning for three nights, remember how Rumpelstiltskin gives the miller's daughter three days to guess his name? In "East of the Sun, West of the Moon", the heroine meets three women who present her with gifts – much like the Magi, the three wise men in the Bible. And then, of course, there's the sacred Trinity in Christianity; and in ancient Egypt, Osiris, Isis and Horus. The ancient Greeks believed in the sacred significance of numbers – Pythagoras and his followers, for instance, believed that three was the number that represented harmony. The Three Fates represent birth, life and death, and Plato saw the number three as symbolic of the simplest spatial shape'—he paused and smiled—'the triangle.'

'But as far as relationships go,' began Pearl, 'two – or, a couple – is still the norm.'

'That's true,' said James, 'but throughout history there have been so many examples of less conventional relationships – among less conventional people – artists, for example. I'm a playwright and it's my job to break down barriers, to offer alternative ways of thinking about things, of viewing the world – of living.' He frowned and heaved a deep sigh. 'It really is a tragedy my play isn't already being performed.'

Pearl considered him. 'It's also a tragedy that Guy Priddey is dead,' she said starkly. Her comment caused James to refocus. 'Of course. I'm sorry,' he said quickly. 'You must think me very egotistical.'

'Does it matter what I think?'

James held Pearl's gaze.

'Yes,' he said finally, as if recognising this for the first time. 'It does matter. In fact, it matters very much.'

He continued to stare intently at Pearl and took a slow step towards her, but a voice was suddenly heard. 'James?'

Turning quickly, Pearl and James saw Tess standing in the shadows on the path behind them. She stepped forward into the moonlight and said to James, 'I've been looking for you.'

Her gaze shifted to Pearl, but it was James who apologised. 'I'm sorry,' he began. 'I just needed to get away from that oaf.'

'I'm sure,' Tess agreed. 'But he's sleeping it off now and everyone's gone to bed. Come on,' she said gently, taking his hand to lead him away. James turned back to Pearl. 'Are you coming too?'

'In a while,' Pearl replied. 'Go on.' She offered a smile and Tess and James turned back towards the house. As they disappeared into the night, Pearl looked back at the oriental bridge, its form now bathed in moonlight. It was real. It existed. Yet somehow in that moment it seemed to Pearl, like so much of this beguiling landscape, to be illusory – much like an enchanting picture from a book of fairy tales . . .

That night, Pearl lay in bed, her curtains open as she considered the view. Beyond the tea terrace, the lights of Faversham twinkled against the night sky, like windows into the heavens, but in the far distance Pearl could also see the mechanical stars of the estuary windfarm reminding her of home. The flashing red lights of the turbines were only a few miles off Whitstable's coast – but still a world away from where Pearl was now. She thought of the view from her own bedroom window at Seaspray Cottage, which looked out on the same night sky and the ever-present silhouette of the Red Sands army fort, which lay nine miles offshore. During the Second World War, soldiers had been based there to protect London from enemy aircraft approaching from the Channel. Many of the servicemen had suffered psychological problems from the isolation, having been stationed like sitting ducks in the middle of the estuary – so near and yet so far away from safety – as Pearl now felt herself to be.

There had been no news of Ian or Kate, although Pearl remained aware that Bowell would have to find more reason to detain them soon or be forced to release them from custody. One part of the mystery had been solved for Pearl – the only clue she possessed. Kate's yellow jacket was proof enough to Pearl that Ian's former fiancée had been in Mount Ephraim's grounds on the night of Guy's murder – and possibly on the next night too when Ian had crossed the lawn to meet her – though the reason for that meeting still eluded her. Dolly was right: it was perfectly possible that Kate may have learned of Ian's arrival at Mount Ephraim from local gossip about Amy's wedding. It was also true he may have resisted meeting Kate and so she had taken it upon herself to visit the estate; but if so, why had she decided to visit him in such a covert way? To Pearl it seemed increasingly likely that, for reasons of her own, Kate had wanted to spy on the proceedings, but could that reason have involved Guy Priddey?

Pearl turned onto her side to try and sleep, but in the next instant her phone rang. Reaching blindly for it, she felt instinctively that it must be McGuire and answered quickly: 'What did you find out?'

Charlie's voice sounded on the end of the line. 'Mum?'

Concerned, Pearl sat up and switched on her bedside light. 'What is it?' she asked.

Charlie's voice sounded flat. 'What are you doing there?'

'I told you last week,' Pearl began. 'I'm . . . here for a wedding.'

'That's what you said.' Charlie paused. 'And now?'

Her son's question brought Pearl up short. On her silence, Charlie continued. 'You're involved in some kind of murder investigation.'

Pearl heaved a sigh. 'Did Gran tell you?'

'No. I ran into Mike today. In Canterbury.' Charlie paused, then: 'Why didn't you tell me?'

'I didn't want you to worry.'

'Worry?' echoed Charlie. 'That you're there, in the middle of the countryside, with a killer?'

'Charlie—'

'No, Mum, I know you got Gran to lie about this. She only told me you were staying on for a few more days.'

'That's true,' said Pearl quickly.

'Because of a murder,' said Charlie pointedly.

Pearl tried to reorganise her thoughts. 'Look, it's complicated. And it's important that this news isn't leaked to the press yet. The police will make a media statement soon—'

'That's not the reason you kept this from me,' said Charlie quietly.

This was true, and Pearl sighed again. 'I wish Mike hadn't told you.'

'Well, I'm glad he did,' said Charlie. 'Don't you care how worried we are about you?'

'There's no need.'

'There's every need. But that's not the point – the fact is, you kept this from me.'

Pearl heard his wounded tone. 'For the best reasons,' she said softly.

'And what if I did the same?' Charlie asked. 'What if I'd gone somewhere and not only put myself in danger but lied to you about it and asked others to do the same? Are you saying you wouldn't feel like I feel right now?'

Pearl had no good answer for that, so she tried to reason with him. 'Look, Amy's my friend,' she said finally.

'Yes,' said Charlie. 'And we're family. I don't want you putting yourself in any danger . . . taking any chances.'

Pearl braced herself. 'I won't, Charlie. I promise. And I will be home soon.'

Pearl heard a sudden click on the line. Hoping it was simply poor mobile reception, she redialled Charlie's number but reached only his voicemail message. She listened to her son's voice on the end of the line then hesitated before she spoke gently, leaving a simple message. 'I love you'.

Switching off her bedside lamp, she allowed the darkness to envelop her, then closed her eyes – feeling more alone than ever.

CHAPTER TWENTY-THREE

'How is he today?' Pearl had called Dolly at the Whitstable Pearl the following morning.

'You don't need to ask that,' said Dolly sagely. 'You already know.'

Pearl frowned, feeling even more troubled than she had felt last night after hearing Charlie's reaction to the news of Guy Priddey's murder. 'Can I talk to him?'

Dolly glanced across her shoulder to see Charlie was busy serving a table of French tourists. 'Not unless you want to distract him from his work,' she said. 'Leave it till the end of his shift – unless, of course, you want to risk him dropping a dozen Whitstable natives down your customers' laps.'

'Well, what can I do?' asked Pearl.

'Come home,' said Dolly bluntly.

'I can't,' Pearl argued, feeling increasingly torn. 'Not yet anyway. I need to talk to Ian once the police release him from custody.'

'You think he and Kate could be involved in Guy's murder?'

'I don't know,' admitted Pearl. 'I trust Ian, but I hardly know Kate.'

'She's a good woman,' Dolly insisted. 'So why on earth would she have wanted to kill Guy? Think about it, Pearl. Even if she's still in love with Ian, Guy was the man who was about to marry Amy and spirit her away from Ian forever!'

'I know,' Pearl agreed. 'It doesn't make sense unless . . . perhaps Kate wanted Amy to experience the kind of heartbreak she'd felt in losing Ian?'

'In that case,' said Dolly, 'she'd have to be unhinged.'

'Maybe all murderers are "unhinged".'

'Perhaps,' said Dolly. 'Bunny boilers do exist.' She paused for a moment. 'Barbara Meadows would never have allowed anyone to come between her and Geoffrey – Amy's dad. And that includes Amy herself.' She went on, 'Some women just can't help themselves. Once they have a man in their sights, nothing can be allowed to get in their way. Barbara was like that with Mary.'

'Who?'

'Mary Boyle. She worked at the bar at the golf club. After Amy's mum died, Geoffrey began hanging around the nineteenth hole for company. Of course, it was only natural he needed a shoulder to cry on – or a bosom – and when it came to the latter, Mary certainly had enough to go round. She also had plenty of heart. She was kind, sympathetic – attractive too.' She heaved a sigh. 'But

Barbara already had Geoffrey in her sights. The poor fellow was widow bait, and Barbara succeeded in chasing Mary off.'

'How?' asked Pearl.

'A complaint to the clubhouse; unsubstantiated, of course, but enough for the club to take action. I don't think anyone quite got to the bottom of it, but Barbara was a long-standing member of the club and Mary was only a part-time member of the bar staff. All that was needed was for a bit of mud to be thrown. It stuck – and the club found a reason to let Mary go.'

'And Babs became the new "bosom" to cry on?'

'She certainly did. She's as ruthless as Lady Macbeth.'

'You think she could have blood on her hands?' asked Pearl darkly.

'If she's the same Barbara Meadows, I wouldn't be at all surprised.'

'Perhaps she's changed?' Pearl suggested.

'If leopards ever do change their spots, then maybe "Babs" Meadows-Young has changed her ways.'

Pearl smiled. 'Amy's on good terms with her now – most of the time.'

'Barbara knows how to manipulate people,' Dolly insisted.

Pearl took this in, and Dolly spoke again. 'Have you talked to McGuire?'

Pearl frowned at the mention of his name. 'I left a message for him this morning. He and I need to talk about Charlie.'

'Pearl—'

'It's no good, Mum,' Pearl cut in. 'I can't have him interfering in my relationship with my son.'

Dolly spoke calmly. 'Charlie has his own relationship with Mike.'

'Maybe,' said Pearl curtly.

'And they're bound to grow even closer,' said Dolly, 'once you get married.' She paused. 'That's if you ever do.'

Pearl responded sharply. 'Why wouldn't we?'

Dolly spoke calmly to defuse the situation. 'Listen to yourself, Pearl. You need to make sense of your feelings before you talk to Mike – *or* Charlie.'

'But—'

'No,' said Dolly. 'You asked *me* not to tell Charlie about the murder, not Mike.'

'But I never expected them to meet up like that.'

'Well, why wouldn't they? They live in the same city. And why should Mike have to lie about this? Come to that, why should I?'

Pearl was speechless.

'I have to go now,' said Dolly. She'd noticed a small army of hikers had just entered the restaurant, sporting camouflage gear and backpacks. 'The SAS have just arrived.'

'Mum?' said Pearl, confused.

But the line went dead in her hand.

Pearl stared at her phone, considering calling Dolly back, when she heard a car drawing up on the gravel path outside. Moving quickly to the window, she squinted against the sunlight and saw DI Jane Bowell stepping out of the passenger door. Sergeant Falconer followed from the driver's side to open a rear door to Ian Soutar. Ian stretched his arms as though relieved to have his freedom. He looked up, and his eyes met Pearl's.

Ten minutes later, DI Bowell had summoned the guests to the garden wing's large sitting room – together with Emma and Ryan, who remained standing at one of the tall windows. Sergeant Falconer stood to attention by the door while DI Bowell took a place at the grand fireplace. Babs had positioned herself beside Simon on the sofa, alongside Amy, while Tess was in an armchair with James perched on its arm. Sarah sat across the room on a smaller sofa with her husband standing behind her. Seated with Ian at the chestnut table, Pearl became aware that all eyes seemed to be trained on him, rather than on the police detective.

'Thank you for your time,' said DI Bowell. 'I think it's only appropriate to let you know where we are with the investigation.'

'In the light of your arrests?' said Toby, raising an eyebrow. Bowell fixed her gaze on Ian and said only: 'Mr Soutar has been helping us with our enquiries.'

'They all say that,' said Toby, unimpressed. Heads turned to him and he responded:

'It's just a euphemism, meaning, "They've got their man – but not enough to charge him".' He looked at Bowell, and James said, 'You arrested *two* people, Inspector – Ian and the woman who attacked Pearl.'

'I wasn't attacked,' said Pearl calmly.

'You were struggling with the woman,' said Tess.

'That's true, but—'

'I'll carry on,' said Bowell, cutting in. 'Ms Parsons has also been released.'

'Nothing on her either,' said Toby with a scowl.

Babs gave a sidelong look at Ian then said to DI Bowell, 'They were a couple once, you know – an engaged couple.'

James frowned at this. 'What was she doing here, Ian?'

All eyes turned back to Ian, who paused before responding. 'As I said in my statement to the police,' he began, 'Kate came here to see me.'

'But why?' asked Amy.

Ian looked troubled but went on to explain. 'She . . . discovered I was here and got in touch.'

'How?' asked Toby brusquely.

'She called me. I didn't respond. Then she left a message telling me she was coming here to Mount Ephraim. I . . . felt I had no choice.' He paused and ran a hand through his dark hair. 'I met her two nights ago – near the cricket pavilion. I told her about Guy's murder, but I also told her not to come to the estate again.' He glanced at DI Bowell. 'I knew this would complicate your investigation. But I honestly didn't think she would come back again.' He paused. 'I was wrong.'

Pearl considered this, then commented, 'I may have

seen Kate in the grounds on the day we all arrived – and that same evening during the firework display.'

Amy frowned, suspicious. 'You didn't mention that.'

'Because I wasn't sure,' said Pearl, 'but I told the inspector that I thought there might have been an intruder. I had no idea it was Kate.'

Amy's eyes narrowed as she looked back at Ian. 'What did she want?'

He gave a shrug. 'Just to talk. It's been a while. I'd . . . broken off communication when I was in London. Suddenly she had my contact details. She'd found a way of getting in touch.' He paused, clearly conflicted. 'I told her not to.'

Ingrid suddenly piped up, raising a manicured hand. 'Let me get this straight. Your old girlfriend shows up here—'

'Fiancée,' said Babs.

DI Bowell eyed Ian. 'To recap, Ms Parsons came to the estate on the day the guests arrived?'

Ian nodded. 'Yes – the same day *I* arrived.'

'But you didn't meet with her until the following night,' Bowell went on.

'After Guy's death,' Ian explained.

'And then she returned again,' said Pearl. 'The night before last?'

Ian nodded once more. 'But I only knew that – I only saw her – *after* you'd found her in the maze.'

Pearl considered him but Bowell announced starkly: 'This is now a murder investigation.'

'No,' said Amy, shaking her head. 'An accident!'

Bowell glanced down at some paperwork. 'Toxicology reports show Mr Priddey took a combination of drugs on the night he died.'

'You mean he committed suicide,' said Toby.

'No!' Amy protested. 'I don't believe it. I won't.' Looking at Bowell, she hammered out a response like rapid gunfire. 'I explained to you: Guy took oxycodone – a prescribed medication. A painkiller.'

Bowell nodded slowly. 'Yes,' she agreed. 'But on the night he died, he also took a large dose of a benzodiazepine. The two drugs would have interacted—'

'You mean,' Sarah broke in, 'Guy was poisoned?'

Bowell considered this question carefully before responding. 'No. But it's likely that the two drugs resulted in effects which could have contributed to his death.'

Tess spoke up. 'What kind of effects?'

'A lack of coordination,' said Bowell. She nodded to Sergeant Falconer, who consulted her notes and listed: 'Disorientation, confusion and respiratory depression.'

'How soon after taking it?' asked Pearl.

Bowell responded, 'Half an hour to an hour.'

'So,' said Pearl, 'After the two drugs had taken effect, Guy would have found it difficult to survive falling into the lake?' She went on. 'There are lots of plants and vegetation growing either side of the bridge where I found his body, so it would be a challenge for anyone to climb out at that spot at the best of times.'

At this, Amy hung her head low.

'What the hell was he doing there?' asked James.

'That,' said Bowell, 'is what I need to ask you – all of you.'

Simon spoke, raising a hand as he did so. 'You mentioned a benzodiazepine? Can I ask which one?'

Bowell checked her notes. 'Diazepam.'

Simon frowned at this. 'Valium.' He shared a look with Babs.

'What is it?' asked Bowell.

Babs appeared panicked. 'My . . . supply has disappeared.'

Simon qualified. 'No, Babs, you just can't find it—'

'Because it's disappeared!' she insisted before turning to Bowell. 'I had it when I first arrived. In the dining room. I mentioned this!'

'I remember,' said Amy.

'So do I,' added Ingrid.

Babs went on as she tried to recall. 'And I had the packet in my hand. I put it on the dining table.'

'That's right,' said Emma, moving forward. 'And I took it off the table, with the cruet, and . . . placed it on the small table near the games room. I didn't move it from there. And I haven't seen it since.' She looked back at Ryan.

'Neither have I,' said Babs sombrely. 'I looked everywhere in my room.' She turned to Simon. 'I told you that yesterday. I assumed *you'd* put them somewhere.' She looked pained. 'But you can't find them either . . .' She trailed off and looked at each of the other guests in turn before asking, 'Where did they go?'

DI Bowell took control. 'I need you to go over your movements again that night.' She surveyed everyone in the room before her gaze settled on Ryan at the back of the room. 'Tell me again – Mr Robson.'

Ryan shrugged, looking uncomfortable. 'I . . . can't tell you any more than I have already. After the firework display,' he began, 'I went off duty, back to our flat.' He turned to Emma who took up the story. 'And I was in the kitchen in the west wing, making sure everything was prepared for breakfast the next day; then I went home to Ryan and wrote some lists so I didn't forget anything.'

Bowell turned to James. 'I turned in early,' he said, 'straight after the fireworks.'

'And I,' said Tess, 'sat on the tea terrace for a while, admiring the topiary.' She glanced across at Pearl. 'You saw me there on your way back to the house.'

Pearl nodded. 'That's right,' she confirmed. 'I remember. We spoke.'

Babs gave Pearl a suspicious look. 'And where had *you* been? I seem to recall you disappeared straight after the fireworks.'

Pearl paused. 'I didn't go far. I took a short walk in the grounds. I realised I'd missed a call and so I returned it as I walked.'

DI Bowell turned to Simon. 'I came straight upstairs,' he said quickly. 'That's after I asked Emma about an iron for Babs's suit. You know what linen's like,' he pursed his lips. 'Creases?'

'And I,' said Babs, grandly, 'followed Simon up shortly after that. After a'—she hesitated for a moment—'chat with my stepdaughter.'

'Chat,' said Tess, 'or argument?' She raised a knowing eyebrow. Babs's mouth dropped open. Amy quickly apologised. 'I'm sorry,' she began. 'I happened to mention it to Tess – and to Pearl – the next morning.' She looked troubled. 'I . . . overreacted,' she explained. 'Wedding nerves.'

Bowell then turned to Sarah and Toby.

'Don't look at me,' said Toby, throwing up his hands. 'If you must know, I went in search of some port in the scullery. Sarah was in bed when I came up.'

Sarah looked from her husband to Bowell. 'And . . . I talked to my brother very briefly before that.'

'Where?' asked Bowell.

'In the gardens right outside.' She threw a glance towards the window. 'Then I went straight to our room in the west wing.'

All eyes now turned to Ian Soutar.

'The last I saw of Guy,' he said, before taking a long pause, 'he was on the stairs in the west wing.'

A shocked murmur went around the room.

'Oh?' said Amy. 'You never said this before.'

'Until last night, I had forgotten,' said Ian. He gave his attention again to DI Bowell. 'I told you, I saw him only very briefly. I'd gone to my car to get some documents from the boot. As I came in, I happened to see Guy going into his suite on that lower landing in the west wing. It was quite late – after midnight. Guy didn't see me.'

DI Bowell exchanged a look with Sergeant Falconer. 'And you're sure it was Mr Priddey?'

Ian nodded confidently. 'It couldn't have been anyone else.'

DI Bowell spoke. 'So, we now have an eyewitness report of Mr Priddey having been seen alive after midnight. But no one heard, or experienced, anything unusual after that?'

'Apart from Simon,' said Pearl.

At this, Babs turned sharply to Simon, who quickly explained, 'It was nothing too "unusual",' he began, 'but I mentioned to Pearl that something woke me. The old clock, I think. I don't know what time it was because it was already chiming away—'

'But it must have been midnight,' said Pearl.

All eyes moved to her. She explained. 'It chimes the hour, so if it had been any later, say, one or two o'clock, you wouldn't have heard it chiming so long. But you said it was chiming while you went to the bathroom?'

Simon nodded. 'That's right. Then I returned to bed and a few minutes later . . .' He trailed off.

Pearl prompted him. 'Your door fell open?'

He nodded again. 'Yes.'

'You didn't close it properly,' said Toby dismissively.

'Someone was there?' asked Amy.

'Probably a draught,' said Ingrid.

'Or a ghost,' said James, looking at Tess. She smiled and remarked, 'Too much imagination, darling.'

'Someone walked past?' suggested Emma.

'Opened his door?' asked Ryan.

'*Created* a draught,' said Pearl.

Bowell took this in, then looked at her notes, searching for a plan of the house.

'The door at the end of that corridor,' she began, 'beyond Mr Mullen's room, leads to a landing in the main house.'

Emma nodded. 'That's right.'

'Fancy that,' said James.

'And?' said Sarah.

Amy suddenly spoke. 'And the landing leads straight to . . . Guy's suite.' She glanced around the room, but Pearl stared across at Emma. 'You said that Guy's door was unlocked that night?'

Emma nodded slowly. 'That's true. I explained how those doors are always left unlocked before a wedding. There's so much to do – it makes access easier for the bride and groom.' She looked at Bowell. 'So someone could have gone into Mr Priddey's room that night.'

'And . . . interfered with his medication,' said Amy.

Ian now looked at Babs. 'Possibly using your pills.'

'What?' gasped Babs.

'Those pills still haven't been found,' said Bowell.

Babs looked at Simon, who shook his head before he froze with a sudden realisation. 'Oh my God,' he said. 'You . . . think the person who passed my room could have been going to—'

'Guy's room,' said James.

A brooding silence fell. Simon looked around the

room. 'If only—' He broke off and then seemed to reorganise his thoughts before beginning again. 'If only I had got up and checked the door when it fell open. I might have seen who it was.'

'But you didn't,' said Babs. 'And whoever it was must have used my pills to . . .'

As Amy lowered her head, Babs trailed off and took Amy's hand. James whispered, 'It was one of us. Someone sitting here.'

Silence fell like a pall before Amy shook her head. 'No. No, I still can't believe that. It's not true!' She sprang to her feet and rushed from the room.

Ingrid got up and went after her while Bowell stared across at Pearl, who gave a nod and followed after Ingrid. She caught up with her in the hallway as Ingrid called up the stairs. 'Amy?'

The door to Amy's room slammed shut like a heavy tome closing. Looking defeated, Ingrid turned back to see Pearl behind her – before she turned on her heels and headed out of the front door.

CHAPTER TWENTY-FOUR

After DI Bowell had left Mount Ephraim, Pearl went in search of Ingrid and found her on the central terrace staring down towards the lake, her mobile phone in hand. As Pearl approached, she heard Ingrid leaving a message.

'Call me as soon as you get this, will you?' Quickly ending the call, Amy's agent stared down at her phone for a moment before she turned back to see Pearl.

'Am I disturbing you?'

Ingrid faltered for a moment at Pearl's question before indicating her phone. 'No, I . . . just had a few calls to make. Business. As usual.' She slipped her mobile in the pocket of the taupe jacket she was wearing.

'This must be very difficult for you.'

'Difficult?' Ingrid's tone was clipped.

'Trying to manage your business from here? I'm presuming you have lots of other clients – apart from Amy?'

For a moment Ingrid said nothing before she finally admitted, 'These days I can count the numbers of clients I have on the fingers of one hand – at least, the ones that are still working.' She eyed Pearl then said in a defeated tone, 'There's no point in me lying to you about that; you could see for yourself if you chose to check my website.' She went on. 'I "streamlined" some time ago. Finding work for hungry features writers can be expensive – not to mention time-consuming. Wining and dining, schmoozing'—she paused—'and often to no avail.' She heaved a sigh and leaned back on the balustrade. 'If you must know, I've lost clients over the years. As soon as they hit the big time, they moved on to pastures greener – though they don't stay green forever.'

Pearl allowed a pause, then said, 'Someone said on the day we arrived that being in the entertainment business can be rewarding but—'

'Insecure,' Ingrid snapped. 'Tell me about it. But that's what *makes* it all the more rewarding when things come together.' She looked at Pearl. 'I've done little else for the past thirty years. I've lived for my clients and their work. They've been like family to me – the family I never had. Work has been everything.' She pushed herself away from the balustrade and strolled across to the area of the terrace that overlooked the wedding pavilion. For a moment, she remained silent.

'Amy has been with me the longest,' she said softly. 'She has talent, but she's also put in the work that makes talent pay. They say you need luck in business, but it's also true that the harder you work, the luckier you get.' She turned back to face Pearl. 'I know what you're thinking; you're a smart woman. You could see how I felt about her giving up writing.'

Pearl nodded. 'You had plans for her.'

'Plans,' echoed Ingrid. 'I have more plans than anything else these days – and too often nothing comes of them. In truth, I've also made some bad decisions.' She took a deep breath. 'If you must know, I ran up expenses, got behind with tax payments . . . and I delayed payouts to some of my clients.' She looked pained.

'That's why you lost some?' Pearl ventured.

Ingrid nodded. 'Partly.' She looked away towards the house. 'For a while I felt like I was trapped in that ditch on the lawn over there. I couldn't see my way out. Just as I managed to scramble up and begin to see some daylight, I'd sink back down again. But Amy stayed. She helped me get out of trouble, and finally I paid what I owed and things have begun looking up again. It's true I was back making plans.'

'For Amy?'

Ingrid looked at Pearl. 'For us both. That was what Thailand was all about. Amy and I are a team.'

'And you profit from her work.'

'I take a percentage of what she earns – from commissions I work hard to get.'

'Commissions which Amy no longer needed once she married Guy.'

Ingrid held Pearl's look. 'So, that makes me a suspect

in your book, does it? You think I could find a way to murder Guy on the eve of his wedding, just so I could keep Amy writing? You really think I'd do that for fifteen per cent of Amy Young's earnings?'

'People have been murdered for less.'

Ingrid turned away but Pearl went on: 'I happened to hear you talking to someone in your room on the night before the wedding. Another business call?'

Ingrid turned slowly to face Pearl, waiting for her to continue. In her own time, Pearl went on. 'You said something about . . . not being able to get through to "her", and there being only one way to change her mind.' She paused. 'I presume you were talking about Amy?'

The question hung between the two women. Finally, Ingrid managed a cynical smile. 'Well, well,' she began. 'You really *are* a regular snoop, Ms Nolan.'

Pearl said nothing, still waiting for a response. Ingrid heaved another sigh. 'If you must know, I was talking to an old friend, the editor of a magazine. She's eager to commission a special feature from Amy.'

'About life with Guy Priddey?'

Ingrid looked away once more. Pearl continued. 'But that isn't going to happen now, is it? Because there isn't going to be any life with Guy – not for Amy, or anyone else.' She paused. 'What *was* the only way you could see to "change her mind"?'

Ingrid's dark eyes flashed up to meet Pearl's gaze. 'I really don't think I need to tell you that.'

'And maybe,' Pearl began, 'you don't need to.'

With that, Pearl turned and began walking away from Ingrid. But after only a moment, Ingrid spoke again. 'I can tell you now,' she called out, 'it wasn't murder.'

Pearl looked back, noting that Ingrid had adopted a confident demeanour and her poker face – which she'd no doubt used many times to bluff a business rival – but she said nothing.

Striding away in the direction of the house, Pearl heard a text arriving on her phone. She took it from her pocket and saw it was from Dolly. It read:

> *Kate Parsons has agreed to see you. This evening.*
> *Standard Quay.*

That evening, after a short drive from Mount Ephraim to Faversham, Pearl found a parking space on the southern bank of the tidal inlet known as the creek. Standard Quay's day trippers had disappeared after exploring the coffee shops and antique bazaars that filled the area, leaving the owners of the craft that moored there in peace. The creek's waters were reasonably shallow but more than adequate for coasting vessels and the tall-masted, brown-sailed barge, known as Greta, which had become part of the local seascape in Whitstable, where it regularly ferried passengers out to the various locations in the bay. Seeing the boat here on its alternative mooring struck a chord for Pearl, and she suddenly wished she was home again, walking along the pebbled beach with McGuire.

She had yet to talk to him about Charlie, but her earlier conversation with Dolly had sown doubts in her mind about her reaction to Charlie's call. It was true Pearl had asked only Dolly, and not McGuire, to keep news of Guy Priddey's murder from Charlie; nevertheless, she resented the fact that McGuire had taken it upon himself to tell Charlie about the murder. She asked herself now if her resentment was justified. Or was she simply looking to shift the blame for her inability to confide in her son? As she walked along the quay, she realised that Dolly was right; she needed to make sense of her own feelings before discussing things with McGuire.

Just as she reached that decision, she saw what she was looking for; a woman was sitting on a bench overlooking the creek at a point where an old dry dock lay between some houseboats, offering a view to green fields across the water. Pearl hesitated for a moment as she observed Kate Parsons, still wearing her bright yellow jacket, hands thrust into her pockets, as she stared absently across the creek. Pearl couldn't be sure if it was guilt or compassion she felt in that moment, or perhaps a mixture of both, but she moved quickly forward, the sound of her footsteps on the gravel path announcing her arrival.

'Thanks for meeting me,' she said gently.

Kate Parsons paused before giving a nod of her head. Pearl sat down beside her and looked out across the creek towards the lowering sun. 'You . . . chose a nice spot.'

'Yes,' Kate agreed. 'I could hardly come and see you at the house.' She turned and gave Pearl a cynical look before glancing away again. 'Not unless I want to get arrested again.'

Pearl considered her. 'I'm sorry,' she said sincerely. 'I had no idea it was you in the grounds, in the maze.'

'No,' said Kate, dully. 'Why would you? I wasn't invited. I was trespassing.'

'But you came to see Ian?'

Kate looked pained at Pearl's question. Unable to speak, she simply nodded.

'You heard he was here in Faversham,' said Pearl. 'Your Aunt Sylvia?'

Kate looked at Pearl. 'She told you?'

'She didn't have to,' said Pearl softly.

Kate looked away again and stood up. 'I should have left things. But I couldn't.' She looked back at Pearl. 'Knowing Ian was back here, so close . . .' She trailed off. 'Once I got his new phone number from my aunt, I asked if we could meet, but he wouldn't. He said there wasn't time. Perhaps I should have taken no for an answer, but I couldn't. I wanted to see him.'

'Ian?' asked Pearl, giving a knowing look. 'Or Amy?'

Kate took her seat again. 'All right,' she said, 'I admit I was curious. Why wouldn't I be? Ian and I were engaged for a long time. We'd planned a future together. A home. A family—' She pressed her eyes tight shut as if trying to dam her tears, then she fell silent again.

'Ian wanted to settle down,' said Pearl gently. 'With you.'

Kate nodded, her eyes still closed. 'But it was no good,' she said finally. 'Somehow, he just couldn't get over her.'

Pearl glanced down and saw that Kate was toying with the ring finger of her left hand, perhaps the space that had once been filled by an engagement ring.

'I can't blame him,' said Kate. 'She's very beautiful, talented and clever.' She turned to Pearl. 'I've never been ambitious. I have nothing to prove. I just fell in love with a man I wanted to be with for the rest of my life – and I thought he felt the same, but . . .' She trailed off once more.

'But what?' asked Pearl. 'What happened?'

Kate shook her head. 'I don't know. I suppose it must have haunted him, the fact that she just couldn't commit to him.' She took on a confused look. 'I never understood why. But neither did he. They were together for some time, but something stopped her from . . . taking things further.'

'Getting married, you mean?'

Kate nodded. 'It was nothing he did. But he once told me that it was like she was harbouring a big secret – something even she didn't quite understand.'

'A secret?' said Pearl. 'About what?'

Kate shook her head again, struggling to explain. 'When I found out about her wedding, at Mount Ephraim, I wanted to see for myself. Who was this man she was marrying? What was so special about him that he could possibly replace Ian?' She paused, her questions unanswered, then went on again. 'I'd always thought that, one day, Amy would come back, recognise her mistake and go back to him.'

'To Ian?'

'Yes; that was why news of this wedding was such a shock.'

Pearl looked away and caught sight of a yacht drifting past on the evening breeze and a rising tide. 'For Ian too,' said Pearl softly as she looked back at Kate. 'So you came to Mount Ephraim . . . on the day we all arrived?'

Kate nodded once more, and Pearl went on. 'I thought I saw you that afternoon near the lake.'

'You did,' Kate admitted. 'I managed to sneak into the grounds from the orchards. I didn't dare cross the lawns in case I was seen, so I used the trees around the lake for cover.' She paused. 'When I saw a woman at the old pump house, I thought it might be Amy, but then you turned, and I quickly made my way up the bank to hide in the little wood. I only realised it was you when you crossed that bridge and I finally saw your face. Pearl Nolan, from the Whitstable Pearl.'

Pearl took this in. 'And later? During the fireworks that evening?'

'I'd asked Ian to meet me at the back of the old cricket pavilion. I said I'd be there.' Kate frowned. 'He told me not to come. But I did anyway.'

'And Ian?'

Kate shook her head. 'He didn't come. But the next day I got a message to meet him in the same place. Late that night, so that we wouldn't be seen.' She paused. 'When he came, he told me about Guy's death. I was so upset, I began crying. It didn't seem possible. It was such a terrible thing – on his wedding day?'

'And you'd primed yourself to think that Ian might have changed his mind about your relationship?'

'Of course,' she said. 'Why wouldn't I? I assumed he'd witnessed Amy getting married that day and thought again about us. I knew nothing about what had happened—'

'Until Ian told you?'

'That's right. I swear.' She paused. 'He told me that Swale Police were investigating the death and that I shouldn't come to the house any more or even admit that I had been there at all, or . . . I might be considered a suspect.' She looked earnestly at Pearl. 'That's what they thought, isn't it? That police inspector? She actually suspected I could have had something to do with Guy Priddey's death? They wouldn't have arrested me otherwise.'

Pearl took a deep breath and organised her thoughts. 'Kate, why *did* you come back to Mount Ephraim again – after Ian had told you about Guy's death and he'd explained why you should stay away?'

'Well, why else?' she asked, nonplussed. 'I was worried about him. How could I possibly stay away knowing he might be in danger?'

Pearl considered Kate's expression – one of helplessness but also of innocence born of love.

'Of course,' Pearl said softly, almost to herself.

Kate continued. 'It's been a mystery to me how he could have ended things with me – walked away like he did, after what we had. Why can't he break loose from the hold she has over him? I need to know. Can you understand that?'

Looking over at Kate, Pearl realised she could be staring at herself – at a woman who couldn't leave a mystery unsolved, and the door to its solution closed . . .

whether this was really true. Apart from her own need to revisit old ambitions and start up Nolan's Detective Agency, Pearl recognised that she had moved on in so many ways. Her relationship with McGuire had set her on a new course that would, given time, become a new life. That was also true of Amy and her relationship with Guy; their marriage would have created new opportunities in a way that her relationship with Ian had not, but why had that former relationship failed? And what was it about the broken engagement that had caused such a problem for Ian – and, in turn, for Kate Parsons – in moving on? Kate had spoken of her need to solve the 'mystery' – not of Guy's death but whatever it was that had produced such an impasse for Ian and Kate – until news of Amy's wedding had signalled an opportunity for momentum. And that chance had faded with the news of Guy's death. Pearl now considered that Amy, Ian and Kate had retreated back to their former positions, creating an odd triangle, and that thought suddenly connected with the concept of James's play featuring a *ménage à trois* – a threesome or triad – three people living under one roof.

The French term always conjured up for Pearl the idea of two women catering for the needs of one man – historically speaking, a king – as the *ménage à trois* had been a common arrangement among European royalty and aristocracy. It also suggested to Pearl the possibility of one person being left out of the triangle because, as Pearl had remarked to James, the conventional relationship still remained a duo: a partnership between two people

– in effect, a marriage. From her schoolgirl French, Pearl knew the word *'ménage'* literally translated as 'household', which suggested more of a domestic situation than a romantic one. In thinking about this now, Pearl realised that her stay at Mount Ephraim had been constantly forcing her to consider weddings – and what they might lead to – even though the reason for her own visit, the wedding of her old friend, Amy, had failed to take place.

Arriving back at the house, she found it in darkness. It seemed clear no one was in a mood to socialise, especially as DI Bowell's earlier visit had confirmed Guy's death as murder. Walking up the path towards the garden wing, Pearl recognised with frustration that, in spite of all she had gleaned, she was still no further forward in discovering the identity of Guy's killer. Glancing towards the terrace, she recalled how she had felt on her arrival: full of expectation for a happy occasion, a celebration and perhaps confirmation of what was to come with her own wedding – in spite of any doubts sown by Dolly that same morning. Now, her mission to right an injustice and find Guy Priddey's murderer was creating friction between Pearl and McGuire – not least because he had been right all along in insisting that the murderer could still lurk among them in this beautiful setting.

Clouds had filled the dark sky and the moon had yet to rise. The silhouettes of tall trees loomed above her as Pearl made her way towards the terrace steps, but before she reached them a figure stepped out from the old porch beneath the terrace. Pearl raised her arm in defence, but a strong hand grasped her wrist. She was powerless in its grip.

'That's no way to say hello,' said McGuire softly before pulling her gently into the old porch. Breathless, Pearl stared up at him, her heart still pounding in her chest.

'What are you doing here?'

McGuire slipped his hand into his breast pocket and pulled out some paperwork. 'Ryan Robson,' he said. 'I found this police report about him suffering an overdose of methadone a few years ago. Seems he has a history of Class A drug dependency.'

McGuire handed her the report and Pearl frowned as she read it. McGuire continued. 'You know that methadone is used as a substitute for heroin?'

Pearl looked up at him and nodded before handing the paperwork back.

'Well?' asked McGuire, confused by her silence.

'I know about Ryan's drug problem,' she said finally.

McGuire looked nonplussed. 'How?'

'Emma told me.'

'And you didn't think to share that with me?'

'I didn't think it was relevant.'

'Really,' said McGuire, unimpressed. 'And is that because she happens to be a friend?'

'Look—' Pearl began guiltily.

But McGuire broke in. 'Why didn't you tell me?' he demanded. Pearl took a moment to organise her thoughts.

'Because it's history,' she said calmly. 'An old drug problem – and Ryan's over it. Emma was open with me about this.'

'No doubt because she knew it would come up.'

'Look, I've seen how hard he works here, how happy they both are—'

'Pearl—'

'There's no motive for murdering Guy.'

'That you know of,' said McGuire. 'But there's certainly opportunity. And someone with Ryan Robson's drug history would know *all* about the effects of prescription opioids like oxycodone.'

Looking at McGuire, Pearl felt conflicted. Knowing he was right, she heaved a sigh, but instead of addressing his point she said only, 'Did you have to tell Charlie about Guy's murder?'

McGuire looked thrown. 'Why wouldn't I?'

'He called me last night. He was upset.'

'I realised that,' said McGuire gently. 'He worries about you – we all do. But I didn't realise I was meant to lie to him.'

Pearl turned sharply. 'I didn't expect you to lie,' she replied in frustration.

'Sorry, Pearl, but how else do you describe not telling the truth?'

She turned away from him once more and shivered from the damp cold of the porch. McGuire's heart went out to her, and he laid a hand gently on her shoulder. 'Pearl, why are we doing this?' he asked. 'Why don't we just let DI Bowell get on with her job?'

'You know why,' said Pearl, looking back at him.

McGuire read the look in her eyes. 'Because you can't stop yourself?'

'Because I owe it to Amy!'

'And what about Charlie?' he asked. 'Or Dolly? Or . . . me?' McGuire paused, then added. 'I've told you, you're here with a killer.'

'A killer who murdered Amy's partner,' said Pearl. 'The man she loved. The man she was about to marry.'

McGuire looked at her and shook his head. 'And you see no irony in that?'

Pearl failed to reply. McGuire moved closer to her, his eyes scanning her face.

'You and I are supposed to be getting married.'

'Are you . . . saying now we won't?'

McGuire continued to hold her gaze. 'I think that depends on you,' he said softly. 'Will you ever stop?'

'Stop?' Pearl's voice sounded faint as a whisper.

'Yes,' said McGuire. 'Stop trying to prove to yourself that you can do my job, or Bowell's, as well as your own?'

'This *is* my job,' said Pearl with conviction.

McGuire slowly shook his head. 'No. It's . . . a mission. I don't think you're ever going to be satisfied. But you wanted information and I've given it to you. And if that wasn't enough maybe this might help.'

This time he handed her a folded newspaper cutting. Pearl took it from him, unfolded it and stared down at a tabloid headline:

DUBLIN WIDOW ROBBED BY CARER'S GAY LOVER

As she read on, Pearl recognised a familiar name. 'Simon?' she asked incredulous.

McGuire looked at her. 'Probably the reason he gave up nursing.'

Pearl turned her attention back to the newspaper story. After reading further, she looked up. 'It says here that there was no case to answer. It was Simon's boyfriend who did this. It mentions . . . "insufficient evidence to link Simon Mullen to the crime".' She looked up at McGuire, who replied, 'That doesn't mean he wasn't involved.' He took the press cutting from her. Pearl thought to herself. 'But surely Babs would have had a police check done before employing Simon?'

McGuire shrugged. 'There was no conviction. And this happened in the Republic of Ireland, several years ago. Simon's not her carer either – you said he's just her "companion"?' He slipped the cutting back into his pocket.

Pearl nodded. 'Yes. So she may not have bothered with a check, even though she trusts him to take charge of her medication.'

'And it was *her* Valium that went missing. I found out she's had repeat prescriptions for years. Five milligram tabs.'

'Her "little helpers",' mused Pearl.

'For "emergencies",' said McGuire. 'Like you say, she's a hypochondriac. But it would have needed only six, at the most, to have had the desired effect on Priddey after he had taken his oxycodone.'

'*And* the brandy,' said Pearl.

McGuire looked at her. 'Motive?'

Pearl met his gaze. 'As Simon's employer, Babs didn't stand to benefit from this marriage – not with the prenup and Amy giving up work – so I don't see how Simon would have done so either.'

'But you only have Guy and Amy's word about those plans.'

'That's true,' said Pearl thoughtfully. 'After the fireworks I heard Guy telling his sister, Sarah, that he would only help her financially if she finally left Toby.' She looked at McGuire. 'But how could he do that if he'd given everything away?'

'Maybe the plan was to somehow keep a good sum set aside – secreted away somewhere?'

Pearl said nothing for a moment.

'What do you want to do?' asked McGuire.

Pearl looked up slowly at him. 'See what Simon has to say.'

She started to move off, but McGuire took hold of her arm.

'Oh no,' he said firmly. 'Not without me.'

Pearl and McGuire entered the garden wing of Mount Ephraim to find the hallway in darkness. The door to the sitting room was open and a fingernail of moon was framed in one of the tall windows. Pearl led the way up the wide wooden staircase and as they turned into the upper corridor, lights were visible beneath three doors; the rooms occupied by Amy, Ingrid, and Tess and James. Looking back at McGuire, Pearl nodded towards the open door that led into the hallway above the main house. As they approached it, she and McGuire saw only darkness beneath Babs's bedroom door, but, next to it, Simon's was partially open. His light was on, and music was sounding softly from inside. After exchanging another look, McGuire nodded and Pearl tapped lightly on Simon's door. No response. Moving closer to the door, Pearl tapped again – louder this time, so it could be heard above the music.

'Simon, are you awake?'

Again, there was no response. McGuire took control and pushed the door wide open, revealing Simon lying on his side in bed, facing away from the door and towards the window as though he might be admiring the silver thread of moon that was hanging in the dark sky. The music appeared to be coming from a smartphone on his bedside cabinet – a track from a Sam Smith album. For a moment, Pearl assumed Simon must be listening on headphones, so she looked back at McGuire, who spoke up loudly. 'All right, Simon, we need to talk.'

Stepping forward, Pearl rounded the bed to find the young man's eyes were still closed, his mouth slightly ajar, as though he was sleeping soundly. She leaned forward and nudged his shoulder to wake him, but as she did so, he rolled back on the bed, exposing that his sheet and pillowcase were drenched with sweat. Pearl whispered his name as McGuire moved in to feel for a carotid pulse in Simon's neck. After only a second, McGuire gave Pearl a grave look, then he pulled his phone from his pocket, dialled and spoke hurriedly into it.

'Police and ambulance. Right away.'

Pearl heard but failed to listen to McGuire giving details of Mount Ephraim's location on the line; instead, her attention was fixed on something lying on the carpet between Simon's bed and the cabinet on which his smartphone still played a plaintive song. Taking a handkerchief from her pocket, she reached down and carefully picked up Simon's glasses from the floor, setting them beside a familiar white pen. The music played on, but as Pearl's gaze remained transfixed on the white pen she heard only Simon's gentle Irish voice sounding in her memory: *'I follow all the rules . . . monitoring my blood sugar regularly and keeping on top of my meds.'*

The image in Pearl's mind of Simon's charming smile transformed into the lifeless body before her, framed by an aura of evil which seemed to grow more powerful with every moment. Looking up, Pearl saw McGuire had finished his call.

'I've been so stupid,' she whispered. 'I should've realised, but . . .' She trailed off before finding renewed purpose. 'We have to talk to Swale Police.'

CHAPTER TWENTY-SIX

A sudden gust of wind splashed a sheet of rain across the tall windows of Mount Ephraim's games room, where the guests had gathered the next morning – perhaps, thought Pearl as she observed them, in an attempt to seek a sense of security. McGuire had left hours ago, but seated at the piano with Tess standing close by, James idly played the melancholy strains of a sonata which seemed to perfectly match the sombre mood. Babs sobbed loudly into a lace handkerchief while Ian studied something on the screen of his smartphone. Sarah stood at the rain-splattered windows, staring out at the gloomiest of days. Ingrid sat on the sofa, her eyes closed as though she was imagining herself to be somewhere else; her manicured fingernails tapped soundlessly against the armrest. Amy's eyes were fixed on Toby, who was taking aim at a white cue ball on the billiard table. Slowly withdrawing his arm, he slammed the ball hard across the green baize then watched it smash into a red, which headed directly for a pocket only to ricochet against its sides before escaping back up the table. Toby shook his head in exasperation then heaved a sigh before addressing James without looking at him: 'Do we have to listen to that morbid cacophony?'

James instantly withdrew his hands from the piano keys as Sarah flinched at the sound of her husband's voice. Then she turned – but said nothing. Ingrid opened her eyes slowly and said to Toby in a slow drawl, 'I happen to find that music rather soothing – especially in the circumstances.' She eyed him. 'Or have you forgotten that a young man died last night?'

Toby met her gaze, but it was Tess who spoke as she laid a hand on James's shoulder. 'Carry on playing.'

As James did so, Babs wailed, 'My poor boy. I *knew* this would happen one day. I warned him!'

Amy shook her head, as though dazed. 'I don't know how it could have happened. Simon managed his condition so well.' She looked up helplessly.

'You're right,' Ian agreed. 'He said so himself. He even showed us that device he used.'

Sarah looked confused. 'What device?'

'Keep up, Sarah,' said Toby, chalking his cue. 'He was diabetic, wasn't he?'

'Yes, and it was no secret,' said Ian. 'The first day we were here, he took a pen from his pocket and said it measured his doses correctly.'

'Doses?' asked Sarah, increasingly bewildered.

Pearl spoke up. 'You remembered.' she said to Ian. 'I'd expect a barrister not to miss a detail like that.'

Ian looked at her with some suspicion. 'What's that supposed to mean?'

'I remembered it too,' said Pearl. 'What Simon showed us that first day was his insulin pen. Clever devices. They carry a cartridge of insulin and a replaceable needle, and from what I understand they're very easy to use – especially for young people who may need to deliver insulin at school or college.' She got up from her chair and moved to stand near the double doors to the dining room, which were open, exposing Emma busy in the kitchen and Ryan bringing in some crates and dumping them on the floor near the Aga.

'As Simon said to us that first day,' said Pearl, 'those pens are painless too; portable and discreet, unlike syringes. He also happened to mention that his own pen delivered an accurate dose – and he was right; it can actually be preset on the dosage dial, which might have been especially handy for him.'

'Why?' asked Babs.

Pearl looked at her. 'Because Simon wore glasses. They were strong lenses, so he must have been quite short-sighted. But if his glasses weren't handy, he could always rely on the pen's preset dosage to give him the precise amount of insulin he needed – just at the right time.' She paused. 'I noticed that his pen was beside him on the bedside cabinet last night.'

Tess looked with suspicion at Pearl. 'And what were you doing in his room?

'I needed to ask him about something.'

'About what?' said Ian.

'Does it matter?' said Toby. 'She clearly didn't get a chance to ask because the guy was already dead.'

'You're right, Toby,' said Pearl. 'I didn't get a chance to ask him.'

Babs wailed again. 'What am I going to do without him?'

Tess wheeled round to face her. 'Is that really all you care about?'

'Tess—' said Amy, trying to placate her. A look passed between the two women, but before either of them could say another word Emma entered through the open doors.

'I'm . . . sorry to interrupt,' she began, 'but I have to know if Simon's family have been notified.'

Ian replied soberly. 'The police will do that.'

Babs shook her head. 'He doesn't have any family. At least, he said he didn't.' Her face crumpled. 'That means there will only be me to mourn him.' She wailed again and burst into tears. Tess sighed with exasperation. 'Why do you have to be so melodramatic?'

Babs stared at her, affronted. 'How can you say that to me?'

'I say it because . . .' Tess trailed off as she glanced across at Amy. Pearl noted how their gaze connected before Tess continued. 'Amy's lost the man she loved,' Tess continued softly, 'but all you're concerned about is who's going to take care of your obsessive needs.'

'Yes,' added Ingrid. 'You were foul to that young man.'

'How dare you!' exclaimed Babs, but James now joined

in. 'It's true.' He pointed at her. 'Those are crocodile tears.'

'James is right,' said Tess. 'For heaven's sake, stop hamming it up!'

'H-h-hamming?' stammered Babs in shock.

'Yes,' said Tess, unashamedly, as she leaned towards Babs. 'You could put the ham in Hamlet.'

Babs gaped in horror. 'You're one to talk!' she screamed to Tess. 'A second-rate actress – or is it third-rate?'

James got up from the piano stool and rubbed his forehead in frustration. 'This really is like a terrible play.'

'One of yours?' asked Toby.

Emma went to leave the room, but Pearl stopped her. 'No. Please, I'd like you to stay and hear something. Ryan too.'

Emma glanced anxiously back at Ryan in the kitchen. Reluctantly he left the grocery supplies and came forward to stand at her side.

'Right,' said Toby, planting the end of his billiard cue firmly on the floor beside him. 'Hear what?'

'What I have to say,' said Pearl, gently. She turned to James. 'You're quite right about this seeming like a play. That's something else we talked about on that first day here. A sense of theatre, the importance of giving a performance – Ian doing so in court, and Tess doing so on stage,' she turned to face the actress, '*and* elsewhere.'

Tess met Pearl's gaze but said nothing. Pearl went on. 'You must spend a lot of time studying people, becoming aware not only of mannerisms but of the signs we all give away; the clues to who we really are – and how we really feel?' Pearl glanced around the room, noting Toby still standing with the billiard cue grasped tightly in his hand while Babs tugged anxiously at her lace handkerchief and Ingrid continued to drum nervous fingertips on the sofa's arm. Amy frowned while Sarah bit her lower lip and Ian raked his hand through his hair. James stroked his beard then held on to it as though it might escape.

Pearl continued addressing Tess. 'James mentioned to me how talented you are but also how hard you work at your "craft". He explained how you only come to inhabit a role when you walk in a character's shoes, literally. I found that fascinating – and clearly so do you, James.' Pearl turned to him as she added: 'As a playwright, you know the importance of this kind of attention to detail. After all, you have to create a whole new convincing world for an audience with just a few characters on stage, speaking your dialogue and following your action.'

James let go of his beard. 'What are you trying to say?'

Pearl turned back to Tess. 'That first night, when I found you in the topiary garden, I asked you about Guy's health, and you lied to me. Of course you would know if Guy was suffering from a serious condition. You'd spent time with Amy and Guy in Thailand, at close quarters – on a yacht – but someone like you, someone intelligent and observant, would have seen the signs. You lied to me.'

Tess opened her mouth, but it was Amy who spoke first.

'Only because I told her not to tell anyone,' she said. Her eyes settled again on Tess as she went on. 'Guy didn't want anyone to know. He didn't want sympathy; but equally, if his health problems were known, it would have affected his ability to raise investment for the salvage operation.' She heaved a sigh. Pearl turned again to Tess.

'So you kept Guy's secret,' she said. 'And it was easy for you. Easy to lie – because you're actually a *first-rate* actress.' She paused. 'But you weren't the only person to know about Guy's health problems. You knew too, Amy, and also . . . Sarah.' As Pearl turned to her, Sarah looked away before admitting, 'Of course I knew. He was my brother.'

'Yes,' agreed Pearl. 'And because of that, and his love for you, he was never happy about your choice of husband, was he?' Pearl now looked at Toby, who gave a shrug, unconcerned. 'Tell me something I don't know. It was no secret. Guy and I never got on.'

'That's right,' said Pearl. 'You were honest, Toby, which is more than I can say for some.' She looked back at Tess. 'Why *were* you sitting in the topiary garden that first night – after James had already gone to bed?'

'I told you,' said Tess. 'It was a nice evening. James hadn't been sleeping very well, but he was tired that night and . . . I thought I'd wait a while before I went up.'

She calmly held Pearl's gaze until Pearl finally turned away to give her attention to Ian. 'I talked to Kate Parsons yesterday.'

Babs frowned. 'The stalker in the maze?'

'Love can make us do strange things,' said Pearl, 'things we're likely to regret – *if* we have a conscience.'

'What do you mean?' Babs asked cagily.

'Causing a kind woman to lose her job at a golf-club bar?'

Babs flushed at this, but Toby huffed as though he had heard enough of Pearl's comments.

'This is very boring,' he announced.

'Toby,' said Sarah, trying to admonish him.

'What? We haven't the faintest idea what she's going on about.' He pointed at Pearl then looked back at Babs. 'Would you at least mind explaining?' He leaned back against the billiard table, his hand still grasping one end of the cue while the heavy end rested on the floor. Neither Babs nor Pearl replied to him, but Pearl sauntered across to the window, where she saw only a hazy green landscape through a pane of rain-smeared glass.

'This time away, here at Mount Ephraim,' she began, 'was for us all to celebrate a marriage – to witness two people in love.' Raindrops coursed down the window like tears. Pearl looked back at Amy, who closed her eyes as if to blot out the truth.

'Do you have to keep going on about that?' said Tess. 'You're only upsetting Amy.'

'I know,' said Pearl, gently. 'And I'm sorry. But news of Amy's wedding actually brought pain to someone else.'

'The stalker, you mean?' said Babs, unrepentant.

'Stop calling her that,' said Ian.

James gave Pearl a wary look. 'Why would that woman be upset about Amy's marriage?'

Pearl explained. 'Kate was upset about something else.'

She turned to Ian. 'The fact that you were back – here in Faversham – and you'd never once been able to properly explain to Kate why you had to end your engagement to her.'

Ian remained silent.

'Why?' asked Ingrid, her curiosity suddenly piqued.

Pearl noted Ian clenching and unclenching his hands, clearly under pressure, though he still failed to respond. Pearl went on. 'I assumed it was because you were still in love with Amy. But that would surely be easy enough to explain. And if Amy knew that to be true, why on earth would she invite you here to witness her marriage to another man?' Pearl glanced back at Amy. 'That was something I found difficult to understand,' she said. 'But it was much more complicated than I thought. In fact, it was only yesterday, after I had been talking to Kate, that I realised this – when I was thinking about your play, James – and the *ménage à trois*.' She paused and held his look. 'Where did you get the idea from?'

James shrugged. 'Why do you want to know? What are you trying to suggest?'

'Perhaps,' said Pearl, 'you felt instinctively that something had gone on. Something involving your partner?'

James slowly turned to look at Tess as Pearl continued. 'Tess met Guy and Amy in Thailand and spent time with them both on Guy's yacht. Just the three of you. A triangle.'

At this, Amy and Tess looked away, but Pearl now turned to Ian.

'And you, Ian, you were part of another triangle – of conflicting emotions. You, Amy and Kate. You felt instinctively that something was wrong. You couldn't accept that Amy didn't love you enough – but that she could love another man—'

'Just drop it,' he ordered.

'Too painful to revisit?' said Pearl. 'The realisation that things were never going to work between you? But then, out of the blue, it appeared Amy *had* found the right man. The perfect partner: rich, attractive, brave, principled, caring – and she was not only marrying him, she was inviting you to the wedding. How could she do that? Had she never understood that her rejection of you, of your future together, had caused you so much trauma you'd been unable to move on or even explain your feelings to Kate?'

Ian sprang to his feet. 'I said drop it! This serves no purpose.'

'Going over old ground?' said Pearl. 'Opening old wounds?'

He looked away, clearly pained. Amy turned to him. 'Ian?'

At the sound of her voice, Ian looked slowly back at her. Amy saw the conflict written on his face and murmured, 'I'm . . . so sorry . . .' Her voice trailed off into silence.

Pearl spoke again, softly this time. 'Someone else now had a place in Amy's heart; someone she described to me on that first day here. A relationship that had caused what sounded to me like a transformation – a Damascene moment in her life.' Pearl looked into Amy's eyes.

'It was,' said Amy. The moment was broken by Babs yelling, '*What* are you trying to say?'

Pearl finally explained. 'I'm saying that on the night before the wedding, Guy realised something – something he needed to set straight. It was the reason he wanted to talk to you, wasn't it, Tess? The reason you had been sitting on the tea terrace late that night. He wanted to see you when all the celebrations were over?'

Tess remained like a stone. James looked at her, confounded. 'Tess?'

'Why are you doing this, Pearl?' asked Amy, helplessly.

'Because I have to,' said Pearl. 'If I don't, the police will,' she said. 'And it's better this way.'

'Yes,' said Tess, finally and calmly. 'Guy asked to see me. That's why I was there on the terrace. It wasn't *just* to admire the topiary,' she said with some irony.

'Why didn't you tell me?' said James.

'Because you didn't need to know,' said Tess, crisply. 'No one needed to know.'

'Not even the police?' asked Pearl.

For a second, doubt flickered across Tess's features – almost imperceptibly, but Pearl caught it. 'Lies,' she said, turning to everyone in the room, 'of one degree or another – and for different reasons. You lied, Ian, about meeting Kate near the cricket pavilion on the night after Guy's murder. You also lied about not having seen Guy enter his suite that night.'

'I didn't lie,' he insisted. 'I . . . forgot. There had been so much going on—'

'Yes,' said Pearl, 'with Kate having come into the grounds, trying to talk to you. But you didn't want to see her, did you? Too many conflicting emotions to deal with—'

'Guy had been found dead!' he said.

'By me,' said Pearl. 'Not far from where I'd stood that same morning with you, Ryan, and the celebrant.' She paused as she held Ryan's look. 'You and Emma are more familiar with Mount Ephraim than any of us. It's your home. You manage this property; you know every inch of it. You have keys to every room. You knew better than any of the guests how the wings connect to the main house and how Guy's suite was easily accessed from the corridor in this wing'—she paused—'just a few steps past your bedroom, Babs.' As Pearl turned to her, Babs slowly lowered her lace handkerchief from her face. 'You're . . . surely not suggesting that I killed Guy?'

'They were *your* pills,' said Toby, looking at her with suspicion.

'But I left them downstairs! Anyone could have taken them.'

'That's true,' said Emma. 'I said before; I saw them on the dining table that first day and I moved them to the small table by the doors here.' She pointed to it. 'When they disappeared, I just assumed you'd taken them upstairs.' She looked at Babs.

'Clearly someone did,' said Pearl.

Ingrid threw up her arms in impatience. 'This is all complete supposition,' she exclaimed, 'going round in circles! I'm sure you can find a reason to suspect every one of us here, but that doesn't mean to say we're guilty.'

Ian turned to Pearl. 'She's right,' he said. 'You're playing amateur detective, Pearl. If the police were here, they wouldn't be very impressed with this.'

'That's true,' Pearl conceded, 'but they're *not* here.' She looked around slowly, her gaze resting on each person in the room in turn. 'I am,' she said. 'And I know what happened.'

CHAPTER TWENTY-SEVEN

All eyes remained on Pearl as she turned once again to the window, gathered her thoughts and looked back at the guests assembled in the games room.

'Just after the firework display,' she began, 'I went into the grounds to make a call. I checked my phone log. I made that call at eleven thirty-six. A short while afterwards I found Tess on the tea terrace.' She looked across at Tess then went on: 'But straight after I finished my call, I was heading back to the house when I heard voices. One was Guy's – and the other, was yours, Sarah.'

Sarah's breath seemed to catch in her throat. 'Me?'

'Yes,' said Pearl. 'I heard you both talking that night.'

'You mean . . . you spied on us?'

Pearl replied calmly. 'I happened to overhear some of your conversation.'

Sarah glanced nervously at her husband then seemed to find the strength to confront Pearl. 'It was a private conversation with my brother.'

Pearl nodded. 'During which Guy made it very clear he wanted you to leave Toby; only then would he support you – *if* you left him.'

Toby shook his head at this. 'And you wonder why we didn't get on?' He jutted out his chin. 'To be honest, I'm glad Guy's gone.'

'Toby!' Amy exclaimed.

'I am,' he continued, unabashed. 'I'm no hypocrite. I've been honest about how I felt about my brother-in-law – the great Guy Priddey. The man who had everything.'

'He was my brother,' said Sarah firmly.

'So you keep reminding me,' said Toby. 'And more's the pity – because if he hadn't been your brother I wouldn't have had to put up with him for so long.' He held Sarah's look for a moment then turned and sent the billiard ball in his hand spinning across the table. It landed squarely in a pocket – which seemed to go some way to placating him.

Pearl continued. 'Amy told me Guy had called her to say goodnight. And I know she was telling the truth because I heard that conversation before I went back up to the house. That's when I saw you, Tess. You were waiting for Guy, but he must have known he needed to take his medication, and so he had gone back up to his room and Ian saw him entering the Sir Edwyn Suite. I was heading into the house when I happened to witness an argument between Babs and Amy. You were both here, in this room, and you, Babs, were making Amy aware of how unhappy you were that she had signed a prenuptial agreement – and that Guy's fortune was to be distributed to good causes.'

'I should have known you'd be snooping!' said Babs. 'And I wasn't "unhappy",' she argued, 'I was just concerned – for Amy.' She turned to her. 'You know I've always had your best interests at heart. We are family.'

Pearl went on. 'Yes. So, you would have felt that, as family, you would naturally benefit from Guy's wealth. Except his "wealth" was now destined for other use.'

'It was a stressful time,' said Babs, 'the eve of the wedding,' she went on. 'It was *no* time to spring such a surprise on us all.'

'Surprise,' echoed Pearl. 'Surely it was a shock to *you*, wasn't it, Ingrid?' she said, turning to Amy's agent. 'Discovering your client was about to stop working for you?'

'Amy doesn't "work" for me,' argued Ingrid. 'I *represent* her. And I've told you before, she's more like family to me than a business client.'

'Yes,' said Pearl, 'but this "family" member was finally leaving home, wasn't she? Deserting you when you most needed her – when the quality commissions were suddenly piling up for Amy because of her relationship with Guy Priddey.'

Ingrid looked away, unable to meet Amy's gaze. Pearl went on. 'Guy had revealed the plans he had made for his fortune once he and Amy were married. Given what they were, why wouldn't someone want to prevent this wedding from taking place?' Pearl looked from the other guests back to Ingrid. 'Is that why you called someone late that night and told them there was only one way to change Amy's mind?' She paused. 'What "way" was that, Ingrid?'

'It was a private conversation,' Ingrid said firmly.

'Yes,' said Pearl, 'which is why I headed to my own room and left you to it.' She thought back to that moment. 'I could hear music coming from Simon's room along the corridor – just like I heard last night.' She left a pause, remembering how she had stood at Simon's door the night before. 'His door was ajar,' she said. 'And he had told me, and told us all, how that same door had opened on the night of Guy's murder.'

'A draught,' said Toby, dismissively. 'We've heard all this before.'

Pearl paused before going on. 'I don't believe Guy's murder was premeditated. Someone had acted very quickly, on the spur of the moment, some time before midnight, taking the Valium from the small table near these doors, then heading upstairs and along the corridor into the main house, and across the galleried landing to Guy's suite. It would have taken only a minute or two. They emptied the pills into his hip flask beside the bed and disappeared. Guy then went upstairs to his suite, took the oxycodone along with brandy from his flask, and then came down – to meet you, Tess.' Pearl stared at her. 'What happened then? You took a walk with him among the topiary?'

Tess looked hunted, then glanced at Amy and finally spoke. 'The Millennium Rose Garden,' she said. 'It's at the end of the tea terrace. Private. Secluded. He didn't want us to be seen.'

Pearl noted a muscle tightening in James's jaw. Tess went on. 'But that had nothing to do with Guy's death,' she insisted.

'Just another "private conversation"?' asked Pearl.

Tess gave a nod. 'Maybe I should have told the police, but—'

'She told me,' said Amy suddenly. 'I . . . told Tess to keep it to herself.'

Ian turned to her. 'Amy?'

'The police inspector would surely have suspected Tess, asked more questions. There was no point.'

She looked back at Tess. Pearl spoke again. 'How long did you talk for?'

'Not long,' said Tess. 'No more than five minutes. And Guy was perfectly fine. What you said about the effects of the drugs . . . He was steady on his feet.'

Pearl took this in, then said, 'And the next morning, the day of the wedding, I overslept. I woke very late, with a thick head. I thought it must have been the champagne, but I realised last night that someone had made sure that I was spiked with the same tranquilliser. That's why I had slept so deeply and woken so late. The diazepam ensured I heard nothing more that night – or saw anything from the windows of my room.' She paused again. 'But one guest had woken. Simon had gone to bed early and had fallen asleep with his phone playing music. He had told me that, but I hadn't given it much thought until last night, when I found him in his bed, with the light on, and music sounding from his phone. But he wasn't asleep last night. Someone had tampered with his insulin pen.'

'What?' gasped Babs.

'How do you know that?' asked Sarah, her eyes narrowing.

'I told you all, I found the pen lying on Simon's bedside cabinet. His glasses were on the floor between the bed and that cabinet. He must have dropped them but thought he'd mislaid them, so he would have trusted the pen to give him the correct dose – as it always did, until last night.' She paused. 'It was set to maximum dose.'

Ingrid frowned. 'You're saying that someone must have—'

'Made sure he overdosed,' said Ian.

'Deliberately?' asked Amy breathlessly.

'Why else?' said Tess.

'To kill him,' said James.

Emma looked at Ryan beside her. 'He was murdered . . .'

'I don't believe it . . .' said Sarah.

'Why would anyone want to kill Simon?' said Babs.

Pearl stepped forward. 'Because of something he said last night.'

'Something?' asked Toby.

Pearl nodded. 'It came to me only when I was in Simon's room last night, when I saw that pen on the bedside cabinet. Yesterday, when we were all in the meeting with DI Bowell,

Simon had explained how on the night before the wedding, his bedroom door had opened.'

'I remember,' said James.

Pearl went on. 'He said *"If only I had got up and checked the door when it fell open. I might have seen who it was."* And then Babs said . . .' Pearl trailed off and looked to Babs for an answer. For a moment, Babs looked confused, then she mumbled, 'I said, *"But you didn't"*?'

Pearl nodded. 'That's right. Simon had signalled to everyone in the room that he could, potentially, have seen who it was who had passed his room that night to reach the main house – if only he had checked his door.'

'I don't understand,' said Toby.

'Don't you?' asked Pearl. 'What Simon was saying must have put someone under great pressure – especially with DI Bowell there at the time. Simon was confirming to you, Babs, that he hadn't seen anyone – so the person who had tampered with Guy's medication might then have relaxed – but perhaps not for long.'

'What do you mean?' asked Amy.

'That same person would have been left with the impression that Simon might well have checked the door and *had* seen who had walked past it to reach Guy's suite. If so, Simon could then have used that knowledge to blackmail the person – if not straight away, then later.'

'So,' said Sarah, her voice lowering to a whisper as she tried to comprehend what Pearl was implying, 'you're saying . . . someone killed Simon to keep him quiet?'

Pearl nodded slowly.

Sarah shook her head slowly. 'No,' she insisted. 'No, I don't believe it.'

'Neither do I,' said Toby. He looked at James. 'This is just more melodrama to add to your play.'

'Will you stop going on about my play,' said James furiously.

Pearl watched Sarah turn back to the window, then she moved closer and asked, 'Are you really saying that those words of Simon's didn't worry you, Sarah?'

Sarah froze – then slowly looked back. Pearl went on. 'You . . . didn't actually mean to kill Guy, did you?'

Amy recoiled as though she had received a sudden blow to her solar plexus. Ian moved quickly to support her. Pearl stepped even closer to Sarah. 'You can tell us now. It's time for the truth. It was you who put the diazepam in Guy's flask – *and* in the water jug by my bed.'

'I—' Sarah broke off, an explanation jammed in her throat.

'Be quiet,' said Toby, fixing her with a determined look. For a moment, Sarah seemed mesmerised, then her eyes began to flicker and her gaze wandered back to Pearl. 'I . . . didn't murder him,' she whispered.

'Of course you didn't,' said Toby, softly but insistently.

But Sarah shook her head slowly, appearing to gain strength as she stepped towards Pearl. 'I couldn't,' she went on. 'He was my brother—' She broke off again, then continued feebly. 'All I wanted to do was . . . sedate him . . . so that he'd miss the wedding and the ceremony couldn't take place. Then we could talk. Things would go back to how they had always been. Guy would change his mind – if not about the wedding, then—'

'About the money?' said Pearl.

Sarah's face crumpled and she broke down in a torrent of tears. Tess moved quickly to comfort her.

'She's upset, unstable,' said Toby. 'She doesn't know what she's saying.' He made a sudden move towards her but broke off as Ian and James barred his way. Finding herself at a distance from her husband, Sarah appeared to find confidence and brought herself up to her full height. 'I should have done what Guy said,' she went on, looking directly at Toby. 'I should have left you. If I had, then Guy would still be alive.'

Toby warned, 'Sarah!'

But she continued, this time looking to Pearl as she pointed to her husband. 'I *told* him what I'd done, and he said it would be all right – that he would go and check on Guy.' She turned to Toby and shook her head, helplessly. 'But you didn't.'

Pearl eyed Toby. 'What happened?' she demanded. 'You lured Guy down to the lake?'

Toby's eyes shifted from Sarah to Pearl then to every other guest in the room before he seemed to make a calculation. Taking a deep breath, he gave a strange, incongruous smile then finally said, 'I didn't have to. It was a "night for truth".' He paused then went on. 'That's what Guy said. He wanted to talk to me, tell me how much he wanted me out of Sarah's life – for good – or he would cut off the money he'd been giving her.'

He glanced across at Sarah. 'Typical Guy Priddey, ordering everyone to do what he wanted. Captain of the ship?' He shook his head. 'Not mine.' His hand tightened on the cue. 'I could see he was already unsteady on his pins. You can't believe what a treat it was for me to see him looking more drunk than I've ever managed to get in my whole life. He always called me an alcoholic but now he was standing there, swaying and reeling . . . he even tried to grab hold of me but then he slipped on the bank near the bridge. The next thing he was mumbling about needing help. Help – Guy Priddey, needing help.' He looked down as if staring once more at a figure in the lake. 'I saw him struggling. And to be honest, I enjoyed it.'

Sarah looked at her husband as though she was viewing a stranger. 'You . . . could have rescued him? You could have got him out!'

'Why should I?' yelled Toby sharply. 'You have no idea what it's been like all these years to live in Guy Priddey's shadow. Everyone's hero – and *your* beloved brother. The one you ran to whenever anything went wrong?' He shook his head. 'Never me. Because I was the dud. The failure. The mistake you married. I'd have been a fool to have saved him after what he said to you that night.' He jerked his head towards Pearl. 'You heard him talking to Sarah?' He paused. 'Well, so did I. You could say, that sealed Guy's fate as far as I was concerned.'

'You . . . let him die?' cried Sarah. 'You let my brother die, but you didn't tell me. You let me believe I was the one who'd killed him. You said I had to keep quiet or

I'd go to prison for murder.' She shook her head once more then slowly looked up again at her husband. 'Then you killed that young man last night . . . just to keep him quiet?'

Toby held her look as he spelled it out for her. 'If he *had* seen you, you *would* have gone to prison – and *I'd* have been left with nothing.'

A moment's silence followed before Amy got to her feet. 'Call the police!'

Ryan moved to dial his phone, but in one swift move Toby took everyone by surprise. He swung the billiard cue out at arm's length, keeping James and Ian at bay. Ryan edged forward but Toby jabbed him back. Pearl eyed Toby, warning him, 'You can't get away.'

'Oh no?' Toby gave a curious smile as he began backing towards the door, still jabbing the sharp end of the cue before him as he quickly felt for the door handle behind him. He allowed his fingers to curl around it before he pushed the door open – and disappeared.

In the next instant, Ryan nodded to Ian and James, and the three men made a rush for the door, followed by Pearl. They found themselves once again in the vast grand hall of the main house. Toby Lawson was backing his way to the main entrance, the heavy end of the cue now facing towards the others in his effort to keep everyone at bay. 'Pearl's right,' said Ian, calmly. 'You won't get away.'

'Oh no?' said Toby. 'Just watch me.' Swinging the cue in a wide arc, Toby struck a porcelain vase, which smashed into fine pieces on the marble floor. He smiled, unconcerned, and continued backing towards the door, a smile still playing on his lips until cars were suddenly heard drawing up on the gravel outside.

His smile faded with the slamming of the cars' doors. Footsteps headed quickly up the steps beneath the pillared entrance. The main door burst open to reveal uniformed police officers, followed by DI Bowell and McGuire. Pearl shared a look with McGuire then saw Toby was now heading towards the cantilevered staircase. He turned, looking around like a hunted animal.

'It's no use,' said DI Bowell. 'There's no way out.'

Ignoring her, Toby's hand clutched the ornate banister and he retreated up the stairs, the cue still in his hand. As he reached the top, Pearl looked up to see him framed by daylight streaming through the glass roof above the galleried landing. Toby searched for another escape route before heading to the door leading to the garden wing. He tugged at the handle and found it locked, so he ran to the door of the west wing, wrenching the handle, but that too was locked. Turning quickly, he stared around. The faces of Mount Ephraim's family ancestors glared back at him as a group of police officers began to approach steadily up the staircase. Increasingly panicked, Toby leaned across the balcony and shouted down, 'Don't come any nearer, you hear!'

At this, DI Bowell signalled for the officers to remain where they were, then nodded to Sergeant Falconer at the entrance. The main door opened once more and someone entered, partially obscured until he stepped fully into the centre of the grand hall. Pearl recognised Simon Mullen as he looked up towards the landing. Toby stared down at Simon as if he was a ghost. 'You . . .' he murmured.

In the next moment, Pearl watched the cue in Toby's hand fall silently through the air, turning a circle until it smashed against the marble floor. Still trying to make sense of what he saw, Toby remained rooted to the spot, unaware of the police officers who now grabbed hold of him. They led him down the elegant sweeping staircase, past Pearl and McGuire – and out of the house. Bowell glanced back at Pearl, then she headed outside with Simon and the rest of her officers while Pearl and McGuire heard a familiar police caution being read to the man who had just been arrested for the murder of Guy Priddey. Pearl turned to McGuire and finally allowed herself to smile as she whispered a single word, 'Snookered.'

CHAPTER TWENTY-EIGHT

Pearl held Dolly's small, framed seascape in her hands. Amy examined it, taking careful note of the shells, dried seaweed and fragments of bleached timber affixed to the canvas. Finally, she shook her head slowly: 'I . . . don't know what to say.'

Pearl smiled at her friend's reaction. 'Good. I'm glad it's not just me.'

'No, I meant I'm really touched that Dolly should have done this for me.'

'Well,' said Pearl, 'I'm only sorry I didn't get to give it to you days ago. But after Guy's death, the time never seemed right.'

'No,' Amy agreed. 'But it is now.' She managed a reassuring smile and set the painting down near her luggage – a suitcase and a few travel bags. Pearl imagined a beautiful wedding dress carefully packed away, perhaps never to be worn again. Amy went on: 'I'm not sure the police would ever have been able to do what you did,' she said, 'provoke an admission like that from Sarah – and in front of witnesses?'

'Yes,' said Pearl, 'McGuire and I thought the same – which is why it had to be carefully stage managed.'

Amy looked at her questioningly, and Pearl went on. 'When we found Simon in his room the other night, it really did seem we were too late. But he was in a coma, and he managed to pull through. After I explained how I'd found that his insulin pen had been set to maximum dose, DI Bowell established with Simon's doctor what the correct level should have been, and we then knew this overdose had been no accident. To keep him safe, we agreed to let everyone believe Simon had died. That allowed me to take note of everyone's reactions.' She paused, then said, 'Everything James had told me about the attention Tess gave to her acting roles had stuck with me.'

Amy frowned. 'Yes. You mentioned people giving away clues, even when they're trying to hide something?'

Pearl nodded. 'Yesterday, I saw that Sarah found it hard even to look at Toby. In truth, she didn't know for sure what he had done, but part of her must have suspected. The problem was she had been victim to Toby's gaslighting for so long, and in denial about his alcoholism and abuse, so she clung to the belief that Toby had nothing to do with Guy's death and that he was simply trying to shield her against the repercussions from spiking Guy's medication. Once I told everyone that Simon had been murdered, on top of everything else I had said about Guy, she couldn't keep quiet much longer. Toby was still confident he could bully his wife into silence, but I felt she might fight back with the truth – *if* she felt safe and we were all there together in one room.'

'So, Sarah's conscience finally got the better of her.'

'You could say the weight of her own guilt about Guy's death proved too much for her to bear.'

'She really did love him,' said Amy.

'I'm sure. And she never intended to kill him—'

'She just didn't want us to get married.'

Pearl paused. 'Not if it meant Guy would be cutting off all the financial assistance he'd been giving her.'

Amy looked at her. 'You're very clever, Pearl. Astute.'

'Am I?'

'You know you are. Everything you said about *ménages à trois*? You made that sound as though Tess and I were both involved in an affair with Guy, but . . .' Pearl finished the sentence for her. 'The truth was far simpler.' She paused. 'You did tell me the truth, Amy, that very first afternoon, here in this room, didn't you? You had met someone who had made your life complete, someone who had answered all the questions you'd ever asked yourself. You were in "the right relationship" at last – but not with Guy. And not with Ian Soutar.' She added gently, 'It was Tess who had rocked your world.'

Amy closed her eyes then opened them once more to meet Pearl's gaze. 'It's true,' she said softly. 'I was with Guy at the time and . . . we were happy. He was a truly remarkable man – an amazingly caring human being – and I really did love him. I enjoyed being with him, but . . . like I said to you that day, I absolutely knew nothing would ever be the same again once I had got together with Tess.' She took a moment to order her thoughts. 'I'd begun to question my sexuality when I was with Ian, but I was young then, and I really needed someone, especially at that time, so we stayed together and got engaged. After Dad married Babs, things became so difficult. I was confused. I felt rejected . . .'

'But you still had Ian.'

Amy nodded. 'But I knew I couldn't spend the rest of my life with him. He was like a good friend. Nothing more.'

'Though he clearly loved you.'

'Yes, but then he got engaged to Kate and I thought he'd moved on.' She looked back at Pearl. 'I never realised I'd left so many unanswered questions for him. I just didn't know how to answer them. It wasn't Ian's fault things ended; it was mine. My relationships with men never worked out.'

'But you still loved Guy enough to marry him. Even after you'd met Tess?'

Amy looked torn. 'I . . . didn't feel I could change course. Guy had so many plans – wonderful ideas about how we could make a difference, do something useful in the world. Together.' She shook her head. 'At the time, that seemed more important, and although I still felt confused I ended things with Tess. But I think Guy suspected something. I missed her so badly when she returned to England. Then I heard she was with James. I called her one night – poured out my heart. Guy must have overheard. He made sure I invited Tess to the wedding, but then he also made sure he got a chance to talk to her.'

'After the fireworks, in the rose garden?'

Amy nodded. 'She told me the next day when she was helping me to get ready, just before you came into the sitting room.'

'I remember.'

'Then Guy went missing and you found his body.' She looked at Pearl. 'I couldn't possibly allow myself to believe he had taken his own life . . . over this.'

Pearl took her friend's hand. 'He didn't,' she said decisively, 'so you have nothing to feel guilty about.'

Amy managed a smile, and at that moment a car horn sounded below. Both women looked out of the window to see Babs sitting in the front passenger seat of James's vintage car. Simon was in the rear, juggling various bags and cases, while James slammed the car boot shut. As James walked to the driver's door, he looked up and saw Amy and Pearl at the window. Amy raised her hand to wave goodbye. For a moment, James didn't react – then his expression softened and he gave a relaxed salute before getting into the driver's seat. Simon looked up and offered a wave while Babs blew a kiss to Amy with a gloved hand.

'They're finally off,' whispered Amy. 'I'll call her later and check how Simon's feeling.'

'He seems well,' said Pearl. 'Fully recovered.'

'I do hope so,' Amy replied, 'but if he's got any sense at all he'll put his feet up and get Babs to take care of him for a change.' She smiled and turned away from the window.

'And Ian?' asked Pearl.

Amy's smile faded. 'We talked this morning. He knows everything. I think it's helped.' She paused before elaborating. 'I should have realised how insensitive I'd been, inviting him to the wedding. It was a mistake. But I only realised that when he left the terrace during the firework display.'

'You went to talk to him that night, didn't you?'

Amy looked at Pearl. 'You knew?'

'It was your door I heard close when I came up to my room. Everyone else in the garden wing had already gone to bed, and if it had been somebody *leaving* their room, I would have seen them in the corridor.'

Amy gave a guilty sigh. 'I should have known I couldn't keep anything from you, Pearl. I didn't tell the inspector in case it incriminated Ian, but I went to his room that night to talk to him . . . and I found him getting ready to leave. I managed to persuade him to stay. I hoped the wedding would give him closure.' She paused and turned to look out of the window. 'I think he has that now. He's gone to visit Kate, and I think he may be staying a little longer in Faversham.' She turned and offered a smile.

'And you?'

'I told Ingrid this morning, before she left, that Tess and I need some time together. We're going away.'

'Far away?'

'I'm not sure yet.'

'And . . . how will you manage?' Pearl asked. 'Financially, I mean? You have Babs to take care of and Simon's salary. Maybe I could help—'

'There's no need,' said Amy. 'After I signed the prenup, Guy said he wanted to give me something, a present. I told him I didn't want anything – I didn't need anything. I had him.' She moved to her bedside table and picked up a book. 'He gave me this.' Sitting down on the bed, Amy handed the book to Pearl. It was the same collection of short stories in which Amy kept the photos of Guy on his yacht. 'Guy loved Hemingway,' she went on. 'He would read *The Old Man and the Sea* when we were sailing.' She slipped the photos from the book once more; Guy sitting at the helm of the *Tranquil C*, nut-brown in the tropical sun. 'Guy said Hemingway was an acquired taste, but it was worth me trying to love his books as much as he did. He then gave me this collection of short stories.' Keeping hold of the photos, Amy nodded to the book in Pearl's hands. 'Take a look.'

Pearl opened the volume, and Amy indicated something on the back of the title page.

'A first edition?' said Pearl.

Amy nodded. 'This was published in 1924. Only three hundred copies were printed for the initial run, and due to an error fewer than two hundred were ever released and sold. The rest were given away to close friends and family or as review copies. *This* is one of the rarest books for collectors.' She paused. 'Almost twenty years ago, a first edition, just like this, sold at a New York auction for over three hundred thousand dollars.' She gave a slow smile. 'Guy liked surprises,' she said. 'And this goes with me everywhere.' She took the book from Pearl and slipped the photos of Guy back inside before holding the volume close to her heart. A moment later, a knock on the door sounded and Tess appeared. 'Am I interrupting?'

Amy shook her head and smiled. Tess moved to her side and placed her arm gently around Amy's shoulder. Sensing she had just walked in at an awkward moment, Tess asked, 'What were you talking about?'

'Books,' said Pearl.

Tess looked back at Amy, who mused, 'Perhaps one day I'll even write one.'

'You really will get back to writing?' asked Pearl.

'Of course,' said Amy. 'It's part of my nature. Just as cooking is for you, Pearl.' She smiled at her old friend before adding, '*And* solving crimes.'

A few minutes later, Pearl descended the stairs to the hallway to find Emma waiting for her. 'Ryan's put your bags in the car,' she said. 'And I've settled a *tarte Tatin* on the back seat – for you, Dolly and Charlie.' She paused then added a sincere 'Thank you, Pearl.'

'For what?'

'For everything.'

Pearl leaned forward and embraced her. As they broke apart, Pearl held Emma's gaze and said, 'I'd love for you and Ryan to come to the Whitstable Pearl on your next evening off. It's high time I cooked for you.'

Emma returned Pearl's smile, but before she could say a word Ryan's voice sounded.

'Pearl?'

Turning, Pearl saw Ryan was standing at the open door. He tipped his head towards the gardens.

'Someone's waiting for you – down by the lake.'

Pearl left the garden wing and set off down the stone steps to the grounds. In the warmth of the sun, the sweet smell of roses clung to the summer air as it drifted across the terraces. Pearl looked back to see Emma and Ryan standing close together on the terrace. They waved across the balustrade and shared a look with one another before heading back into the garden wing.

Pearl allowed herself to enjoy one last look at the beautiful old manor house set in its Edwardian gardens in the heart of an eight-hundred-acre estate, then she stared away in the direction of the Miz Maze, the medieval labyrinth comprised of hedges and flowering plants, and then towards Snowdrop Bank. Pearl knew that the gardens had become overgrown during the Second World War, but once the chaos of conflict was finally over they had been restored by the family that had occupied Mount Ephraim for over three centuries. That family's initials were embedded in the iron gates and in the stone plaques of the two pavilions on the lower terrace – one of which Amy Young was to have been married in. With that thought in mind, Pearl continued on past the yew hedges and the stone bench on which she had overheard the final conversation between a brother and sister. Then she took the well-trodden path alongside the Japanese rock garden, where the sight of McGuire brought her up short. He stood facing away from her as he stared down towards the lake and the old pump house across the water. Coming up behind him, Pearl finally spoke.

'It's a magical setting, isn't it?'

McGuire turned and looked taken aback at the sight of her; Pearl's long dark curls were draped across one shoulder, her beautiful grey eyes animated, skin tanned, high cheekbones beginning to flush – perhaps at the sight of him. McGuire smiled. His gaze shifted to the oriental bridge with its stone lanterns while his mind returned to the photographs he had seen on a website on his smartphone. 'I'm guessing plenty of couples have stood there over the years.' He took Pearl's hand and led her over to the bridge.

'You'd be guessing right,' she said. 'A bridge is appropriate for a wedding,' she went on. 'After all, it takes you from one side to another.' She looked into McGuire's blue eyes. 'From being alone . . . to being together.'

Once they found themselves standing at the centre of the bridge, McGuire laid his palm gently against Pearl's cheek. 'From being Ms . . . to Mrs?' His eyes searched hers before he suddenly looked away, his smile fading.

'You said you thought you might have had a premonition on that first day you were here – before you found Guy's body?'

Pearl nodded slowly. 'And maybe I did. Or maybe'— she looked around—'this place was trying to lead me to the truth.'

McGuire looked back at her. 'If you *are* able to see into the future,' he said, 'what does it hold for us?'

Pearl paused, then: 'A wedding?'

'Here?'

'Here would be idyllic,' she replied, 'for Emma and Ryan.'

McGuire frowned. 'But not for us?'

Pearl took a deep breath and tried to explain. 'I want things to be perfect. I don't want them to fall apart – like they did for Amy.'

'And you think that might happen? You think . . . we . . . could fall apart?'

Pearl held his look then shook her head, assured. 'No. But I realise what I've put you all through. You, Mum, Charlie . . .' She moved even closer. 'I've had time to think about things.'

'And?'

'And I think you work too hard – and you need to book a few weeks off from all that leave you have stored up.'

'Oh?' said McGuire, taken aback.

'I think we could plan our wedding – *after* we've had a honeymoon.'

'After?'

Pearl nodded. 'Why not?'

McGuire looked sidelong at her. 'Trust you to do everything the wrong way round, Ms Nolan.'

'As long as it works, I don't much care. Do you?'

McGuire stared deep into her moonstone-grey eyes and moved in to kiss her – but a ringing phone broke the moment. McGuire recognised its distinctive tone. 'That's the mobile you use for Nolan's.'

'You're right,' said Pearl. 'A good detective!'

She took the mobile from her pocket and hesitated for a moment – before rejecting the call. Switching the phone to its camera mode, she handed it to McGuire and smiled. McGuire got the message. Holding the mobile at arm's length, he carefully framed them both in the camera lens and took a single shot before he opened his arms and allowed Pearl to fall into his embrace.

'Honeymoon it is,' he said softly, leaning in to kiss Pearl while a clamour of rooks glided silently overhead, high above two figures standing close together on a Japanese bridge, within a magical landscape – in a world of their own.

The End

ACKNOWLEDGEMENTS

Murder at Mount Ephraim was written during the Covid-19 pandemic, when lockdowns and various tier restrictions in Kent made it very difficult for me to do any of my usual location research. However, I remain indebted to the Dawes family, especially to Lucy Dawes and her father, Sandys Dawes, for safely accommodating me during two wonderful research stays at Mount Ephraim and providing me with fascinating and invaluable historical and logistical details about their beautiful ancestral home. I am also very grateful to Mount Ephraim's former Accommodation Manager, Amy Baxter, for all her care and attention during those stays.

The idea of featuring Mount Ephraim as the setting for a traditional closed-circle murder mystery came to me after the main house had appeared as a location in the TV series *Whitstable Pearl*, filmed October 2020 to March 2021 by production company, Buccaneer, for the streaming channel Acorn TV. Based on my Whitstable Pearl Mystery novels, the first season of this TV series began airing in May 2021, starring Kerry Godliman as Pearl, Howard Charles as McGuire, and Frances Barber as Dolly. I am immensely thankful to both companies and to all the cast and crew members for bringing my characters to the small screen in such a gripping and entertaining series, and I am thrilled that a second season of *Whitstable Pearl* has now been commissioned by Acorn TV, with filming having begun in February 2022.

I am also extremely grateful to my friends, Dr Howard Stoate, for his help with medical research, and fellow author and real-life police detective, Lisa Cutts, for her advice on police procedure.

As ever, sincere thanks go to Constable's publishing director, Krystyna Green, who, in 2015 commissioned the first Whitstable Pearl Mysteries for publication and has been my editor ever since. I am also grateful to Anna Boatman and the team at Little, Brown Book Group for all their hard work. Special thanks go to my agent, Michelle Kass, who has been a rock for me throughout the last thirty years – together with all her dedicated associates.

Finally, a big thank you to all my readers, whose appreciation and support for these books has resulted in what could be described as a lovely string of Pearls.